The
Magnolia
Sisters

Also by Michelle Major

The Magnolia Reunion

For a complete list of Michelle Major's books,
check out her website at www.michellemajor.com.

MICHELLE MAJOR

The
Magnolia
Sisters

HQN

ISBN-13: 978-1-335-01328-6

The Magnolia Sisters

Recycling programs
for this product may
not exist in your area.

This edition published by arrangement with Harlequin Books S.A.

For questions and comments about the quality of this book, please contact us at CustomerService@Harlequin.com.

HQN
22 Adelaide St. West, 40th Floor
Toronto, Ontario M5H 4E3, Canada
www.Harlequin.com

Printed in U.S.A.

For Matt. Thank you for believing in me. XOXO

Dear Reader,

I'm thrilled to welcome you to Magnolia, North Carolina, and to introduce you to the three sisters who have made this setting so special for me. Avery Keller's life is on the rocks when she drives into the quaint town of Magnolia for the will reading of a father she never knew. Her plan is to collect whatever inheritance he left her and start over someplace new. But first she'll have to work with her half sisters to clean up their father's mess. In the process, Avery discovers a connection to them she hadn't expected along with a surprising attraction to the sexy single dad who lives next door.

Gray Atwell has his hands more than full with his work as a firefighter and being a dad to his precious and precocious daughter, Violet. Avery shouldn't be his type at all, except the spunky newcomer to his hometown quickly captures his heart. If only he can convince her to stay.

Avery must decide if this new life—and love—in Magnolia is the one that will finally give her the sense of happiness and home she's always craved.

I hope you love Avery and Gray's story, and be sure to check out *A Magnolia Reunion*, a prequel novella for this series. I always love to hear from readers, so please reach out!

All the best,

Michelle

CHAPTER ONE

HOW DID ANY sane person survive the South's oppressive humidity?

As Avery Keller surveyed the landscape surrounding the gas station just outside Magnolia, North Carolina, she tried to draw in a deep breath. It felt like sucking air from a hot oven. Thick forest bordered the concrete parking lot, the trees more the pine variety than the town's namesake. She glanced up at the water tower looming in the distance, the word *Magnolia* emblazoned on it in thick block letters. The bold designation mocked her, a lofty reminder that her past had been here waiting, even if she'd known nothing of it until a few days prior.

Almost a week now. One late-August week to process that the story of her life had been a lie because the truth was too callous, even for her aloof and ambitious mother. Avery had struggled with her identity as the daughter of a single mom, whose reckless decision had left her pregnant from a one-night stand with a nameless, random hookup.

Or not so random after all. As it turned out, Avery's father knew about her, at least enough to leave her an inheritance after he died.

Maybe the humidity wasn't to blame for the prickly heat crawling under her skin. More likely the bitterness that had festered like an open sore on her cross-country trek for the reading of the will. She would have preferred to ignore the summons, to remain unaffected by the news that she wasn't the fatherless, unwanted girl she'd thought herself to be.

Fatherless, no. Unwanted, most definitely.

She shoved the gas pump nozzle into the tank of her Lexus sedan and stalked toward the convenience store, needing caffeine and chocolate in equal measure.

The stale air inside the shop carried the scent of hot dogs and processed nacho cheese, but it was blessedly cool. She reached for a water but changed her mind at the last moment and pulled a Diet Mountain Dew from the commercial refrigerator at the back of the store, immediately shoving the bottle under her shirt. She gasped at the bite of cold plastic against her skin.

"Normally people drink that stuff," a deep voice said from a few feet away. "Although, the color's too reminiscent of antifreeze for my taste."

She rolled her head to glare at whoever was offering an unwanted opinion and stifled another gasp. Over six feet of gorgeous man stared back at her. As if the thick brown hair, piercing green eyes and rock-hard body weren't enough, he was wearing the crisp blue uniform of a firefighter. Avery had always been a sucker for a man in uniform, although she wasn't about to admit that now.

Apparently she didn't need to because one side of his sexy mouth pulled up, like his effect on the fairer sex was a given. No doubt, which only fueled Avery's irritation. She'd spent the past two and a half days on the road, steaming asphalt and satellite radio her only companions. She'd given up the guise of healthy choices midway across Missouri, and she wasn't in the mood to take crap from anyone.

She made a show of studying the slim container of beef jerky dangling between his fingers. "Those who live in meat-stick houses shouldn't throw stones."

His half smile widened into a full grin. "Now, darlin'," he drawled, "I don't even know your name. Seems a bit premature for you to be discussing my meat stick."

She felt her cheeks flame at the blatant innuendo but managed only a lame "in your dreams" as a response.

He chuckled. "Sorry," he said, shaking his head. "I don't get out much anymore."

"Shocker," she muttered before heading for the cash register. She added a pack of M&M's—the peanut variety for protein—and paid the gum-smacking attendant. Halfway to her car, Mr. Beef Jerky caught up with her.

"I really am sorry for the lousy joke," he said, matching his stride to hers. His voice was gravelly, the vowels drawn out in typical Southern fashion, and she fought the immediate prick of attraction skittering along her skin at the unnecessary apology for some silly teasing.

The unsolicited bit of kindness didn't make him a decent guy and shouldn't matter either way. She was here to discover why the father she never knew had reached out to her now when he'd never bothered to during his life. And collect her inheritance and put this tiny dot on the map in her rearview mirror.

Too bad she had no plan for what came next. She'd essentially blown apart her entire life a month ago with her stupid choices. One particular choice involving one specific man.

Avery wanted to believe she hadn't inherited her mom's self-destructive streak when it came to men. The facts—and the lives ruined in her wake—told a different story. She wasn't about to take a chance again, even for a moment of harmless flirting.

She stopped next to her car and turned to face him. "Listen, Jim-Bob or Billy-Bob or Bubba or whatever your redneck name is," she began, loosening the reins on the anger, irritation and misplaced grief she'd been tamping down for days, "you might be hot but I'm not interested in some good ol' boy who thinks he's God's gift to women."

He cocked a thick brow, but she continued before he could speak. "So why don't you just saunter off to whatever god-awful watering hole this town has to offer and ply your tired charms on a woman who's too drunk to care whether this—" she wagged a finger up and down in front of him "—is all you have to offer."

When his eyes flashed with something that looked like pain before narrowing, she sucked in a ragged breath. Oh, no. She'd just ripped into a perfect stranger who didn't deserve her unbridled animosity. Talk about kicking the dog. Shame and regret bubbled up inside her, as familiar as a worn pair of shoes. She opened her mouth to apologize, but he held up a hand.

"It's ten in the morning and I'm on duty," he said, his tone stony. The Southern drawl sounded even more pronounced when laced with temper. "But I sure do appreciate the advice and I'll keep it in mind for later, darlin'. This was just the reminder I needed of why women like you are a bad bet."

Women like her.

Ouch. She didn't understand the exact meaning of his words, but they were obviously an insult of the highest order. And one she deserved more than he could realize.

Which was why she didn't go after him when he stalked toward the hulking black truck parked near the front of the building, even though guilt ate at her insides. Let him believe she was a raving bitch. Most people from her old life did.

She glanced at her watch and stifled a groan. She was late for the meeting at the attorney's office. After her outburst with the hottie firefighter, she had half a mind to skip the reading of the will. With the maelstrom of emotions rioting through her, there was no telling what kind of trouble she'd get into next.

She put away the gas nozzle, then climbed into the car, leaning into the dash as the air from the vents turned cool once again. Blond hair clung to her sticky neck, and she took the elastic band off her wrist and pulled her hair into a messy ponytail. She'd woken today at a hotel in Raleigh and gotten ready like she was heading to the most important business meeting of her life.

She'd ruthlessly straightened her hair, although she quickly realized how much of a waste of time that had been. No amount of product was going to beat the impact of the late-August heat and humidity. The Calvin Klein pantsuit that normally made her feel confident now seemed like overkill, especially as sweat beaded at the backs of her knees and trickled between her shoulder blades.

She turned out of the service station parking lot, following the route programmed into the car's GPS. She'd done her research on Niall Reed. He was commercially successful, critically eviscerated and not man enough to claim his bastard daughter while he was alive.

Her stomach twisted as she pulled to the curb in front of a brick building near the center of downtown Magnolia. Although the town was picturesque, with colorful flowers bursting from planter boxes along the sidewalk and a predominance of Greek Revival architecture that showcased the area's history, the streets seemed almost deserted.

Avery didn't bother to fix her messy ponytail or reapply makeup. At this point, what did it matter? She took another swig of Mountain Dew and walked toward the redbrick building, clutching the Italian leather portfolio she'd splurged on after her first promotion. The knots in her stomach tightened with each step.

An older woman with a cotton-ball head of hair looked up from her desk as Avery entered. The receptionist gave her a long once-over, then pointed to a closed office door. "They're waiting for you."

"I'm Avery Keller," Avery told her automatically.

"Yes, dear," the woman agreed. "I know who you are."

Of course she did. Avery stared at the door like it was a portal to hell. She was being ridiculous. Her life had already been smashed to bits. One meeting wasn't going to change things that much. Maybe she'd get money. Maybe a painting or two. Perhaps her father left a letter for her, something that would explain why—

"They're waiting," the receptionist repeated. "Mr. Damon has to be at the courthouse at eleven."

"Right." Avery straightened her shoulders and moved forward, entering the office as quietly as possible. Not that it mattered. Three sets of eyes turned to her.

Douglas Damon sat behind an enormous mahogany desk, files piled high on the credenza behind him. He was roughly sixty years old, with a meaty build and salt-and-pepper hair. He stood, pulling a pair of reading glasses from his nose. "You must be Avery."

She nodded.

"Have a seat," he told her, indicating the empty chair in front of his desk. Avery had never been sent to the principal's office growing up, but she imagined it felt very much like this moment. Why was she so nervous? She'd done nothing wrong.

Maybe it was the two women glaring at her from where they sat on either side of the unoccupied chair. But why were there two?

She recognized Carrie Reed from her photos on the internet. Based on Avery's research, Niall's legitimate daughter had served as his assistant and the manager of his art gallery here in Magnolia. Carrie was her half sister. It felt odd…even though Avery had always wanted a sibling. She wasn't what she'd pictured, a woman with shoulder-length chestnut hair and a pinched mouth who clearly wanted this meeting as much as Avery did. Had Carrie known about her father's other daughter?

Who was the third woman? Unlike Avery in her stifling suit and Carrie, who wore a flowing, flowery skirt and soft peasant blouse, the petite brunette wasn't dressed up for this meeting. On the contrary, her rumpled T-shirt, jeans and heavy-duty work boots seemed like a thumb of the nose to the formality of Douglas Damon's office. Avery hadn't discovered anything about a third sister but got the impression that Carrie and the other woman weren't complete strangers. So what was going on?

She could feel each of the women throwing some wicked side-eye as she lowered herself into the chair. Her skin itched like it was suddenly a size too small for her body, as if she were shrinking under the weight of the critical stares from these two strangers.

But Avery wasn't about to show weakness. Not now. Not when she'd held her head high through the scandal in San Francisco. Through Tony's wife confronting her in the office, hurling vile accusations. Through the public humiliation of being reprimanded in front of her entire risk assessment department at Pierce and Chambers, the financial firm where she'd been so proud to work. Through the tragedy of what came next.

She kept her gaze fixed on a spot beyond Damon's left shoulder as his words washed over her. Apparently the attorney had been her father's closest friend in addition to his attorney so he'd been named executor of the will and would shepherd the estate through probate. He talked about Reed's accomplishments, his mistakes and regrets and the hope he'd had that his three daughters would come together after his death to preserve his legacy.

Three. Daughters.

Both of these women were her sisters—half sisters. To Avery, who'd grown up alone, the fact that she shared only one parent with each of them hardly counted. Rage swept through her at all the potential withheld from her. Of course, there was no guarantee knowing her father and sisters would have changed anything. But it remained a possibility.

One Niall Reed had stolen from her.

Blood roared in her head as the attorney detailed the terms of the will. It was difficult for Avery to follow along with her emotions threatening to take over. Her focus sharpened when Carrie let out a tiny gasp.

"I get his gallery?" Avery asked, forcing herself to take a steadying breath.

"No," Carrie whispered next to her.

Douglas Damon nodded. "Along with a sizable mortgage. Unfortunately, the house and the commercial buildings both come with a tremendous amount of debt attached. Julie Martindale over at the bank will discuss the particulars, but the colloquial phrase to describe the situation would be 'mortgaged to the hilt.'"

A snort came from Avery's left as the other sister leaned forward. "How about the phrase 'he screwed us'?"

"Meredith, don't," Carrie muttered through clenched teeth.

"I understand this is a shock," Damon said, looking down his nose at the woman called Meredith. "But your father did try to clean up his finances before he passed. In all likelihood, the stress of that is what—"

Avery gripped the arms of the wingback chair as Meredith bolted up and stalked to the window. "I don't give a rat's ass about Niall's stress or the fact that he kicked it." When Carrie drew in a sharp breath, Meredith whirled on her. "Did you know? All these years of playing the town princess, did you know about me?" She jabbed a finger in Avery's direction. "Or her?"

Carrie shook her head, a strand of silky hair falling against her cheek. "Of course not."

"Why should anyone believe you?" Meredith demanded. "His dutiful daughter, staying by his side even when your mother finally got smart enough to cut and run."

"I didn't know," Carrie insisted quietly, twin spots of angry color blooming on her cheeks.

The attorney shifted in his chair and leveled a disapproving glare at Meredith. "Histrionics won't help anyone at this point."

"I don't want the house," Meredith responded, crossing her arms over her chest. "Give me the beach property. It's where I—"

"The terms of the will are clear," Damon interrupted. "Meredith, you inherit the Reed family home. Avery, the gallery and other commercial space he owned downtown. The ranch belongs to Carrie now."

Meredith narrowed her eyes. "Like hell it does."

"Sit down," Damon told the fiery brunette.

"You don't tell me what to do." Meredith's voice cracked on the last word, and she swallowed hard. "I'm out of here. Niall didn't care about me when he was alive. Why should I care about his wishes now that he's gone?"

Before anyone could stop her, Meredith fled the room. The door to the office banged against the wall in her wake.

Damon looked toward Carrie, sympathy and compassion filling his tired gaze. "It's worse than we thought. He owed a lot of money to a lot of people, Carrie."

She gave a shaky nod. "I'll deal with it," she promised. "Give me some time." She rose from her chair and turned to Avery. "I have an appointment right now but will be at the gallery after one. Come by and we'll talk about…next steps."

Then she left, as well. Avery wanted to follow but felt rooted in place. A man she didn't know—her father—had left her his art gallery along with some overmortgaged real estate. She'd never even seen one of his paintings in person. She had two half sisters, who seemed to hate each other in equal measure to their ambivalence toward her. Just when she thought life couldn't get worse, it did.

"We can talk in more detail about the assets and debts

Niall left behind when you've had time to process everything," the attorney said, the words a clear dismissal.

She tucked a strand of hair behind her ear. "I thought I'd be here for a day at the most."

He chuckled. "Niall didn't make things easy—not when he was alive and not now. It will take a while to even begin to sort this out. Welcome to Magnolia."

CHAPTER TWO

AVERY WALKED THROUGH the door of The Reed Gallery later that afternoon, not sure what she expected to find but surprised just the same.

The space was clean and bright, with wide-plank floors and large windows looking out to Magnolia's quiet main street. The walls were painted antique white with simple Craftsman trim around the high doorways. She could smell the scent of a candle burning, and soft music played from speakers built into the ceiling.

Somehow the place still seemed...sad. In his heyday, Niall Reed had been a force of nature and an expert at branding, turning out overtly nostalgic paintings of American life and cloyingly sentimental works of the country's famed landscape. One particular critic had likened him to a sorry mix of Norman Rockwell, Thomas Kinkade and Barney, if the giant children's television dinosaur learned to paint. It had seemed an odd combination but standing in front of a wall of canvases, Avery understood the comparison.

The scene depicted was the beach, maybe one on the North Carolina coast, although the colors and brushstrokes made it appear like something out of a dream. That had been Niall's gift and shtick, depending on the viewpoint of the critic or consumer. A mother and daughter took center stage, holding hands and gazing at each other the way Avery had always wanted her mom to look at her. She resisted the sudden sentimentality squeezing her chest, feeling as if she'd somehow been coerced into the emotion.

"A lot of people get that dismissive curl to their lip when they first see his work."

Avery turned as Carrie entered the open space, hands clasped tightly in front of her. Her prim and proper manner was at odds with the bohemian mode of dressing, and Avery was unable to get a true read on her new half sister. At one time, Avery had prided herself on her ability to assess a person's character, but after the mess she'd made of her life, she no longer trusted her instincts.

"I don't see what's so special," Avery admitted, moving closer to one of the paintings.

"He hadn't done his best work for several years," Carrie answered. "I can show you photos of some of his older pieces, the ones that made him a household name."

"The ones that paid the bills?" Avery asked.

"For a long time, yes." The tight line of Carrie's mouth pursed even further. "I knew he'd made some bad investments but not the extent of the financial risks he'd taken."

"You're not to blame for that." Avery shifted her gaze to study the willowy beauty. Carrie was tall and almost model thin, although it was somewhat difficult to discern her true figure under the shapeless clothes. Her features were classic—wide-set eyes and an upturned nose but Avery got the impression Carrie couldn't see her own beauty.

A strange concept since Avery's mom had long been an advocate for using whatever assets she had at hand to get ahead in life. Avery had been taught to wield her beauty like a blade, slicing through any obstacles to meet her end goal. It was all she'd known until the collateral damage she'd left in her wake became too much.

"I was his assistant, and in more recent years, his manager. He was the artist. My duty was to take care of the rest of his life. I failed."

"Your father's keeper," Avery murmured, finding it difficult to muster the resentment she needed to remain emotionally uninvolved. Carrie already seemed so close to broken. Who was Avery to add to that?

She glanced from her sister to the far wall, on which hung a series of photographs of Niall Reed at different ages. Several of the photos showed him with Carrie, as a baby and then as she grew into a lanky girl with caramel-colored hair down to the middle of her back. Another featured Carrie in a cap and gown, Niall's arm draped over her shoulder as he smiled proudly.

Anger came surging back, like a sudden riptide that pulled her under until she had trouble drawing in a breath. "So we find a buyer for the space and try to recoup some of the losses. Can you recommend a Realtor—"

"No. I won't sell this place. I can't."

"You don't have any say," Avery answered. "The gallery belongs to me."

"He owned the whole block." Carrie's voice held no emotion.

Avery's heart plummeted to her stomach. "Excuse me?"

"All of the buildings on this side of the street." Carrie squeezed shut her eyes for a moment.

"You have rental income, then? Some kind of cash flow?"

"Things have been tough in Magnolia lately," Carrie answered, cringing. "Back in the late nineties, people flocked to the town to see Dad paint. He'd give demonstrations of his technique and held workshops and open houses at the gallery and his studio space next door."

"What does that have to do with your tenants?"

"The town came to rely on the tourism dollars his reputation afforded the local businesses. When people stopped visiting, it impacted that revenue."

"Are you telling me Magnolia was built on one man's popularity?"

"The town has plenty of other things to offer, but it became tied to Dad's legacy. Once that began to falter, so did the town. He felt a great responsibility—"

"Too bad he didn't feel the same sort of responsibility toward his other two daughters."

"Yes, well…" Carrie's blue gaze met Avery's. "He hasn't collected rent for several years."

"What kind of an idiot was your father?" Avery pressed her palm to her forehead.

"He was your father, too," Carrie countered. It was the first time Avery heard any real emotion in her voice. To her shock, Carrie sounded angry, as if she'd been the one slighted in this whole deal.

"He means nothing to me," Avery lied. Niall Reed might be a stranger, but his impact on her life couldn't be denied. "Tell me about the other one. Meredith… What's her last name?"

"Meredith Ventner." Carrie's features went stony. "I didn't know about her, either."

"But you *know* her?"

"We both grew up in Magnolia," Carrie said with a nod. "She's a year younger than me."

"How old are you?"

"Twenty-eight."

Avery sucked in a breath. "I turn thirty next month. I'm the oldest."

A few beats of silence filled the space as they each absorbed that added detail to their new reality.

"Do you have brothers and sisters?" Carrie asked, then frowned. "I mean, besides Meredith and me."

Avery shook her head.

"Me neither. Meredith is the youngest of three. She has two older brothers."

"And now two older sisters."

"She'll never claim us as family. She likes being angry too much."

"From where I'm standing, she has good reason. We both do."

"We *all* do," Carrie said. "He never gave any hint that I wasn't his only child."

"Did your mom know?" Avery couldn't help her curiosity.

Carrie wrapped her arms more tightly around her waist. "I'm not sure. She and I haven't spoken in a while."

Avery felt her mouth drop open. Her relationship with her mother was tumultuous, but she'd never gone more than a few days without a call or text from Melissa Keller.

"When she divorced my…" Carrie cleared her throat. "Our father," she amended, "my mom gave me an ultimatum. She thought he was too controlling of both of us and wanted me to leave with her."

"But you stayed?"

Carrie shrugged. "He needed me."

"What about now?"

Another shrug, and that brief lift and lowering of Carrie's shoulder seemed weighted with far more than indecision about calling her mother. Why had Avery thought this trip to Magnolia would be simple?

"I've made another appointment with Douglas Damon for tomorrow and left a message for the banker he referred to in the meeting."

"Julie Martindale," Carrie supplied, scrunching up her nose when Avery narrowed her eyes. "It's a small town."

"Right."

"How long do you plan to stay?"

"Mr. Damon said it could take a while to settle things. I'm hoping by *a while* he means a week or two."

Carrie's large eyes widened further. "You'll be here the whole time?"

"Is that a problem?" Avery felt her hackles rise. Not that she expected a warm welcome, but she wasn't ready to be run out of town so soon.

"No. I just assumed you had a life to return to."

"I…I mean… Of course I have a life." Avery willed away the color she felt rising to her cheeks. "But I can take some time away from it. You don't know what it was like to grow up thinking your father was a nameless one-night stand. I might hate Niall Reed for not claiming me, but it doesn't change the fact that he's part of who I am."

"You could come by his house," Carrie offered, then clasped a hand to her mouth. "Meredith's house now, although it still doesn't make any sense that he left it to her."

"You lived with your dad?"

Carrie let out a delicate snort. "Not for a few years. I've been staying there since he died while I work on cleaning it out. Dad became a bit of a pack rat recently. Do you need a place to stay?"

"Yes," Avery admitted, "but it isn't going to be at Niall's house. That's too weird for me right now."

"I can give you the keys to my apartment. It's a carriage house, actually. I still have my stuff there, but you can use it while you're in town."

"Why would you do that? You don't even know me."

"You're my sister," Carrie said simply.

Oh.

Unfamiliar emotion clogged Avery's throat. "That's a concept that will take some getting used to, I suppose."

"Give me your phone and I'll put the address into it. I don't ever lock the place. Crime isn't really an issue in Magnolia."

Avery automatically pulled the phone from her purse but hesitated before handing it to Carrie.

"If that's still too much," Carrie told her, "I can recommend a couple of hotels nearby."

An image of the statement from Avery's dwindling bank account filled her mind. "I appreciate you letting me stay there," she said as she gave the other woman— her sister—the phone.

"VIOLET, I KNOW you're in here."

Grayson Atwell glanced around the quiet carriage house at the back of his property as he entered later that evening.

"I'm not," a tiny voice called out from the far side of the couch.

Gray ran a hand through his hair and threw a longing glance at the refrigerator sitting in the small kitchenette. Carrie kept it stocked with his favorite brand of beer, and he could use one right now.

His shift had been hectic, but he'd agreed to a few hours of overtime because his ex-wife was supposed to pick up their daughter from school for an overnight at her house. Stacy hadn't shown, and his mom had stayed with Violet until he'd found someone to cover the rest of his shift.

True to form, Stacy hadn't answered any of his calls or returned his messages demanding to know what the hell she was thinking flaking out on their five-year-old daughter. He'd finally gotten a terse text from her as he pulled into the driveway minutes earlier. She'd had an emergency at the office.

He didn't bother to wonder what constituted an emergency for a cosmetic dermatologist. This wasn't the first time she'd made plans with Violet only to cancel at the last minute or not show at all. It was the clichéd trauma of children from divorced families everywhere, and it burned like acid in his gut that his daughter had to deal with it.

His mom meant well but had the unfortunate—if understandable—habit of talking trash about his ex to Violet. Gray knew his daughter was hurt by her mother's callous treatment, but she was still loyal to her mom. Nana's reminders of how much Stacy didn't care only hurt her more.

Violet often retreated to the carriage house behind the two-story Victorian he'd bought after the divorce.

Carrie Reed, his easygoing tenant, always made the girl feel better. From baking cookies to painting nails, Carrie had an effortless way of distracting Violet from the pain of her mother's indifference.

But Carrie had been staying at her childhood home for the past week, so Gray was on his own with no domestic or personal beauty skills to help ease the sting of Stacy's latest stunt.

He came around the edge of the sofa and lowered himself to the carpet next to Violet. "Nana said you wouldn't eat dinner tonight."

"She put broccoli in the mac 'n' cheese," Violet told him, as if that explained everything. Which it kind of did.

"Yuck."

"Did she do that when you were little?"

"Probably," Gray admitted. "Your nana was always trying to get Uncle Chase and me to eat healthier. Just so you know, she does it because she loves you."

His heart pinched as the girl's chin trembled. "Why doesn't Mommy love me?"

"She does, sweetie." He opened his arms and she climbed in, burying her face against the front of his T-shirt. "Your mom loves you so much, but you know how busy she gets at work. It doesn't have anything to do with you."

A statement both true and not. Stacy was selfish to the point of narcissism, which was completely out of his and his daughter's control. But that didn't mean a five-year-old could or would understand. To Violet, it felt like a rejection and Gray hated his ex-wife for it.

"She was going to fancy braid my hair tomorrow."

Violet sniffed. "Margo's mommy can do a Dutch braid, and I told her mine could braid even better."

"Better than a Dutch braid?" Gray whistled appreciatively even though he had no idea what a Dutch braid was. His mom had raised two boys and still sported the same low-maintenance bob from his childhood. He couldn't imagine she'd be any help. "That's a tall order. Maybe I can try in the morning?"

Violet lifted her head and gazed up at him with those melted chocolate eyes. "Daddy, you're a terrible braider." She patted his cheek and the soft touch practically undid him. If it took an entire night of watching YouTube videos, he'd learn to braid. "When is Carrie coming back?"

He had no doubt his neighbor could have helped with the hair dilemma, although he hated relying on her. He'd known Carrie since kindergarten, and there had never been a spark of attraction on either of their parts in all these years. She was sweet and generous with Violet because it was her nature, but he didn't want to take advantage. Carrie already had plenty of that in her life.

"I don't think—"

His answer was interrupted by the sound of the carriage house's door opening.

"Carrie!" his daughter shouted and jumped up from his lap. "Who are you?" she demanded a moment later, her feathery brows furrowing.

"Who are *you*?" a feminine voice answered, somehow familiar to Gray but definitely not Carrie.

He quickly straightened and felt his jaw go slack at the sight of the woman glaring at him from inside the front door. The same woman who'd given him hell at the gas station this morning.

Glancing from her face to the pocket-sized can of pepper spray she'd pulled from her purse, Gray tugged Violet closer to his side. "You're not Carrie," he said and mentally congratulated himself for his mastery of the obvious.

"But this is *her* place," she answered. "What are you doing here?"

"My daddy owns this house," Violet said, her jaw jutting forward. "Carrie is our friend. You can't be here."

Gray stifled a groan. Violet usually redirected her anger toward Stacy at Gray or his mother, and they were both adept at defusing the girl's temper. Apparently, it was now transferring to this stranger, and by the way her sea-glass-blue eyes narrowed, she wasn't in the mood to be so patient.

"There's clearly been a misunderstanding," he said, lifting his arms, palms out.

"Are you Carrie's landlord?" the woman demanded.

"I am."

"And her boyfriend?"

He shook his head. "Not at all."

She gave a sharp laugh as if she didn't believe him, and he wasn't sure why that bothered him so much. "Then get out."

"*You* get out," Violet shot back. "Carrie lives here. Not you."

"I don't owe you an explanation, pipsqueak…" The woman moved forward, yanking an oversized suitcase across the threshold. "But Carrie said I could stay here."

"You can't," Violet insisted, her voice shaky. "Carrie is coming back."

"Not tonight," the woman said.

"Violet, let's go back to the house. It's time for your bath."

"Kick her out, Daddy," the girl pleaded, tugging on his hand. "She shouldn't be here. She doesn't belong."

"Smartest thing anyone has said all day," the woman muttered.

Gray pressed two fingers to his suddenly pounding head. He lifted Violet into his arms. "This *nice* lady must be Carrie's friend," he told the girl. "That means she's our friend, too."

"I most certainly am *not* your friend," the woman said, her tone as sharp and decisive as it had been earlier. "I'm not Carrie's friend, either."

"See, Daddy. I told you. She's—"

"I'm her sister," the woman clarified, and the shock on Violet's face reflected his own surprise. The news wasn't exactly a bombshell. Carrie didn't share many details of her life, but he'd heard the rumors swirling around town about Niall's will. He knew Meredith Ventner had been outed as one of the eccentric artist's previously unknown daughters. He'd heard the news had come as a surprise to Meredith but not her former marine father, Carl.

It explained this woman's sudden appearance in Magnolia. She didn't look the type for a road trip to a sleepy Southern town. Even after what had to be a trying day, with her suit rumpled and wisps of golden blond hair escaping her low ponytail, her cool beauty and obvious poise weren't diminished in the least.

She looked like someone who would be friends with his ex-wife, definitely not a mark in her favor. The fact that she and Violet were currently engaged in a stare down didn't speak well of her, either, although his first instinct was to give her a break given her current circumstances.

As stony as she appeared, he sensed she was holding on to her composure by a thin thread. He could appreciate a good defensive mechanism, even when aimed in his direction. But he'd always been too soft when it came to women.

"If you need anything," he said, moving toward the cozy guesthouse's front door, "just holler."

She arched a brow. "I don't 'holler.'"

His gaze slammed into hers as a dozen innuendoes crowded his mind. All of them revolved around what he would do to provoke her to lose control enough to shout—preferably his name in the throes of passion. A blush stained the woman's cheeks—hell, he didn't even know her name—like she could read every one of his inappropriate thoughts.

Why did she have this effect on him? He hadn't been on a single date since his divorce, let alone had time for any sort of sexual dalliances. Violet was his world and every choice he made was to protect her. He didn't care about what he might be missing when it came to women.

Especially not with a woman who had taken an immediate aversion to him.

"Then have a good night," he told her, and pressed a hand to his daughter's thin back as he walked out the door.

CHAPTER THREE

AVERY AWOKE TO the sound of chattering, giggling voices. She glanced at the bedroom's open window, wondering if some middle-school social club was holding a meeting in front of the carriage house.

Although the house had central cooling, she'd cracked the window sometime in the middle of the night when she couldn't sleep. Eventually, the hum of crickets from the woods bordering the property and the scent of the fresh air calmed her enough to get a few hours of rest.

Rubbing sleep from her eyes, she walked to the window, ready to call down a scathing rebuke to the group of girls. One lone child sat at the picnic table situated in the grass between the main house and her place. Violet, whose hostile welcome last night had felt somehow comforting.

Kids had never really liked Avery. On a day when Avery's world had been turned even more upside down than she thought possible, Violet's animosity had reassured her she hadn't dropped into some strange alternate universe.

The girl focused on the iPad propped in front of her as she reached two twig-like arms around the back of her head, fingers tugging at her long, dark hair.

Another round of giggles drifted up from whatever

video was playing. Her far too attractive firefighter daddy needed to buy his daughter a pair of headphones.

The girl let out a frustrated cry and slammed the brush she held against the iPad, sending it hurtling off the picnic table and onto the grass.

Avery sighed, lifting her gaze toward the painted Victorian house and wondering where the girl's dad was at the moment. And what about a mom? She hated that her stomach clenched at the thought of Carrie's landlord with another woman. What did she care about her sexy neighbor? He was a complication her already complicated life didn't need.

She tugged on the hem of the tank she'd worn to bed and padded downstairs. Carrie had decorated the small house with overstuffed furniture, shelves filled with all sorts of books and small knickknacks, and a variety of colorful art posters hanging on the walls. Avery was somewhat surprised none of Niall's paintings hung in the house. If she hadn't known it for a fact, she never would have guessed that the daughter of the famous artist lived here.

The coffeepot on the counter called her name, but she bypassed the kitchen and let herself out the door, walking across the thick lawn. It was only seven thirty, but already the muggy air and bright sun hinted at the record-breaking summer heat forecasted for the day.

"iPads don't grow on trees," she said, bending to pick up the device from the ground before sliding onto the bench across from Violet.

The girl's mouth took on a mulish pout. "I hate my hair," she whispered.

"We could cut it off," Avery offered conversationally. "I bet you'd be cute with it shaped around your ears. There're probably scissors in Carrie's place. If you come with me—"

"You're not cutting it," the girl interrupted, sounding scandalized. "I'll look like a boy."

"You could never look like a boy," Avery told her. It was true. Avery might not like kids much, but she could appreciate that Violet had won the genetic lottery. Her skin was creamy against her rich brown hair, her dark eyes framed by long lashes—the kind grown women used copious amounts of mascara to achieve. The girl's father had the same lashes.

"Why are you staying at Carrie's?" Violet demanded.

"I'm in town visiting and she offered it to me."

"What's your name?"

"Avery."

The girl studied her for a long moment. "I don't like you."

"I can live with that," Avery answered, nodding.

They sat in silence for several moments until Avery finally reached out and tapped a finger against the iPad's screen. "Why are you watching out here? Is it a show your dad won't let you see?"

Violet shook her head. "It wasn't a show. I was learning how to braid my hair. Margo always has her hair done at school, and I told her I was going to do something real good with mine. I was s'posed to stay at Mommy's last night. She forgot about me. Daddy thinks he can do hair, but he's bad." The girl picked up the iPad and climbed off the picnic bench. "I didn't want him to get hurty feelings so I tried to learn. I'm bad, too."

She turned and walked away, and Avery felt an unfamiliar flood of warmth for the girl. Avery knew all about trying to make do on her own and failing miserably, but that didn't explain the urge to wrap her arms around Violet's bony shoulders and pull her close. Avery didn't do that kind of affection. One day in Magnolia was already messing with her head.

"I can braid hair," she called as the girl started up the steps to the main house.

Violet returned to the picnic table. "I just told you I don't like you," she said, clutching the iPad to her chest. "Why would you do my hair?"

"Your friend Margo sounds like a real brat," Avery answered, earning the barest hint of a smile from the girl.

"You aren't supposed to call kids brats."

Avery also wasn't supposed to fall in love with a married man and get blamed for tearing his family apart and his son ending up in the hospital. She wasn't proud of it, but name-calling a kindergartner was low on her list of no-nos. Besides, based on Violet's reaction, this Margo seemed to be getting a jump on her mean-girl status. Avery had never been able to tolerate a mean girl. "Do you want your hair done or not?"

"Can you do a Dutch braid?" Violet walked around the picnic table and positioned herself in front of Avery.

"How about crisscross Dutch?"

The girl sucked in a breath and gave a small squeal of delight. "Yes," she breathed.

Avery cocked a brow.

"Yes, please," Violet amended. She handed over the brush and turned so that Avery could access her long hair.

Avery smiled as she began to braid, a sense of contentment filling her for the first time in months.

"AVERY BRAIDED MY HAIR, Daddy."

Gray blinked at the excitement in his daughter's voice. Normally it took at least a day or two for her mood to rebound after being disappointed by her mother.

He'd gotten dressed in jeans and a UNC T-shirt after his shower, panic seizing him when Violet didn't answer his calls. At five years old, she was fine unsupervised for a few minutes, but he was on constant alert for anything that could be perceived by a court as him not being a fit parent. Misplacing his kid would definitely qualify.

Then he'd glanced out the window above the kitchen sink to see her with Carrie's newfound sister. The woman hadn't seemed like a fan of kids last night, or at least of Violet, so he didn't exactly trust her to be alone with his daughter.

He'd rushed out the back door, both females turning as the screen slammed. But instead of having to step in as mediator the way he'd expected, Violet bounded over to him with a huge grin on her adorable face.

"It's a crisscross Dutch," she reported, spinning so she was facing away from him. "She's so good at braids." He'd stayed awake until midnight and then set his alarm for six to watch braiding tutorial videos, ineptly practicing on Violet's American Girl doll. It would have taken years for him to get proficient enough to create the intricate style she sported.

"I love it," he told her, lifting his gaze from the back of her head to the woman—Avery—now coming around the edge of the picnic table. Gray felt like he'd been clubbed in the head with a steel pipe. She wore a pair of loose boxer shorts and a thin tank top, her blond hair falling over bare shoulders. Yesterday she'd been all about stuffy attitude and a prim sort of beauty, even after a day in the North Carolina heat had taken its toll.

But casual and unadorned, she was beyond gorgeous, despite it being an aspect of herself she clearly wasn't comfortable sharing. She wrapped one arm across her chest and tugged on the bottom of the shorts with her free hand, like she wanted to hide from his gaze.

"Thanks," he mouthed, and she responded with the barest hint of a nod.

"She thinks kids are useless and smelly," his daughter reported, lifting one braid and smiling with satisfaction as she examined it. "She told me."

He lifted a brow. "Really?"

"I didn't say those exact words." Avery rolled her eyes. "But you can't blame me for being crusty. Someone woke me up with the lack of iPad volume control. I haven't even had a cup of coffee."

"Daddy makes coffee with the timer the night before. Like he does my lunch." Violet turned to her. "I still don't like you, but you can come in and get a cup since you do such good braids."

"What a generous invitation," Avery muttered.

"Violet, you can't tell people you don't like them." He crouched down and cupped his daughter's soft cheeks in his palms. "We've talked about manners."

"Avery doesn't care." Violet shifted to look over her shoulder. "Do you?"

"Nope," Avery admitted.

Gray patted her cheek. "I expect you to be polite."

"I said thank you and told her she could drink your coffee," his daughter replied. "I have to get dressed for school. Margo is going to be so jealous of my crisscross."

He straightened as she skipped toward the house.

"I don't know what your deal is with kids," he told Avery. "But you made her whole morning and got me off the hook."

"Braiding is easy."

"Tell that to the American Girl doll with knots in her hair after a night with me."

"You're into sleeping with dolls?" Avery asked, deadpan. "That's a super creepy fetish."

He chuckled at her dry humor, and the sound felt rusty in his throat. "The offer for coffee was real. I can even throw in a banana nut muffin to sweeten the deal. My mom brought them over yesterday."

It was obvious she wanted to refuse, but then she nodded, making Gray feel like he'd won some sort of neighbor lottery. "Banana nut is my favorite," she said as they walked toward his house, like she wanted him to understand her acceptance had nothing to do with him.

Fine.

"I'm Gray Atwell, by the way." He held the screen open with one hand and offered her his other.

"Avery Keller," she murmured but moved into the house without shaking his hand.

"You and Carrie are sisters?"

"Half sisters."

"She's a good person." He moved toward the cabinets and took out two mugs. "Always has been. The whole town loves Carrie. We went to school together from kindergarten through high school graduation."

"But you two aren't dating?"

He frowned as he poured the coffee, not quite understanding her preoccupation with his and Carrie's relationship. "We've always been friends, but never anything more."

"Did you know Niall?"

He handed her a mug and grabbed the container of muffins his mom had left. "Sure. Magnolia's a tight-knit community and Niall was our most famous resident, even after his art fell out of favor. He gave a lot back to the town during the height of his fame. He funded the revamping of the main park and a walking trail along Indian Creek, which runs through downtown."

"A real stand-up guy." Avery grabbed a muffin. "He turns himself into a local hero while ignoring the fact that he has two extra daughters, one of whom grew up in Magnolia."

"You have a point." Gray massaged a hand over his neck. "He left all three of you in a bad position."

"Meredith didn't seem to be in any hurry to create long-lasting family ties."

"Are you?" He took a drink of coffee as she pondered her answer. It would be better if she said no. Better for him anyway. He wasn't sure where this strange connection he felt toward her came from, but he knew enough at this point not to trust it.

She might be beautifully rumpled at the moment, but he guessed that yesterday's cool perfection swept closer to the truth of Avery Keller. He'd been there and done that with a sophisticated woman out of his blue-collar league. It had left him with a broken heart and a daughter to raise almost exclusively on his own.

"We need to work out some things with Niall's assets."

Gray nodded. "He owned a big chunk of down-town."

"I own that chunk now," she revealed, biting down on her full lower lip. "But his finances are in bad shape according to the attorney."

"And Magnolia is long past its heyday," he added. "But why you and not Carrie?"

"You think she's more entitled?"

"To the gallery?" He inclined his head. "She's dedicated most of her adult life to her father's legacy, completely giving up her own art along the way."

Avery's blue eyes widened. "Carrie's an artist?"

"She was back in high school, but I don't think Niall approved. Probably because she was more talented than him."

He watched her mull over that information and regretted that he'd shared it. If Avery had as much in common with his ex-wife as he suspected from her manner, she'd use any detail she could gather to her own advantage.

"You'll figure it out," he said, grabbing Violet's lunch box from the refrigerator. She'd be down any minute and ready to head out to show off her new braids.

"Why did Violet's mother stand her up last night?" Avery asked softly.

"She was busy," he mumbled, disgust at his ex's maternal apathy squirming along his skin like a thousand cockroaches. Making excuses for Stacy was becoming second nature. "She's a doctor and had a patient with an emergency."

"What kind of doctor?"

"A cosmetic dermatologist."

"Emergency Botox?" she asked with a sniff.

Despite his anger, Gray chuckled. "Maybe. She's a real piece of work."

"How long have you been divorced?"

"Over a year." He placed his mug on the counter when he felt his fingers begin to shake. "But things were off track longer than that. My fault. Stacy didn't want…" He broke off, shook his head. "It doesn't matter now and you probably don't care about the details of my broken marriage."

Her chest rose and fell as if she was having trouble catching her breath. When her mouth opened, he wanted her to contradict him—to tell him that she did care. Stupid on his part. He'd been on his own too long if he had to imagine a bond with a woman who wasn't in town under the best of circumstances. Not to mention that she didn't seem to like kids and Violet was the most important thing in his world.

She set down her mug and flashed the sorriest excuse for a smile he'd ever seen. "Not really," she said airily. "But thanks for the coffee. I'm not sure how long I'll be staying here but try to keep your kid out of the carriage house while I'm around. Unlike my sister, I'm not sweet or the type to be universally loved."

No doubt, Gray thought as he nodded. He should have been relieved by her caustic words. Her bad attitude would make it easy to keep his distance. But, damn, if he didn't hate watching her walk away.

CHAPTER FOUR

AVERY PULLED INTO the driveway of the enormous, almost antebellum-style house, checking the Fig Street address Carrie had given to her one more time.

She wasn't sure what she'd expected of Niall Reed's home, but this structure seemed like a smaller, slightly more cared-for cousin of the famous Grey Gardens mansion. Vines trailed around the balusters of the front porch and the yard was badly in need of mowing. The stately home was painted a pale cream, or perhaps the color would be more aptly described as dingy white.

The bones of the house were still impressive, with columns framing the porch and black shutters flanking the tall windows. She could imagine the house had once been the jewel of the town. From what she was coming to understand about her biological father, she had no doubt he reveled in what the house communicated about his status in the community.

This was where Carrie had been raised. Jealousy spiked in Avery, even though she knew Niall's one legitimate daughter was as much of a victim as her and Meredith. That was difficult to remember as she stepped into the quiet of this picturesque street.

Growing up in a sterile condo in downtown San Francisco, Avery had always wished for a yard and trees to climb. She'd imagined having a swing hanging from a hundred-year-old tree branch, much like the one sway-ing slightly in the breeze in the center of the yard.

Her father had owned her dream house, or close to it. Granted, the style was a bit lord-of-the-manor for her taste, as well as something of a cliché, since the home had been built atop a gently sloping hill. That put it higher than the other houses in the neighborhood, as if Niall had been the king of everyone around him. She could imagine that fit well with his image of himself.

Had she gotten her taste for traditional style and overly romanticized daydreams from her father? As a kid, it seemed normal that she'd fantasize about mani-cured lawns and white picket fences. Weren't those the stuff of the American dream? Not that Avery's child-hood had lacked any of the necessities.

Her mother worked long hours as a neurosurgeon, pushing to raise the glass ceiling at her hospital, and providing Avery with a world-class education, the best nannies money could hire and a million-dollar view of San Francisco Bay. But there had been no running through backyard sprinklers or neighborhood sledding hills. Avery hadn't been allowed to have friends over who might drip juice on the impeccable white carpet her mother favored. Everything had been perfect and pristine, and all the while Avery had longed for some-thing she'd never known was within reach. All the while Carrie had been given this bucolic childhood. It was so damn unfair.

Avery thought of what Gray had let slip about Car-rie giving up her art to take care of Niall. She didn't want to feel any sympathy for her sister. Carrie had lost a hobby. Avery felt like she'd been robbed of ev-erything.

Now she'd been given a block of failing businesses in this sleepy town, the home she'd always dreamed of still not part of her reality.

It would be comical if it wasn't so pathetic.

She moved toward the front door, careful of the flagstone walkway that had seen better days. The cracked pieces of stone had grown uneven as tree roots infringed on their path. No one answered when she rang the doorbell, and then she heard a grunt and a crash from the back of the house.

If the front of the house was mildly neglected, the back upped the ante to almost hoarder levels. Heaps of scrap metal and piles of decaying wooden pallets littered the lawn. She could see that the yard might have once been lovely. Tall maple trees canopied the edges and a wrought-iron fence had been erected around one section that looked like an overgrown garden.

How could Niall have let this beautiful property fall to ruin?

A scraping sound interrupted her musings, and she turned to see Carrie about ten feet away, balanced precariously on the highest rung of a ladder—the rung that Avery knew the instructions advised not to use.

Carrie had on denim shorts, a thin T-shirt and beat-up sneakers, her hair pulled into a high bun on her head. She wore thick leatherwork gloves and made low-throated grunts of effort as she scraped a handheld shovel along the house's gutter, flipping hunks of decaying leaves and debris onto the cobblestone porch below.

"Are you trying to break your neck?" Avery called conversationally when Carrie paused in her heaving.

Her new half sister gave a little shout of shock, and

Avery rushed forward when it looked like Carrie might lose her footing.

By the time Avery got to the ladder, Carrie had righted herself and was climbing down. "Are you trying to kill me?" she asked when she got to the ground, rounding on Avery.

"No way." Avery held up her hands, palms out. "I don't want to deal with Niall's mess on my own."

"Then maybe don't sneak up on a person." Carrie wiped a hand across her forehead. She was covered in flecks of dirt and who knew what else.

"What are you doing anyway?"

"Cleaning the gutters. What does it look like?"

Avery gestured to the cluttered backyard. "This place is the second coming of the *Sanford and Son* junkyard. Why bother with the gutters? It's like focusing on a splinter in your toe when your leg is broken."

Carrie frowned. "Who are Sanford and his son? Should I know them?"

"Never mind." Avery huffed out a laugh. "I watched too many reruns as a kid."

"Dad wouldn't let us have a television," Carrie told her, peeling off the leather gloves. "He wondered why I always wanted to go to my friends' houses and not have them here."

"Once again I feel the need to mention…" Avery inclined her head toward the weed-infested lawn. "You're telling me the lack of TV was your biggest deterrent to having people over?"

Carrie followed her gaze and sighed. "It wasn't like this back then. The yard was beautiful. My mom loved to garden, and she was OCD in her cleaning. It was another thing that drove her crazy about Dad. He was a bit of a slob."

"I think the word you're looking for is *hoarder*."

"That happened more recently," Carrie said quietly. "I moved out five years ago and basically stopped coming to the house. I didn't realize how bad it had gotten."

"The neighbors didn't complain?"

"I'm sure they talked about him and his collections, as he liked to call them. No one would say anything to his face. Dad still wielded a lot of power around here, and he wasn't opposed to making life difficult for someone who got on his bad side."

"Such an utterly charming man."

"Yes, when he wanted to be," Carrie said, purposely ignoring Avery's sarcasm. "What are you doing here?"

"I thought I'd check out the house."

"What happened to it being weird?" Judgment laced Carrie's soft tone.

"I'm not moving in," Avery said, not bothering to hide her defensiveness. "But I figure we need to take stock of all the assets before the meeting at the bank. It will help if I know what kind of work needs to be done on each property."

"The house doesn't belong to you," Carrie countered, brushing at the front of her T-shirt.

"I get that." Avery tried to imbue her tone with an equal mix of patience and empathy. "I thought I could spearhead the effort to sell."

"What if Meredith doesn't want to sell the house?"

"Why wouldn't she? She doesn't seem to want anything to do with our new sisterly connection."

"She wants the ranch, which belongs to me now.

Maybe I'll ask her to trade the house for the land out by the beach."

"So it's a ranch, or is it beach property?" Avery asked.

"Both." Carrie placed the gloves on one of the rungs of the ladder. "There are photos of Last Acre in the house. You might as well come in since you're here, but I'll warn you it's not pretty."

"Based on the backyard, I don't expect it to be."

Carrie arched a delicate brow. "It's worse than you think."

Before Avery could answer, her sister moved past her toward a set of French doors at the far end of the patio, under an awning attached to the house that, like most everything else belonging to Niall Reed, had seen better days.

She noticed that heavy curtains covered every window on the ground floor, blocking the view into the house.

"Was Niall a vampire, as well?" She lifted her sunglasses to the top of her head as she entered the back door.

"Of course not. Don't move forward until I get a light turned on."

"Then why is it so dark?" She squinted as her eyes tried to adjust to the difference between the glaring sun outside and the gloomy interior.

"Less overwhelming that way. Ready?"

A chandelier flicked on overhead, and Avery gasped. "What happened here?" she whispered.

"I told you I hadn't been to the house in years. Dad and I argued, and it was easier for both of us to see each other at the gallery or my place." Carrie's voice was apologetic, as if the mess that surrounded them was her fault. "He'd always been a pack rat. Things got out of hand."

"You think?" Avery shook her head. It was like she'd walked into an episode of a hoarding show on cable television. Newspapers and old magazines were piled in four-foot-high stacks all around the room, which looked like it had functioned as a den at one time. In addition to the piles of paper, there were art supplies, old easels and a variety of antiques jumbled on every available surface.

A slightly hysterical laugh burst from Carrie, and she clasped a hand over her mouth. "I know it's silly, but that's why I'm working on the gutters. The rest of this is too overwhelming. I tried to start in the dining room the morning after he died, but hours later it was still so full of stuff."

"You need to call the junk people." Avery walked forward carefully. A narrow path had been carved out amid the hoard. It felt like walking through a cave, only instead of the walls being formed by rocks they were made from paper and miscellaneous household items.

"I can't." Carrie shook her head. "First, it would kill Dad for everyone to know this is what his life had come to at the end. I don't expect you to understand, but he was a proud man."

"It's difficult to kill someone who's already dead," Avery couldn't help but point out.

"Besides," Carrie continued as if Avery hadn't spoken, "I've found journal entries and sketches tucked into every pile I went through. Those need to be saved and preserved."

"Why?" Avery reached out to run her fingers along the edge of a stack of decades-old *Life* magazines. Suddenly her mother's antiseptically clean condo didn't seem so awful. Carrie claimed Niall had only developed this problem recently, but he'd probably always been a hoarder at heart. Maybe her half sister hadn't lived the charmed life Avery wanted to resent her for after all.

"His work was important. It might not have been appreciated during his lifetime, but Niall Reed's legacy will endure."

"I never met the guy," Avery said softly, "but I can imagine those words coming out of his mouth."

Carrie's nostrils flared and she turned and disappeared into the next room. Avery followed her into the kitchen. At least that room was somewhat clean. Vitamin bottles of all shapes and sizes littered the counter, but there were no dirty dishes filling the sink or rotting food left out to draw bugs.

"They aren't his words." Carrie pulled two glasses from the cabinet. The ice maker in the refrigerator scraped for several seconds before dispensing cubes into first one and then the other. "No one knows more about his art than me. I can tell you he'll be remembered."

"Great," Avery agreed. "Maybe his art will increase in value posthumously, and we'll be able to afford to fix up the place before we sell."

"I'm not selling." Carrie handed her a glass of water with a little more force than necessary.

"It's not up to you."

"Or you," her sister shot back. "You don't know anything about him or this place. Or me."

The long sip of water Avery took felt cool on her throat. Cool and clean, a contrast to the heavy weight of this house. "I'm working on that." She tipped her glass in Carrie's direction. "I heard you were an artist."

"Who told you that?"

"Is it true that your dad—our dad—discouraged you because you had too much talent?"

Carrie barked out a laugh. "You're a real piece of work. You come careening into town with a massive chip on your shoulders, and suddenly you want to know everything."

"I want to know about *you*." The words were as much of a shock to Avery as they seemed to be for Carrie. She *did* want to know. This place—her history—was like a puzzle she couldn't quite piece together. She didn't want to believe it had anything to do with the yearning to belong that had always been her darkest secret. If Niall hadn't wanted to acknowledge all three of his daughters when he was alive, why had he thrown them together in this way as part of his will?

"I took art classes in high school," Carrie said, wiping an invisible crumb from the counter. "Like lots of other kids. There was nothing special about me."

Avery knew the other woman was lying but didn't push the subject. There was plenty of time for that. Time. The concept felt unfamiliar in Magnolia. In her old life, Avery stalked time like a ruthless predator, always trying to get the upper hand. Work more. Work harder. Prove that she deserved the success that came her way.

"If you say so. Tell me about the beach ranch and why it's so special to Meredith."

Carrie closed her eyes for a moment, pain shifting across her features like the waning light of afternoon making its way across the grass.

Avery started to take a step forward before stopping herself. "What's wrong?"

"It must have been horrible not to know who your father was," she said after a moment. "I can't imagine why Niall and your mother kept that from you."

Avery's mouth thinned. It was one thing to offer sympathy but quite another to accept it.

"Meredith grew up here. She knew Niall. Her family hated him." She shook her head, a strand of loose hair falling across her cheek. "I never understood why, but now I get it. Her dad must have known the whole time."

"He never confronted Niall?"

Carrie shrugged. "I don't know, but it's complicated and the house at the beach is part of that."

"How?"

"The property sits on twenty acres of waterfront property. The Ventners owned it for generations."

"That's Meredith's last name," Avery murmured.

"It had been her father's family ranch." Carrie shook her head. "The man she knew as her father. Carl is a former marine. He had some issues with PTSD after the Gulf War. Meredith has two older brothers, and everyone knew things were rough for the family. When her parents divorced, the mom moved to Florida but left the kids with Carl. Dad bought the ranch from Meredith's grandma before she died. Carl didn't know about the sale until after it went through. He was livid because he'd expected to inherit. But his mother put the money in a trust for the kids' college. Meredith's brothers, who were a few years older, left Magnolia and haven't returned."

"So she was raised by a dad who wasn't really her dad?"

Carrie drew in a breath. "Carl eventually cleaned up his act. He owns a garage and auto parts store in town. Meredith was really into animals. She became a vet tech and works for the local animal hospital. A couple of years ago, she came to my dad—her dad—wanting to lease the property out by the beach for an animal rescue organization."

"She didn't know she was asking her biological father to lease her the house that had belonged to the family of the father who raised her?"

"No." Carrie shook her head. "Looking at it from this side of knowledge, I wonder what Niall was thinking. It's kind of…"

"Sick and twisted," Avery supplied.

"Exactly."

Neither said anything for several moments. They stood in the silence of the kitchen, dust motes dancing across the sunlight that filtered in from the window above the sink. It wasn't too late, Avery mused. She could still walk away. Even though she had nothing to return to, surely starting over someplace else would be easier than slogging her way through the family drama that was certain to ensue in the wake of Niall's death.

She'd been furious with her mom for keeping this secret. Now it occurred to her that, for once, Melissa might have acted with Avery's best interest at heart. Probably unintentional but the result was the same.

Then she noticed a single tear track down Carrie's smooth cheek. Her sister. Despite everything else, she yearned for a connection. For a family. Carrie and Meredith shared her DNA, and she couldn't turn her back on that.

"Can I see the rest of the place?" she asked. "Even if

you can convince us not to sell, it's going to take a ton of work to clean out the house."

Carrie swallowed and flashed a grateful smile. "Sure. The upstairs isn't quite as bad as down here."

Not quite, but close. A cloying sense of frustration grew heavier on Avery's shoulders as Carrie gave her the tour. Furniture, knickknacks and stacks of newspapers were crammed in every room.

"Why did he buy all this stuff?"

"I recognize some pieces from his more recent paintings," Carrie told her. "I'm guessing he was looking for inspiration in the antiques or reminders of a time in his life that felt happier. We'll need to get Meredith here, whether she likes it or not. It all belongs to her in theory."

"And I thought I got the raw end of the deal with the tenants who pay no rent."

Carrie started down the steps again, but Avery paused at the top. "Is this an attic?" She placed her hand on the antique brass knob of the three-panel door.

"Don't go up there," Carrie snapped, the sharp edge of her tone a surprise.

Avery lifted a brow in question.

"It's just storage," her sister explained quickly. "There's nothing but junk, and the floor isn't stable in a few areas. Part of the roof was destroyed by a storm a few years back. There's water damage that hasn't been fixed."

"Why don't I believe you?" Avery glanced between Carrie and the closed door but didn't take her hand off the knob. "Is that where you keep the art you don't want to talk about?"

"I told you it's storage space," Carrie said, trying and failing to sound nonchalant. "Seriously, it's hotter than

Hades. I need to have a contractor come out and look at the floor before anyone can go up there."

Avery studied Carrie. She wasn't sure why Gray's comment about Carrie being a talented artist stuck with her. As far as she was concerned, Niall Reed had been the artistic version of a snake oil salesman. He'd been better at marketing his vision than creating it. But her gut told her that his effervescently sentimental paintings masked a man with some deep insecurities and possibly an inferiority complex.

Avery's mom might not have been the chocolate-chip-cookie-baking type, but she'd wanted her daughter to be successful.

"I'm going up," she announced, quickly opening the door and bounding up the steep steps before Carrie could stop her.

"No," Carrie shouted but Avery was already at the top. She flipped on the light switch, expecting to see another space crowded with more junk.

Instead, the long, narrow room was practically empty, covered in a layer of fine dust but otherwise untouched by the passing of years.

But what caught and held her attention were the canvases leaning against the far wall. So many of them, the largest at least four feet in length and five feet tall. It looked like they were stacked eight deep in some of the rows she counted.

They weren't Niall's commercialized works. These paintings were done in a style that was a fascinating combination of modern and impressionism. Ordinary objects painted with an attention to light and shadow that made Avery's breath catch in her throat despite years of dust obscuring them.

"Are they yours?" she whispered, glancing over her shoulder to where Carrie had stopped at the top of the steps, arms folded tightly across her stomach.

"He wouldn't let me take them when I moved out," she answered tightly. "That was what we argued about. It doesn't matter now. They're going to the dump."

"What are you talking about?" Avery took a step forward. It felt like she was discovering something magical in this moment, like she'd stumbled upon an artistic version of Narnia in this dusty attic. "These are amazing." She turned to face her sister. "Were they all done while you were in high school?"

Carrie gave a barely perceptible nod. "Mostly. I was putting together a portfolio for my college application. I had my heart set on New York City. It was a long shot at best."

"You're undeniably talented," Avery countered. "Any art school would have wanted you."

"I doubt that," Carrie said. "Although, I guess I'll never know. Mom left at the end of my junior year, and after that it was clear Dad needed me."

"We could sell these at the gallery."

"No way. Come on, Avery. This is private and I wasn't joking about the water damage in the floor. No one has been up here in years. It's not safe."

"Seems fine to me." Avery turned back toward the paintings. She wanted to clean off the canvases and see them in natural light, not just under the glow of the dim fixture hanging from the center of the attic's ceiling. She moved toward the dormers near the front of the house, their windows covered with heavy drapes. If she could just convince Carrie—

A loud keening sound split the air, much like a

glacier calving. Avery screamed as the floor beneath her suddenly gave way. Life in Magnolia was full of surprises, and most of them were turning out to be unwanted.

CHAPTER FIVE

TEN MINUTES LATER, Gray threw his truck into Park, grabbed his tool bag from the passenger seat and ran up the front lawn toward the old Reed house. In all the years he'd been friends with Carrie, he'd never been in her father's home. That privilege had been saved for denizens of the community back in Niall's heyday, when he and his ex-wife had hosted parties for society types who came to Magnolia just to meet the eccentric painter.

Carrie appeared in the doorway as he approached, gesturing him in with a frantic wave of her arm. "I don't think she's badly injured," his friend told him. "But I can tell she's in pain."

"Show me."

With a nod she turned and led him through the house. He registered the furniture, stacks of paper and general clutter that seemed to cover every square inch, but his attention remained focused on getting to Avery.

"There are too many heavy pieces in the spare bedroom for me to get a ladder under her," Carrie explained, reiterating what she'd told him on the phone.

He'd been at the station when she called, now thankful for a slow morning. As Carrie hurried up the main staircase and into a room lined with built-in bookshelves but crammed with tables and chairs piled up like the makings of a bonfire, he saw the pair of shapely legs clad in dark jeans dangling from a hole in the ceiling. Tufts of pink insulation clung to her hips.

The house was one of the oldest in Magnolia, with ten-foot ceilings even on the second floor. That fact gave the room an open feel, despite how crowded it was. But it wasn't going to make it any easier to get Avery unstuck.

"Gray's here," Carrie called, and Gray saw the legs go tense.

"I'm fine." Avery's tone was exasperated but he could hear the thread of pain in it. "I don't need help."

"Where's the attic?" he asked Carrie.

She backed out of the bedroom and pointed to an open doorway across from the main staircase. "I warned her not to go up there."

"This isn't the time for 'I told you so,'" Avery shouted.

Carrie gave him a look and lowered her voice. "Get her out, Gray. She's irritating as hell, but I can't have her hurt in this mess of a house."

"She'll be fine," he reassured her. "I'm going to try to make this work from above instead of below. I'll need reinforcements if we're going to move the furniture. That'll take too long."

He climbed the steps, waving a hand in front of his face until the dust that filled the air cleared.

"You sure know how to make your mark on a place," he said casually as he surveyed the scene.

"I don't need your help," she snapped. "Doesn't Carrie have a helpful neighbor she could call?"

"She called me," he answered simply. He kind of

liked Avery Keller's attitude and admired her calm in the situation, but right now he was all business. "Can you tell if the floor joists around you will hold my weight or are they too damaged?"

"The ones in front of me will give," she answered. "I'm wedged in here tight and when I try to shift my weight to lift myself up, everything feels like it's sagging."

"Then don't move."

"Thanks for the tip," she muttered. "In case you care, I also have a piece of splintered wood lodged in my left arm. So I can only use the right one at the moment."

His gut tightened at the thought of her in pain. "Do you think anything's broken?" He stepped gingerly toward her, making sure to test each section of floorboard before he moved. He couldn't very well help her if he ended up in the same predicament.

"Bruised," she admitted, "but not broken. Do you think Clark Griswold knew how lucky he was to land on that bunk bed?"

"That's the Hollywood version of this scenario. This is real life."

"Does that mean I'm not going to get a happy ending?"

"You're going to be fine," he told her, placing his tool bag on the floor and pulling out a small saw.

"You must practice that commanding tone at the firehouse." She laughed softly. "It's weirdly reassuring."

"My job is rescuing people. I'm good at it."

"Great." For the first time since he'd encountered her at the convenience store, Avery sounded defeated.

It bothered him more than he cared to admit.

He began talking her through his plan, mostly making it up as he went along. The floor joists behind her seemed to be structurally sound, but he wasn't going to risk putting the weight of his entire two hundred pounds on them.

"Can you get her out?" Carrie called from below them. "I climbed over the mess in here and I've got pillows to cushion a fall just in case."

"I'm glad I didn't wear a skirt today," Avery said through clenched teeth.

"Nothing I haven't seen before," he reassured her, earning a snort.

She shifted to look over her shoulder at him, and the floor around her heaved.

He heard Avery's gasp, along with Carrie's worried cry from the bedroom.

"Stay still," he commanded, then called to Carrie, "Don't stand directly underneath her."

"I don't want to fall," Avery said, more to herself than to him.

He answered anyway. "You're not going to fall."

She drew in a ragged breath. "I might be starting to panic. I don't usually panic."

"No reason to." He bent to his knees, then crawled forward, stretching out to reach her. The ideal way to handle this would be clearing out the spare bedroom and having some of his crew supporting her from below. But there was no guarantee that more of the floor wouldn't give way while they waited for backup to arrive. Plus she was in pain, and he wanted her safe on solid ground as soon as he could manage it.

"I'm right behind you," he said as he got closer. "I'm going to cut the piece of wood that's got you wedged in here."

"I feel like a chicken skewer."

One side of his mouth curved, and he inched forward. Narrating his movements for her, he managed to saw through the splintering section of wood.

Avery let out a sigh when it fell away from her arm. She had a deep cut, but it wasn't bleeding badly at the moment.

"Now I'm going to lift you back toward me. Use your elbows to brace on the joists on either side of you."

"I can do three pull-ups in my CrossFit class," she announced. "Who knew all my upper body strength would come in so handy?"

"Exactly," he agreed, knowing it was fear driving her seemingly casual chatter. "Do you upend tires, too?"

"Sometimes. Mostly it's a lot of burpees and suicides."

"I hate burpees." He positioned his hands under her arms. "You're strong, Avery. You've done a great job holding steady. Just a few more seconds and..." He half lifted, half dragged her up out of the hole, quickly moving both of them away from the water-damaged section of the attic.

"You did it," Carrie shouted from the bedroom below.

"You did it," Avery echoed in a hoarse whisper.

"*We* did it," he corrected. He had the crazy urge to wrap his arms around her and pull her close, holding her to him until the tremors he felt rippling through her body subsided. The notion was odd and out of character. He'd rescued plenty of people in his years as a firefighter.

Hell, just last week, he'd come to the aid of Kenneth Masminster when he'd locked himself in his tool shed. But a seventy-five-year-old gardener who smelled like menthol and mothballs hadn't elicited near the emotional reaction that Avery did. Avery, with her shiny hair and manicured nails, and the scent of expensive perfume on her skin that was at odds with the hot, dusty attic. A scent that should put him off. As appealing as it was, what the scent conveyed about the woman who wore it made her all wrong for him.

"Thank you," she said into the front of his uniform shirt. She seemed as unwilling to let go as he was.

Carrie's footsteps sounded on the attic stairs, and Avery pushed away.

"I have the first-aid kit," Carrie said, holding up a red vinyl bag.

"I'm fine," Avery said, then winced as Gray touched her arm.

"You need that bandaged. A trip to the ER isn't a bad idea. We need to make sure there are no splinters left in the wound."

"I'll wash it out here," she told him, shaking her head.

"Are you sure?" Carrie asked.

"Yeah. But first I'd like to get out of this attic."

"I'll boil water," Carrie offered with almost manic enthusiasm. "And get out the hydrogen peroxide. Meet you in the kitchen." She turned and hurried down the steps again.

"She does like taking care of people." Avery smoothed a hand over the front of her wrinkled and torn shirt.

"You should see a doctor."

"Nope. Niall has already given the people of Magnolia too much reason to talk about me. I'm not adding more to it." She glanced at her arm. "I don't need stitches, so I'd prefer no one else know about this little catastrophe. There's plenty of work to be done on the house without everyone thinking it's dangerous, as well."

"Most people know not to walk through a decaying attic," he pointed out.

"I was distracted," she said, moving carefully toward the staircase.

Gray kept a steadying hand on her back, and it spoke volumes about her current state of mind that she didn't shrug off his touch.

"By the moldy insulation?" he asked with a chuckle.

"Check out the far wall, funny man."

After ensuring she made it to the top of the steps, he turned back to the dimly lit space. "Carrie's paintings," he said softly. He hadn't noticed them when he came up, his attention focused solely on getting Avery to safety.

"I'm not sure if she or Niall shoved them up here," Avery said. "We didn't get to that before my accident. She was too busy shouting at me to ignore them."

"I told you she was talented."

"An understatement."

He nodded.

"She should be using her talent."

He inclined his head to study her. "That comment makes it sound suspiciously like you care."

She lifted an arm to wave off his comment, then grimaced. "She's a potential revenue stream. We need money for repairs. Don't make me out to be some would-be saint. I'm not Carrie."

The bite in her tone ripped into him like getting caught on a jagged rock outcropping. It was exactly the reminder he needed to keep his distance—both emotional and physical—from this woman.

"She's waiting in the kitchen," he said. "I can stay, too, if you need me."

Something flashed in Avery's blue eyes. Vulnerability and perhaps disappointment, like she'd wanted him to argue with her assessment of herself.

"Carrie will take care of things. It's fine." Then she nodded and headed down the steps.

Gray followed with a sigh. The vague sense of regret rippling through his veins was the reason he kept his life simple. Complications only caused trouble.

AVERY THUMPED HER head to the shiny linoleum that covered the tabletop in the quiet corner of The Bean Bandito before looking across the table at her two half sisters. "Could he have made dividing his estate any more complicated?"

"You shouldn't bang your head that way." Carrie offered a compassionate smile. "Falling through the ceiling might have jumbled your brain."

"My brain is fine." She rubbed her fingers over the bandage wrapped around her arm. "I got a little scraped up. That's all."

"At least eat something."

"Or better yet, gulp down another margarita," Meredith suggested. "Maybe that will help Niall's insanity make more sense." She flicked a glance at Carrie. "He was a lunatic, you know?"

Carrie's perfectly shaped lips thinned. "Artists are known to be eccentric."

Meredith snorted and ran a hand through her chin-length bob. "You have to admit your father royally screwed us."

"He's your father, too."

"Don't say that." Meredith slapped a hand on the top of the table. "I have a dad. Yours is just a guy who fooled around with my mom and was too stupid or selfish to wear a condom. One more reason for me to hate both of them."

Carrie recoiled from Meredith's anger as if she'd been slapped. "He helped you when you came to him needing a property for the animal rescue."

"If he'd really wanted to help, he would have left me the ranch. I don't need his crumbling hoarder-paradise house."

"Oh, look," Avery said brightly. "The waitress is here with our food." She smiled at the young woman who set Fiestaware plates filled with chicken enchiladas, a burrito and tacos onto the table. "Your timing is perfect. Some of us were getting a little hangry."

"I'm not hangry," Meredith snapped. "I'll be just as pissed with a full belly."

"Lucky us," Carrie muttered.

Meredith looked like she wanted to punch someone. Possibly Avery. Definitely Carrie.

Why had it seemed like a good idea to include Meredith in tonight's dinner discussion about a plan for Niall's estate? Carrie might not like the idea of selling the properties, but Avery believed she could convince her that it was for the best. Meredith remained a wild card, feigning indifference but obviously emotionally wrecked by her new reality.

That made her dangerous. Who knew what she might do or say to sabotage Avery's plan to unload their father's assets? According to Douglas, the whole of the estate needed to be settled before any of the properties could be put on the market. Niall had several thousand dollars in credit card debt and had taken out a second mortgage on the Fig Street house. In fact, the beach-front ranch was the only property he owned outright, which made it the most valuable.

Carrie owned it, but Meredith needed it.

Her two sisters would have to find a way to work together. Helping them to do that felt like Avery's only choice.

After the waitress checked their orders and it was just the three of them again, Avery leaned across the table. "We need a plan."

"First we have to get through the memorial service this weekend."

"Excuse me?" Avery paused with the fork halfway to her mouth. Melted cheese dripped toward the plate, but suddenly she couldn't imagine taking a bite of the gooey enchiladas. A lead ball of dread had just ripped a hole through her stomach.

"There's no way I'm going to that," Meredith said, biting into a crunchy taco.

"What are you talking about?" Avery set down the fork. "Surely you've had the service already?"

Carrie shook her head. "Dad left specific instructions that a service celebrating his life should be planned for the fourth Saturday of August."

Meredith exhaled a caustic laugh as she took another bite of taco. "It also happens to be the morning of the kickoff parade for Summer Fair, which is one of the biggest events Magnolia hosts all year. Of course he'd want to hijack the weekend to make it all about him."

She leveled a look at Avery. "It's a wonder he didn't get himself fitted for a crown back in the day. He always walked around like he was king of this town."

"He loved this place," Carrie whispered.

"Spoken like a true princess," Meredith countered.

"It would have been easier if you'd just been hangry," Avery told her youngest sister. Youngest. She was the oldest of three sisters. The family she'd always wanted.

Be careful what you wish for and all that.

"Are you planning the service?" she asked Carrie.

"No." Carrie looked toward Meredith. "There's a committee of volunteers from the downtown business district. I'd hoped to keep things low-key, but they're making his memorial part of the kickoff for the festival on Saturday morning. The parade will start at the elementary school like it always does, but instead of ending on the steps of town hall, it will finish at the gallery. They're setting up a grandstand on the street and—"

"A grandstand?" Avery's voice came out as a squeak. "Like a stage?"

Carrie nodded, looking almost sheepish as pink flushed her cheeks. "For the mayor to give his speech and Dad's eulogy."

Meredith looked as stunned as Avery felt. "Don't you think you might have mentioned this?"

"I totally forgot," Carrie told them, pushing away her barely touched burrito. "Between finding out about the two of you—"

"She says," Meredith muttered, "in the same way someone would talk about discovering they had a communicable disease."

"That's not how I said it," Carrie argued weakly. "It was a shock, as was the state of Dad's house."

Meredith picked up her fork and pointed toward the green-chili-smothered burrito. "Are you going to eat that?"

Carrie shook her head, and Meredith pulled the plate closer.

"How are you so tiny?" Avery asked the pixie-sized woman. "You eat like a team of linebackers."

"Good metabolism," Meredith told her after shoveling in a bite. "I get it from my…" She shook her head. "I always thought I got it from my dad's side of the family, but I guess that's not the case."

Both Avery and Meredith looked at Carrie.

"The Reeds have good metabolisms," she said with a nod. "Dad's family came from Scotland. His great-grandfather was a blacksmith. He settled in Cambridge and met my—our—grandmother when her family moved into the house across the street. Childhood sweethearts."

"Did Niall have brothers and sisters?" Avery asked, unable to completely squash her curiosity about the man whose DNA she carried.

"A brother who was five years younger," Carrie confirmed. "He died in a car accident when he was twelve. It destroyed their family. Gram and Gramps got divorced, and Dad didn't stay close to either of them." She shrugged. "He always said his unhappy childhood inspired the joy in the scenes he painted. He was trying to capture the ideal version of a family he never had."

"And chose not to create for himself," Avery added.

"Oh, he created it." Meredith dabbed at one corner of her mouth with a napkin. "With his perfect wife and perfect daughter. I'm not exaggerating when I say they were like royalty around here. Only no one knew he had a whole below-stairs story going on at the same time."

Avery could tell Carrie wanted to argue but she only said, "Looks can be deceiving."

"Right." Meredith rolled her eyes. "Even knowing what a two-timing jerk he was, the town is still giving him the celebrity treatment. His paintings haven't sold well in years. He's a laughingstock in the real art community, but we're going to treat him like a fallen hero at the memorial."

Finally, Avery'd had enough. "Are you about done with the pity party?" she asked Meredith, whose mouth dropped open.

"Did you seriously just ask me that? Do you know what I've been through with all this? How my life—"

"Welcome to the club, sister." Avery leaned forward. "I mean that literally. Sister. We *are* sisters."

"Half," Meredith muttered under her breath.

"Sisters," Avery repeated.

"Sisters," Carrie said with conviction.

When Meredith didn't respond, Avery shrugged. "We can debate which of us has been more wronged and who gets to be the most resentful until we're old and gray. You don't have to like it or either of us. I understand Niall gave you plenty of reasons for your bitterness. But who is it helping at this point?"

Meredith slugged back the rest of her margarita but gave no answer.

"Exactly. For better or worse, we're in this together.

At least until we can figure out what to do with the messed-up, debt-riddled nightmare of an inheritance he left us."

Meredith cracked the barest hint of a smile as she asked, "How do you really feel?"

"Angry, confused and slightly panicked. My life was already half off the tracks and this has pushed me even closer to the edge. I don't like it any more than you do. I don't want this to be my reality. Our father didn't leave us much of a choice."

"You have a choice," Carrie said, inclining her head toward Avery. "This town isn't your home."

Avery swallowed, hating the emotion that clogged her throat and definitely not willing to admit she didn't have a home anymore. "I know."

"Don't you have a life to get back to?" Meredith asked. "What do you mean 'half off the tracks'?"

Suddenly Avery wondered why she'd bothered to attempt to bridge the gap between these two. The last thing she needed was having them find solidarity by putting her in the hot seat. So far she'd been able to avoid revealing any details about the mess she'd made of her life, and she wanted to keep it that way.

"My company went through a downsizing," she said, her features schooled. No need to explain that the only person downsized was her when she'd been given the choice to quit or be fired. "I was getting ready to start a new job when I got the letter about Niall."

If by *job* she meant watching reality television and ordering Chinese takeout like it was her job, she wasn't exactly lying. "I can put things on hold while we figure this out."

The other two women watched her like they didn't believe a word of what she told them, but neither called her out on the flimsy fabrication.

"That's good," Carrie said after the awkward silence stretched almost too long to bear. "We'll need to work together to get the house in order."

"We also need a plan for the real estate downtown," Avery added. "There's no way the bank is going to continue to let us slide on mortgage payments now that Niall's gone." She leveled her gaze at Carrie. "Which means we can no longer let the local businesses get away with not paying rent."

"The ranch is paid for," Meredith said, nodding as if congratulating herself. "That means my rescue has no threat of closing."

"We can sell it to pay for renovations on the house," Carrie said, surprising Avery with the vehemence of her tone.

"No way," Meredith argued. "I need that property. You wouldn't dare—"

"Don't get your panties in a bunch," Carrie interrupted. "I don't want to sell anything."

"Why not?" Avery demanded. "That's the only option that makes sense for all of us."

"It sure sounds like you wanted to sell," Meredith grumbled.

Carrie inched her chair closer to Meredith's. "We're going to have to work together." She looked between the two of them. "The house needs renovations. The buildings downtown are mortgaged to the hilt and we're already behind on payments. Meredith wants to keep the beach house. Each of us owns a property, but we need one another to find the right solution. A solution that will benefit all three of us."

They sat in a weighted silence for a minute while the waitress cleared the plates and brought the check. Carrie held up a hand when Avery and Meredith reached for their wallets and pulled out a heavy bag of coins from her tote bag.

"I found two dozen beer growlers filled with coins in the master bedroom closet."

Meredith arched a brow. "Do I officially own those since they were in the house?"

"I've loaded and hauled four truckloads of old newspapers to the recycling center over in Kirby since last week. Let's call it even."

Carrie started digging out quarters, then paused when she realized Meredith was grinning at her. "What?"

"You're different than when we were kids," Meredith told her. "I like you better without so much shine and polish."

"I like you better now that you aren't slamming me into lockers," Carrie said.

Avery gasped. "You bullied her?"

Meredith sniffed but looked faintly embarrassed. "My dad hated Niall Reed. Being mean to his daughter felt like family loyalty."

"We're a mess." Avery dropped her head onto the table again. When she lifted it, both Carrie and Meredith grinned.

"Speak for yourself." Meredith handed her a napkin. "Wipe the guacamole off your forehead while you're at it."

With a groan, Avery took the napkin and blotted her forehead.

"At least we're not in this mess alone." Carrie offered an encouraging smile.

"True," Avery said, and even Meredith nodded in agreement.

A Magnolia mess but one she didn't have to face on her own.

Maybe that was enough for now.

CHAPTER SIX

GRAY KNOCKED ON the door of the carriage house after Violet fell asleep, trying to convince himself he was just being neighborly.

He'd heard Avery arrive home an hour earlier, not that he'd kept the family room window cracked to listen.

She opened the door a moment later, brandishing a packaged roll of cookie dough in his direction. "I've got it under control," she said by way of greeting.

He opened his mouth to tell her he had no idea what she was talking about when the scent of something charred—cookies if he had to guess—hit him.

"Are you trying to burn down my guesthouse?"

She batted her eyelashes. "Just looking for an excuse to have the hot firefighter next door come over and check out my oven."

"You wouldn't be the first," he told her with a laugh.

She swatted him on the shoulder with the cookie dough log. "I'd invite you in, but I'm not sure your ego could fit through the door."

He plucked the log out of her hand. "I'll fit," he said, dropping his voice to a low growl, laughing again when color rose to her cheeks. "Such an easy target."

She stuck out her tongue, then turned and walked back into the house. She didn't shut the door in his face, which he took as a good sign, and he followed her.

"Did you seriously smell smoke?" she asked, leading the way to the small kitchen area.

Grimacing as he took in the scorched remains of a dozen cookies on a baking tray, he shook his head. "No. I stopped by to make sure your arm was okay."

"It hurts less after a couple of margaritas." She picked up the baking sheet and scraped the burnt cookies into the trash can next to the refrigerator. "It's not a great idea to drink and bake," she told him.

"I'll remember that. Did you drive home?"

"Home," she murmured with an almost sad laugh. "Home to my sister's apartment in a town I didn't even know existed a few weeks ago. I don't have a home, Mr. Hottie Firefighter."

"You like to call me hot."

She pointed a finger as if accusing him of something. "It's the truth. Despite what you might have heard, I'm not a liar." She placed the baking tray in the sink with a clatter. "Or a drunk driver. I got a ride home. I'll pick up my car tomorrow morning."

"Glad to hear it. Can I see your arm?"

She studied him for a moment, and even with her gaze slightly blurry, her hair coming out of the messy knot on the back of her head and a smear of chocolate down the front of her loose-fitting sweater, she was gorgeous and still unabashedly ladylike. "You rescued me today." She sounded bitter, which made him smile.

"You would have figured out how to get down eventually."

She shook her head, then walked toward the small four-person table in the dinette. Plopping into a chair, she yanked the hair tie from the back of her head, blond hair tumbling over her shoulders. She flipped it away from her face, then pulled the sweater over her head, revealing a pale pink ribbed tank top underneath.

"You're like an honest-to-God hero."

"The way you say it makes me feel like I should apologize."

"I'm just unaccustomed to stand-up guys."

Gray moved closer, thoroughly intrigued by this version of Avery Keller. "How many margaritas did you have?"

"A couple," she answered. "But I don't usually drink. I like to be in control."

He drew a chair next to her and lowered himself into it. "I can just imagine."

"How's your rug rat?" she asked as he unwound the bandage from her arm.

"Violet's asleep."

"Duh. I mean, how was her day? Was that bi-otch friend of hers impressed by the braids?"

"I don't think you're supposed to refer to little girls that way."

"I won't tell if you won't. What happened? Did it go well?"

"Yes," he answered. "Apparently she saved a seat for Violet at lunch."

Avery groaned, and Gray stilled. "Does it hurt?"

She turned her head to look at him, her face close enough that he could feel her breath on his cheek. "My arm is fine. What hurts is remembering the politics of the lunchroom in elementary school."

"She's in kindergarten." He examined her cut, touched the edge of it. "There are no politics."

"Don't fool yourself. Girls can be brutal, and from

what Violet told me her new lunch-table friend has gotten a jump on her queen-bee status."

"I can't believe she shared more with you than she has with me."

"It's hard to talk to a dad about girl drama. Or I assume it would be. I didn't have that option."

"Violet has me forever, but most times I feel like a two-bit stand-in for the type of parent she really needs."

"She needs someone who loves her unconditionally," Avery said quietly. "You'll do."

The words could barely be considered a compliment, but they resonated through Gray like he'd just been awarded a Congressional medal. "Your arm looks good. Put a fresh bandage on it in the morning."

"Thanks." She turned to face him more fully, her bare knee brushing his leg and sending a jolt of awareness through his veins that felt like the heat from a shot of straight whiskey.

Damn, he needed to get out more.

"Have you heard about the deal with Niall's memorial service on Saturday?"

"Yep. The station's ladder truck is part of the parade every year. I guess Mal is hoping to get some national press coverage—honoring the memory of a town hero and all that. It may bring more tourists into town for the end of the summer season."

"Who's Mal?"

"Our mayor," he clarified. "Malcolm Grimes. He was elected last year and is doing his best to revive things around here. For all Niall's purported devotion to Magnolia, he didn't make it easy."

"What do you mean?"

Gray sighed. He wasn't one to speak ill of the dead and didn't relish getting involved in an already complicated situation. "Even after his art stopped selling, Niall held a lot of sway in town. He wanted things done a certain way, mostly in a way that made him look good. Any ideas for events or tourist campaigns that drew notice away from Niall Reed as the center of attention... Well, he managed to get most of them shot down by his cronies on town council."

"The more I learn about him, the less I like."

"He had his moments of bigheartedness, and he loved this place in his own way. At the end of the day, he was a narcissist. I don't think he had it in him to see beyond himself."

"Carrie, Meredith and I inherited a veritable Poopapalooza."

"You'll find a way to make it work."

"Like you have with Violet?"

"Not the same thing." He closed his eyes for a moment, thinking of Stacy and her skewed priorities. "But yes."

"Your daughter is lucky to have you."

"My ex-wife would disagree."

"Is it appropriate to use the word *bi-otch* for a grown woman who doesn't do right by her kid?"

He felt a muscle tick in his jaw. Normally he wouldn't allow himself to think disparaging thoughts toward his ex. He didn't want to color Violet's opinion of her mom. His life was all about what was best for his daughter. Fostering a solid relationship with her mom was part of that. But in the quiet of this moment, with a woman who had no knowledge of his past or any reason to lie to him, he could admit the truth.

"Absolutely," he said, relief at being able to drop his mask for even a few moments cresting in him like a wave.

Avery lifted her hand to his face, smoothing out the tension he held there with her soft fingers. Need tumbled through him as her gaze dropped to his mouth. It felt like the most natural thing in the world to brush his lips against hers.

He expected the heightened jolt of desire and the yearning for more, but what surprised him was the emotional respite of touching her. The contact soothed him in ways he hadn't expected. Kissing her was like finding a soft place to land at the end of a plummeting fall.

Gray savored the sensation, nipping at the corner of her mouth and then tracing his tongue along the seam of her lips. It had been a long time since he'd kissed a woman this way. Had he ever experienced this kind of kiss? It could go on forever, and he'd never get enough of the teasing exploration.

She cupped his face, then moved her hands to the back of his neck, gently pulling him closer. Oh, yeah. Avery was a woman who liked to be in control, and he let her take it.

So much of his life was responsibility and managing things, from his life and Violet's to ongoing custody negotiations with his ex. There was the work at the station and dealing with his family. So much.

To give sway to someone else and let himself enjoy the ride was another kind of gift. He kept his hands at his sides, knowing that if he touched her, his need might get the best of him. This was too good to hurry.

They kissed like people with no past or future, totally enveloped in the moment and the pleasure of each other.

She smelled like shampoo, not expensive perfume, and tasted sweet and tangy from the margaritas and cookie dough. Their tongues mingled as she deepened the kiss, and finally Gray couldn't stand it any longer. His whole body tingled with the need for more. He lifted his hands, first sifting his fingers through the long strands of her light hair before wrapping his arms around her back.

A moment later she was in his lap, and the weight and warmth of her set him on fire. She fit perfectly against him, her soft curves dulling his edges. They'd grown and multiplied since the heartbreak of his ruined marriage until he didn't recognize himself as anything but a flinty automaton. He'd forgotten how good it felt to hold a woman in his arms. Or maybe he'd blocked out the bone-deep knowing because it was too difficult given the bleak state of his love life.

Avery was a revelation. How could a woman who looked so uptight kiss with such abandon? He never wanted this moment to end.

As if she recognized the force of his desire, and how close he was to losing control, she wrenched her mouth from his and scrambled off his lap.

"Mistake," she whispered, her eyes wide and panicky as she moved away, tripping over one of the chair legs.

He wanted to contradict her but couldn't make his mouth form a retort. The word ricocheted through him like a bullet tearing through layers of flesh. Stacy had called their marriage a mistake on the night he'd moved out of the house they shared. But he'd known what she was really saying. *He* was the mistake. She'd been wrong to get involved with a man whose background and future were so different than the life she wanted for herself.

Avery was new to Magnolia, but it was clear she didn't belong in the close-knit town. Or his life.

His bed might be a different story, but Gray had never been a fan of casual sex. He was wired for commitment. Too bad that intrinsic need came back to bite him in the ass every time.

"It's not a big deal," he said, rising from the chair. "I'm a single dad with no social life. You're drunk. We kissed."

She drew in a sharp breath. "Are you saying you used me?"

"I don't think we got far enough for a claim like that on either side." He wanted to touch her again but forced himself to offer a casual smile. "Keep it in mind, though, the next time you go drinking with your sisters. You know where to find me."

"There won't be a next time."

He could tell by the way Avery's chin trembled that emotions were starting to get the best of her. He understood and couldn't blame her. She wouldn't want to break down in front of him, and he wasn't going to push her over the precipice. As much as he wanted to offer comfort, he flashed a cocky smile.

"Your loss," he said as he walked by her and out the door.

WHEN THE KNOCK sounded on the door the next morning, Avery glanced at the clock on the nightstand, then groaned. "Go away, Violet," she called, but not loud enough for anyone to hear.

She might not be a morning person, but she also wasn't as heartless as she wanted the girl to believe. Seven o'clock was early for any sort of eye-hand coordination, even the rudimentary amount it took for braiding. She hoped like hell Gray was awake and had sent his daughter over with coffee.

Or that he was with Violet, preferably shirtless. Possibly even sans pants. She gave herself a soft smack on the cheek as she headed to the door. She did not want to see Gray Atwell without his clothes. Right. Just like she didn't have a monthly craving for a huge bowl of rocky road ice cream.

The comparison actually gave her some comfort. Avery was a master of willpower. She could withstand the temptation of chocolate and sugar so surely she could keep her hormones in check when it came to her sexy neighbor.

She'd told him their kiss was a mistake. Avery didn't like making mistakes, especially since her last one involving a man had resulted in several lives being destroyed.

Focus, she told herself. Braids. Braids and coffee she could handle.

But it wasn't Violet standing on the other side of her front door. Or Gray.

"What took you so long?" Meredith asked, adjusting her grip on the animal wriggling in her arms.

"I was sleeping. It's what normal people do." Avery raised a brow. "Is that a miniature cow?"

"It's a dog."

"Nope. It's a black-and-white spotted sausage."

"Can I come in?"

"Do you have coffee?"

"I'll make a pot."

Avery stepped back to allow her youngest half sister to enter.

Meredith kicked the door closed behind her, then lowered the tiny cow dog to the floor.

"It's as wide as it is long."

"She," Meredith corrected, crouching down to unclip the dog's leash, then giving it a quick scratch behind the ears. The animal immediately rolled to its back, stubby legs high in the air like it was playing dead. "Her name is Spot."

"Spot needs to cut back on the kibble."

"I knew you'd want to help." Meredith pointed a finger at Avery before moving toward the kitchen. "This place is cute. What do you think about Gray?"

"He's fine," Avery said, making sure her tone remained bland.

Meredith snorted. "He's *fine*, alright."

"I didn't mean it like that. He's not my type."

"Are you a lesbian?" Meredith asked conversationally as she filled the coffeepot with water from the tap.

"No, but—"

"Then he's your type. A man that gorgeous is everyone's type."

"Have you dated him?"

"He doesn't date." Meredith dumped some grounds in the filter, hit the button to start the coffee brewing and turned to face Avery. "Grayson Atwell does *relationships*. He's a serial monogamist, or he used to be. He was older than me but all the girls knew Gray. I don't think he's gone out with a woman since his divorce. Word on the street is his ex did a real number on him."

"Oh." Avery tried to sound uninterested but based on the smile Meredith flashed, she wasn't doing a great job of it.

"A man like that could bring all the o's," Meredith said with an eyebrow wiggle.

"Enough about Gray." Avery nudged the dog still sprawled on the hardwood floor with her toe. "What's the deal with Snort?"

Meredith took two mugs from a cabinet as the scent of brewing coffee filled the air. "Her name is Spot."

The dog turned to her belly at the sound of her name but didn't get up.

"You're a good girl," Meredith cooed.

"Wow," Avery whispered at the look of unabashed love that came into her sister's eyes. The softening was instantaneous and transformed Meredith from a cute pixie to ethereally beautiful. "Having a heart agrees with you."

Meredith stuck out her tongue. "I picked up Spot yesterday from the family of an elderly woman who'd died over in Winthrop. The kids don't want to keep her, even though she was their mother's constant and loyal companion in the last years of her life."

"But you run an animal rescue, so you'll find a new home for her." Avery flicked another glance at the dog. Spot's eyes were lowered to half-mast and the tip of a pink tongue lolled out of her mouth like she was exhausted. Avery had yet to see the dog walk two steps.

"Eventually," Meredith said slowly with a sweet smile that looked awkward on her. "She needs to lose weight first."

"Don't you have a whole ranch where she can run around?"

"Sort of." Meredith shrugged. "The property is twenty acres, and I have four separate fenced exercise enclosures."

"Why do I feel like Spot's rear end isn't the biggest 'but' in the room right now?"

"She's self-conscious."

Avery snorted. "She's a fat dog."

"Don't say that," Meredith scolded. "You'll give her even more of a complex."

Avery glanced down at the dog. Spot gave a lazy wag of her tail. "Is that possible?"

"It's like when a morbidly obese person starts a fitness program. Haven't you watched *My 600-lb Life*?"

"Not once."

"The Biggest Loser?"

"Nope."

"Spot knows she can't keep up with the other dogs, so she won't try. She's not very social. She needs to get in better shape on her own. It's a self-confidence thing."

It said a lot about Avery's life since coming to Magnolia that this was, in no way, the strangest conversation she'd had. "What does that have to do with me?"

"I thought you'd make a good foster family."

"Wow," Avery repeated. "That sounds great."

Meredith let out a relieved sigh. "Really?"

"No," Avery yelled, throwing out her hands. "Are you crazy?"

Meredith crossed her arms over her chest and jutted out a hip. "Come on, Avs."

"No one calls me Avs."

"I just did."

"Don't do it again."

"Say you'll keep Spot."

Avery shook her head. "You said you needed a family. I'm one person."

"Good enough for Spot."

"I'm not keeping the dog."

"She's great on a leash and potty trained. Hardly ever barks. She needs love and a lot of exercise."

"Also, less kibble."

Meredith gave her an awkwardly enthusiastic thumbs-up. "See? You're already a natural."

"No."

"Just for a couple of weeks? She'll be a distraction for you."

"I don't need a distraction," Avery answered. "I need to focus so we can get Niall's estate figured out."

Meredith studied her for a long moment. "If you keep the dog, I'll be more helpful. I'll work on my attitude and pitch in cleaning out his house."

"It's your house now."

"Don't remind me."

"I thought you were going to work on your attitude."

"Will you foster Spot?"

Avery looked at the dog again. Spot had fallen asleep and was snoring softly. "Can't you find someone else?"

"She's a special case. I need a person I trust."

"You trust me?" Avery stifled a disbelieving laugh.

Meredith took a step toward her. "You're my sister," she answered, almost reluctantly. "I don't know why that means something since we're practically strangers, but it does."

"It does to me, too," Avery agreed, then laughed softly. "Have you always been this good at manipulating people?"

"I grew up with older brothers. I'm a master manipulator."

"Two weeks," Avery muttered after a moment. "I'll keep her for two weeks."

"I'll take it." Meredith pumped her fist in the air. "She really is sweet. You can help her."

"I can barely help myself." Avery rolled her eyes. "But I'll do better if you pour me a cup of coffee."

"You pour the coffee," Meredith said. "I'm going to my truck to get Spot's supplies and the donuts I picked up."

"You've been holding out on me, sis."

"I wasn't going to give them to you unless you agreed."

"You really are a master."

Meredith beamed like she'd been given a huge compliment, then walked toward the door, stepping over the sleeping dog.

Avery poured the coffee and took a long swig, so desperate for caffeine she didn't bother with creamer.

She stared at the dog, wondering exactly what she'd gotten herself into. Her mother had never allowed pets when Avery was a girl. Too messy and too much work, she'd said. As an adult, Avery had taken much the same stance. But her life in Magnolia was different than it had been in California. She no longer had a seventy-hour-a-week job or a standing appointment with a personal trainer at the local gym. She no longer had much of anything.

Except now she had a dog. Temporarily.

Meredith returned with the donuts and a bag of dog supplies.

"I brought enough diet dog food to last a week. I have more out at the rescue."

"Okay," Avery said absently as she opened the box and released the sweet, doughy scent of the donuts.

"Do you have any questions?"

"Glazed or jelly?"

"Glazed," Meredith told her. "I'm a purist."

Avery placed a glazed donut on a napkin and handed it to Meredith, then picked up a chocolate-iced one for herself. Suddenly the little dog sleeping near the front door woke with a start. Spot sniffed the air, then trundled over to the kitchen.

"No people food," Meredith told both Avery and the dog.

Spot ignored her rescuer, plopping down at Avery's feet with a plaintive whine. "You heard her," Avery said. "It's for your own good."

The dog barked.

Avery raised a brow and glanced at Meredith. "I thought you said she didn't do that."

"It's the donuts."

"In that case," Avery said to the animal, "I don't blame you, but you're not getting fatter on my watch."

"Thank you." Meredith wiped her fingertips on the napkin. "For agreeing to keep her."

"Like you gave me a choice." Avery took another bite of donut, then placed the remaining half on the counter. "I expect to see you Saturday at the memorial service."

"Weekends are busy at the rescue," Meredith answered immediately.

"You promised to be helpful," Avery reminded her.

"By helpful I assume you mean letting me boss you around."

Meredith sniffed. "Hardly, but I'll try to make it on Saturday. Right now I have to get to the day job. The office opens at eight."

"I'm meeting with some of Niall's tenants in town this morning. I'll take Spot for a walk first."

"She'll love it."

"I doubt that."

"Good luck with your tenants."

Her tenants. Avery's stomach pitched thinking of the difficult conversations she was bound to have.

After Meredith left, Avery put the remaining donuts in a resealable container and loaded the mugs into the dishwasher. Spot didn't move but continued to watch her with baleful eyes.

"New plan," Avery said to the dog. "You're coming with me to town. How upset can people get with me while I've got a furry, spotted sausage roll on the other end of the leash? Maybe a distraction isn't such a bad idea after all."

CHAPTER SEVEN

"THAT DOG DOESN'T look right."

Avery gritted her teeth at the not-so-helpful observation delivered in a slow Southern drawl. "She's fine," she said without turning around. Instead she concentrated on Spot. "I've got a whole bunch of treats in my pocket. Who wants a treat?"

She tugged on the leash, but Spot didn't budge. The dog had made it about twenty-five feet across the grassy park in the center of town before dropping to the ground and refusing to walk any farther.

Avery had purposely parked on the far side of the park to give Spot a bit of the exercise she desperately needed. She'd planned to take the dog for a walk before leaving, but instead she'd taken a minute to check email and her social media accounts, and gotten sucked down the online rabbit hole.

Spot hadn't seemed to mind. The dog had nudged her leg until she'd bent and picked her up. Meredith said no people food but hadn't mentioned rules about dogs on furniture. Spot had scooted closer on the sofa, then curled into a ball at Avery's side.

The dog's presence had been surprisingly comforting as Avery surreptitiously snooped on the Facebook account of the wife of her ex-boyfriend. Sofia posted updates on their young son, Mark, who'd been seriously injured in a car accident that Avery still felt responsible for.

She hadn't let herself check up on Tony's family since she'd fled San Francisco, but somehow Spot's warmth and rhythmic breathing next to her made her feel like she wasn't so alone. She and the dog had stayed together long enough that Avery barely had time to shower before she needed to be downtown.

"You think a dog treat's a smart plan? Seems to me someone's already been a bit too generous with the biscuits."

"It wasn't me," Avery said, realizing she sounded defensive. "And I'm not really going to give her a treat." She straightened and turned to find a tall, well-dressed man standing behind her, a straw fedora perched on his head. The man's skin was the color of a perfect latte with a salt-and-pepper beard covering his jaw.

"So you're lying to that animal?"

Something about the teasing note in his tone made Avery smile, despite her frustration with the heat and with Spot. "Do you think she cares?"

"Nope." He held out a hand. "I'm Malcolm Grimes, mayor of Magnolia. You're Avery Reed from—"

"Keller," she corrected quickly. "Avery Keller. My mom raised me on her own, so I have her family name. How do you know who I am?"

Malcolm nodded solemnly. "I was raised by my granny, so I know all about strong women taking care of business on their own. Everyone around here knows who you are. And I googled you."

"What did people do before the internet?"

"Used the phone book a lot more, for one thing."

Spot made a soft grunting sound, lifting her head to sniff the air.

"She caught the scent of the Bagel Buggy," Malcolm said with a laugh.

"What's a Bagel Buggy?" Avery's stomach rumbled as the warm breeze carried the smell of fresh-baked bread to her.

"Magnolia's version of a food truck. They're more like food 'carts' but they work for us. We have a bur- rito, bagel and pizza buggy. Cyrus, who runs the Bagel Buggy, usually opens first. He does breakfast sand- wiches in addition to a lunch menu. We'll have to make a date for lunch one of these afternoons. As mayor it's my duty to welcome new residents to our town."

Avery frowned. The offer was friendly, not flirty, and she didn't get any weird "pickup" vibes from the older man. "I'm not staying in town," she told him hon- estly. "I'm a waste of a good bagel sandwich."

"The Bagel Buggy is never a waste." He inclined his head. "Don't be so sure about what you mean to this town or what we might come to mean to you."

"I'm here for family business," Avery said, glanc- ing at her watch. After giving Spot's leash another tug, which the dog ignored, she bent and scooped the chunky fur ball into her arms. "Nice to meet you, Mayor, but I'm late for a meeting."

"I'll walk to Josie's with you," he offered, falling into step beside her. "You understand the Reeds have been a big part of this town and our history for many years now. Niall committed himself to—"

"How did you know I was heading to the dance stu- dio?" Josie Trumbell owned Josie's School of Dance. It was one of several businesses in the buildings Avery now owned that hadn't paid rent for several years according to the financial records she found in the office at the gallery. She threw him a sidelong glance as he cleared his throat.

"Lucky guess?"

"Try again."

"Josie, Phil and Stuart asked me to talk to you," he admitted. "They're worried about how you're going to handle their leases."

"Are they also concerned that they've been riding the coattails of Niall's misplaced generosity for far too long?"

"Your father understood the importance of a thriving downtown. He was willing to help support others for the good of the community."

"How is downtown thriving if the shops and business owners aren't bringing in enough revenue to pay the bills?"

"Things changed around here when tourists stopped coming to visit the gallery and the workshops Niall sponsored. But Magnolia is a great place with good people. We're all doing what we can to turn things around."

Avery didn't like the frisson of responsibility that skittered along her skin. She owed nothing to this town or its well-intentioned mayor. Maybe Niall Reed should have paid more attention to his own life and less to his reputation as Magnolia's guardian angel, especially when he no longer had the financial means for that sort of largesse.

"Ignoring reality doesn't help anyone," she told Malcolm, not slowing her pace. "It didn't do much for either of my sisters or me. I'm not sure what you hope or expect from me..."

"I don't want to see Josie's studio close," Malcolm answered without hesitation. "Or Phil's hardware store or the bookshop Stuart's family has owned since his great-grandma retired as the school librarian over thirty years ago."

Avery stopped walking, and Spot wiggled in her arms. Finally, something positive about this morning. The dog wanted some exercise. She lowered the animal to the ground, and Spot quickly trotted over to where someone had dropped a half-eaten breakfast sandwich. The dog gobbled up bites of egg and sausage like she was an Olympic competitor.

"Spot, no." Avery yanked the leash, half dragging the dog away from the food. So much for positive.

"Listen, Mr. Mayor," she said, turning to Malcolm. "As sympathetic as I might be to the plight of a struggling small town, there's nothing I can do to help your friends."

"Are you sympathetic?" His face brightened. "Did you grow up in a small town?"

"No." Avery waved the hand that wasn't holding the leash. "I was raised in San Francisco. We lived in a high-rise downtown, and my mom worked a lot. She's a surgeon. It was a very important job. But I watched *Gilmore Girls* back in the day. I get small towns."

Malcolm threw back his head and laughed, a cackling sound of joy and disbelief. "Lordy, girl. Watching a television show about small-town life is like seeing a photo of cotton candy. It looks good but you sure can't understand the sweet scent or the joy of spun sugar melting on your tongue unless you experience it firsthand."

Avery bent down and picked up Spot again. "I've never had cotton candy."

"Excuse me?"

She shrugged. "My mom didn't believe in sugary treats."

"What's a treat without sugar?" Malcolm shook his head.

"I don't like things that are messy. Like cotton candy. Or children."

"Small-town life is messy," Malcolm said gently. "*Life* is messy."

"Not mine," Avery told him and resumed walking. "It never has been, and I'm not starting now." She spoke the words, hoping the confidence of her tone would convince them both. Her world in the past month barely resembled the life she knew. "I couldn't help the business owners even if I wanted to."

She held up a hand when he would have spoken. "Which I don't. I don't have the money to float them or the clout Niall apparently had with the bank. They aren't going to allow me to continue skipping mortgage payments."

"These are good people, Ms. Keller," Malcolm said, and there was no mistaking the plea in his voice.

"I'm not arguing that point. I wish there was more I could offer."

Did she? This town and the people in it meant nothing to Avery. If she had the ability to help the businesses turn things around, would she take it?

She shook off the thought. It didn't matter because there would be no opportunity for her to help. "I appreciate you taking the time to introduce yourself," she told Malcolm. "I hope whatever happens to Magnolia after I sell Niall's property ends up being for the best."

"Me, too," he agreed, not sounding at all convinced.

"It's a beautiful area," she said, unsure why she felt the need to give him some hope but unable to stop herself. "My background is in business management, and for my senior project in college I did a marketing plan for a small town in northern California. It was just outside wine country so it needed marketing and advertising that would entice tourists to make the stop." She shrugged. "You have so much to offer here. It's past time to look beyond Niall Reed's reputation as a draw for Magnolia. That might have worked a decade ago, but it's not enough."

"I like the way your mind works," Malcolm told her. "We need some innovative thinking around these parts. In fact, you could help—"

"Not me," she said, holding up a hand to cut him off. "I've already told you I'm not staying in town. Now I need to get to the meeting. Have a nice day, Mr. Grimes." She readjusted Spot in her arms and started across the street.

"Call me Malcolm," the mayor shouted as she got to the other side. "All my friends do."

"Bye, Malcolm," she said, waving over her shoulder.

She'd planned to stop in the gallery but bypassed it and headed directly toward the dance studio next door. As she opened the door to enter, Carrie emerged from the gallery.

"I need to talk to you," Carrie called, motioning her away from the door.

Avery glanced toward the front of the gallery and lifted a hand. "Late for my meeting. I'll stop by after," she said and walked into Josie's dance studio.

Spot gave a tiny yip, and Avery felt her mouth drop open as she took in the lobby crowded with people, all of whom seemed to be staring straight at her. "Um... hello," she said softly.

"You're here. Late, but here. Thank heavens." A tall woman who might have had a dancer's build at one time hurried forward. Her graying hair was pulled back into a low bun and she had pale skin and ruby-red lips. Despite being at least twenty pounds overweight, she moved with the innate grace of someone who'd spent her life at a barre. "I'm Josie Trumbell and you must be Avery."

Avery gave a slight nod.

Josie waved toward the people smiling hopefully at the two of them. "We've been waiting."

"I thought we had a meeting scheduled." Avery noticed that Josie seemed intent on not making eye contact with her. "To talk about your lease," she added even though they both knew why they were supposed to meet.

"Tried to warn you," Carrie muttered from behind Avery's left shoulder. She hadn't noticed her sister enter the dance studio behind her.

"And who is this adorable creature?" Josie reached out her red-tipped fingers to scratch between Spot's ears. The dog preened like the attention was her due.

"This is Spot." Avery leaned closer to Josie. "Why are these people here?"

"They're the parents of my students," Josie explained in a voice that carried. "The children have something special planned. As many who could make it came in early just for you."

"Oh, no." Avery tucked Spot under one arm and held up her free hand. "This is a business meeting."

"How can we discuss the studio's future until you understand what my classes mean to this community?"

"I'm sure they mean a great deal. I just don't ca—" Avery broke off when the crowd surrounding them seemed to surge forward at her words. She had the sneaking suspicion she might be subjected to an old-fashioned tarring and feathering if she didn't make time for whatever Josie had planned.

This wasn't fair. How could she be expected to care about a bunch of people she didn't know? Magnolia wasn't her town, and she hadn't made the mess of Niall's finances. From what she understood, he'd raked in plenty of profits from his art back in the day. Maybe if he'd been more responsible with how he handled his money, the people who'd depended on him wouldn't be in this predicament now.

She glanced at the faces of the parents in the lobby, a sick pit opening in her stomach. She didn't want to be the bad guy again, especially not in this situation. Her gaze snagged on a pair of green eyes. Gray Atwell gave her an almost imperceptible smile along with an encouraging nod. Was Violet part of this stunt?

Had he known Avery was being set up this way? Not that he owed her any loyalty, but it still stung.

"I don't have a lot of time," she lied to Josie. All Avery had was time. Time and a growing balance of credit card debt.

"Then let's get started." The older woman took Avery's hand in hers. Josie's grip was sure, her skin soft in the same way Avery remembered from her mother. "Available students in each class, from the tiny toes to the teens, have put together a short demonstration of their current program. It will be like a mini recital."

"Oh, joy," Avery muttered.

Josie squeezed her fingers, tucking Avery and Spot closer against her side. She smelled like some sort of overflowery perfume or lotion and Avery could just imagine the multitude of wee dancers in Magnolia who'd grown up only to have the scent of roses carry them back to their childhood. She almost laughed at the fact that this woman holding her hand had reminded Avery of her mother. Melissa Keller didn't hold hands. She rarely showed any sort of physical affection, unless straightening Avery's school uniform counted.

Josie and Avery walked into the open dance studio, which was bright and welcoming with large windows, polished floors in honey-colored wood and a row of ballet barres in front of a wall of shiny mirrors. "We hold our seasonal recitals at the elementary school," Josie explained. "But this will do for today."

"It isn't going to change anything." Avery felt compelled to say the words out loud.

"Maybe not," Josie agreed with a sad smile. "But the kids wanted to try."

Avery plastered a smile on her face as Josie led her to a row of chairs situated against the far wall. What else was she supposed to do? The parents followed, filling in the seats around her, although no one sat directly beside her until Carrie and Gray approached. Her sister took the seat to Avery's left and Gray to her right. Spot remained in her arms, happy to be cradled like a baby. Avery tried to take comfort in the dog's steady heartbeat. At least someone was happy with this turn of events.

"Sorry," Carrie mouthed, patting Avery's leg as she tucked her purse under the chair.

"Nice mini cow," Gray told her. He reached out to scratch Spot's back, earning a soft snuffle from the animal.

"Did you know about this?" Avery demanded under her breath.

He shook his head. "Not until one of the moms called me to say she was picking up a few of the dance class girls early from school."

His words eased a bit of the tension spiraling through her. "It's ridiculous," she whispered.

"Josie has a special way with the kids," he countered gently. "She's an institution around here."

"I'm not debating that. But—"

She broke off as Josie introduced the first group of dancers. Five young girls and two boys filed out from a door at the other side of the studio. They couldn't have been more than three years old. The girls wore pale pink leotards with tulle tutus, tights and soft ballet slippers. Several of them looked nervous while a couple of the girls offered gapped-tooth grins to the audience. One of the boys, a skinny towhead, waved at his parents.

Spot perked up, shifting in Avery's arms as if intrigued by the performance. They watched as the kids began to move through the choreographed positions. Avery had expected it to be adorable. She wasn't completely unaware of the charm of children even if she typically remained immune to it.

But Gray had been correct. Josie was amazing with the kids. Her love for dance and teaching it was palpable. None of the kids was going to give Misty Copeland a run for her money, but each of them danced with an infectious joy that couldn't be denied.

After a few minutes, the music ended. The first

group of dancers bowed and then filed out of the room, replaced by the next class. Violet appeared, still sporting Avery's braids from yesterday. She waved to her father, beamed at Carrie and then shot Avery an angry death glare.

Avery tugged on the ends of her hair and mouthed, "Nice braids," earning an eye roll from the girl.

"You know she's five," Gray whispered, leaning in. "You're supposed to be the adult."

Oh, yeah, Avery's girlie parts wanted to shout as Gray's heat and masculine scent washed over her. All grown woman right here.

"Kids shouldn't be coddled," she answered instead, then bit the inside of cheek, hating that she sounded like her mother.

"Dad used to say the same thing," Carrie told them both. "That's a strange coincidence."

"Stop distracting me. I'm pretending to care." Avery ignored both Carrie and Gray, even when she felt them share a look behind her back.

She'd never admit it, but she did care. It was infuriating to have her emotions manipulated by a financially strapped dance teacher and her students, but Avery couldn't help it.

Of course she still didn't believe she could help Josie. Maybe that explained the tears that pricked the backs of her eyes when the final students, three awkward and lovely preteen girls, took their bows.

As the parents clapped, Josie glided toward Avery with a triumphant smile. "Well?" she demanded. "Weren't they magnificent?"

"Yes," Avery said simply. Maybe she wouldn't have chosen the word *magnificent* to describe the dancers, but the show of solidarity and the attempt to sway her from a path she hadn't chosen was something to behold.

"Does this make you change your mind about selling the building?" Josie asked, her tone so hopeful it made Avery's heart lurch.

The children had followed their beloved teacher, and Avery felt her cheeks burn as everyone in the room seemed to hold a collective breath waiting for her answer.

"I can't... There isn't..." She shook her head. "I don't—"

"We don't have a plan yet," Carrie said, jumping to her feet and taking Avery's hand. "But Avery, Meredith and I are working on one. Our father loved this town, and Avery already sees how special it is."

"I don't," Avery protested, teeth grinding at the gasps of horror that went up around her at those blasphemous words. "I *do* see that Magnolia is special," she amended. "But I'm not—"

"Ready to give up on Dad's dream just yet," Carrie supplied.

Avery pinched the back of Carrie's arm so hard the other woman yelped.

"Thank you," Josie said, wiping tears from her eyes. "I know you'll think of a way to save us. It's what your father would have wanted."

"I'm not anyone's savior," Avery said quickly. "Clearly neither was Niall. Despite what Carrie has led you to believe—"

"Can I pet your cow?" a girl asked, moving forward.

"She's a dog," Avery clarified.

Spot wriggled and licked the child's hand as she rubbed her freckled nose.

"She's cute," another girl said, joining her friend.

A moment later, Avery was surrounded. She cringed as the dancers pummeled her with questions and invitations for Spot to have playdates with their various pets.

"Dogs don't do playdates," she muttered, eyes narrowing at the sound of Gray's deep chuckle next to her. She sent him a desperate glance. "Help me."

"Looks like you and Spot have got this one covered," he answered, moving away from the sea of pink tulle.

Spot was shockingly in her element, so animated Avery wondered if the dog might have a heart attack from all the excitement. She lowered the animal to the wood floor, and Spot did her back-flop trick, much to the delight of the pint-sized ballerinas.

"Come to the gallery when you're finished here," Carrie said, giving her shoulder a squeeze. "We'll work on a plan."

"The plan is selling the buildings."

"Good luck with that," Carrie offered, then made her way out of the crowd.

Luck was just what she needed, Avery thought, wincing as several dancers shrieked when Spot let out a loud dog fart.

Luck and a giant bottle of headache medicine.

CHAPTER EIGHT

GRAY CLENCHED AND unclenched his fists as he sat in the upscale waiting room of the medical office in downtown Raleigh.

"She shouldn't be too much longer," the receptionist offered with an apologetic smile. "Are you sure I can't get you a bottle of water?"

"I'm fine, Tammy. Thanks." Tammy Brooks had been his ex-wife's receptionist since Stacy started her practice. Although loyal to her boss, Tammy had always been kind to Gray, even through the tensest moments of the divorce. She was also unfailingly kind to Violet, who often spent time waiting for Stacy to finish with clients.

"It's Voss, if that makes a difference."

Gray didn't bother to hide his confusion. "Should it?"

"She pays a lot of money for it. People say it's really fresh and clean like…"

"Water?" he prompted.

Tammy grinned. "I guess."

"I'm partial to tap water," he admitted.

"Then let me get you a glass of tap water."

He gritted his teeth, then flashed a smile. "You're a sweetheart. A glass of plain old tap would be great."

The slim redhead jumped up like she'd just been handed the Olympic torch. "How about ice?"

"Your call," he told her and she disappeared down the hall toward the break room.

He leaned back in his chair and studied the photographs that lined the wall on the opposite side of the waiting room. Various portraits of his ex-wife, several of them with clients and two outdoors in a local park with Violet. The images displayed a maternal warmth he was surprised Stacy managed to muster, even for the camera.

No, that wasn't fair. Stacy could be wonderful when she set her mind to it. Gray had fallen for her fast and hard when they'd first met. He'd been a newly minted firefighter in Raleigh, out celebrating with his buddies and she was part of a bachelorette party at the same bar. With her dark hair, pale skin and luminescent blue eyes, she'd been one of the most beautiful women he'd ever seen. She'd held herself apart from her friends and the other patrons, and Gray had wanted her instantly, much like a coveted toy just out of reach.

Stacy was seven years older than him, a new doctor in town and intent on becoming the most sought-after dermatologist in North Carolina. Her ambition fascinated him. Although he understood he was just a physical diversion for her, he hadn't cared. His mom had warned him as a kid not to grasp for a life above his station, and he should have heeded her advice. But within a month, Stacy was pregnant and Gray had been all too happy to marry her and start their future together.

His parents had been married until his dad was killed on the job by a random bullet. From what Gray remembered, his father had loved being a cop, but his devotion to the force had led to a marriage fraught with turmoil. Gray's parents had fought and manipulated one another, their relationship vacillating between random moments of pure bliss to long spans of flaring tempers. As a young boy, he'd grown used to the feeling of his stomach in knots. His mother had loved his dad, but it was a sort of dysfunctional love that wore at them both. Then, after a tragic altercation during a routine traffic stop, Gray's father was gone and they never had the chance at any kind of future.

Gray wanted to create something better in his own marriage, even if its start had been unplanned. It soon became clear that he and Violet weren't the life Stacy wanted. He resisted her pleas to go to work for her father's insurance firm. His career as a firefighter and passion for the job meant nothing to her. It often felt like being a mother to Violet meant just as little.

He tried to understand. Her dad had given her the capital to start her own practice and she devoted all of her time and energy to building her client base. Well, not all of her time. When Violet was three, Gray discovered Stacy was having an affair with the architect who'd designed her office space. He filed for divorce a week later.

It might have been a relief to them both, and he'd believed her when she told him she wanted to be partners in co-parenting. Hollywood types might be the experts on "conscious uncoupling" but Gray had been determined to create a harmonious relationship with his ex for the sake of their daughter. Only Stacy wasn't always a good mother. She ignored Violet a fair bit of the time, forgetting to pick her up on their scheduled weekends, or dragging her to speaking engagements or private Botox parties in the city's wealthier neighborhoods.

So Gray was working on a plan to go back to court

and file for sole custody. He didn't want to keep Stacy from her daughter, but he needed to protect Violet.

"Here's that water." Tammy handed him a tall glass.

"Thanks."

"Are we out of Voss?" Stacy asked as she entered the waiting room from her office.

"He wanted tap," Tammy answered, then retreated behind her desk.

"Figures," his ex-wife muttered.

Gray placed the glass on the table in front of him, trying not to let his mouth gape open as he stood. "What the hell happened to your face?"

Stacy looked like she'd been on the losing end of a fight with Mike Tyson in his heyday. Her entire face was swollen and red, with dark bruises shadowing both of her eyes.

Her lips pressed together. At least he thought that was what happened. He couldn't be quite sure.

"I don't have any more clients for the week so I did a couple of nonsurgical treatments on myself."

"You did that to yourself on purpose?" He couldn't hide his disbelief.

"Don't be ridiculous, Gray. This isn't the end result. Within forty-eight hours the swelling will go down and I'll look ten years younger."

"You don't need it, Stacy."

"I'm almost thirty-six."

"And still gorgeous," he told her. He might not like his ex-wife, but no one could deny her beauty.

She stared at him for several moments before shaking her head. "It's a shame you have no ambition. We could have been something special."

He laughed without humor. "Once upon a time, I thought we were."

She took a step back as if he'd thrown a punch, then steadied herself. "What do you want?"

"I'd like to keep Violet this weekend."

"She's scheduled to be with me."

"I realize that, but tomorrow is the kickoff for Summer Fair in Magnolia. It's the last big festival of the season. Her Dragonfly troupe is marching in the parade. She wants to be a part of it."

"No," Stacy said without hesitation.

"Why?"

"I don't have to give you a reason."

"This isn't about me, Stace."

"Of course not. It's about your precious town."

"She wants to be with her friends. I'll bring her to you in the afternoon if that's what it will take. I'm not asking for much."

"You could have called or texted about this."

True, but he knew she never would have entertained the idea of letting him change the custody schedule unless he subjected himself to a decent amount of groveling. That was easier to do in person.

"Please, Stacy. I'll make it up to you. If you need to adjust the calendar or want an extra weekend, we can work it out."

"Violet and I had plans for the weekend."

Liar, he wanted to shout. Stacy almost always slept late on weekends. Violet would often call him from her mother's phone while she ate a bowl of cereal in front of the television.

"Please," he said again.

"I'll think about it," she finally relented. "Right now I want to go home and put my feet up. I'll text you later."

The urge to argue almost overwhelmed him. But Stacy liked a fight too much to give her that satisfaction. Gray hated fighting. It reminded him of his parents.

"Thank you for considering it," he said, making the gratitude in his tone overt. "I hope your face…" He ran a hand through his hair, still baffled by the lengths women went through to preserve their youth. "Turns out the way you want."

"It will," she answered with a shrill laugh. "I'm the best."

"Of course." He nodded. "I'll wait to hear from you. Thanks for the water, Tammy."

"Sure thing," the receptionist called.

He didn't even care that the other woman had witnessed him begging his ex-wife for something she should be willing to freely give. Hell, Stacy could have offered to bring Violet to the parade if the schedule was so important to her.

His stomach knotted and churned as he walked toward his truck, parked at the end of the block. The late-summer heat wave had finally broken. The unseasonable temperatures gave way to a pleasant cool front accompanied by a gentle breeze.

He'd lived in Raleigh for several years, having packed his beater truck to hightail it out of Magnolia as soon as he'd turned eighteen. At that point small-town life had been like a heavy wool blanket, oppressive and scratchy, weighing him down and chafing at his younger self. Then Violet was born, and suddenly he understood the appeal of a close-knit community.

Even his relationship with his mother had changed,

softening in a way he never could have expected. He appreciated what she'd sacrificed for him and his brother growing up. Life and an unhappy marriage had molded her into the woman he'd known and resented all through his childhood.

Parenthood was a great equalizer.

So when his marriage imploded, it had been the most natural thing in the world to return to Magnolia. As a single dad, he needed the support of a community. He needed to know he wasn't alone.

His hometown was only forty minutes from Raleigh, but it felt like a world away. It also felt like the place he belonged, and he was grateful to the people who had known him forever for taking his daughter into their hearts.

Nothing was more important than Violet and her happiness.

Which was why he forced himself to take several deep breaths and then climb into his truck. As much as he wanted to stalk back to Stacy's office, picking a fight that would end with both of them going for blood, that kind of verbal sparring would do nothing for his girl. He hoped his ex would see her way to agreeing to the parade. But if she didn't, he'd get Violet through the disappointment. He'd make it okay for her because she was everything to him.

"WHAT HAVE YOU done to that dog?"

Avery looked down at Spot, who was nosing around one of the planters of colorful flowers outside the gallery on Saturday morning, then smiled up at Meredith, who approached from around the corner. Avery could feel the stares from the people beginning to line the street along the parade route. She kept her focus on Meredith and Spot.

"I gave her a makeover."

"She's a dog," Meredith muttered. "Not a fashion model."

"I think she looks cute," Carrie offered from where she stood in the gallery's doorway. "Like Olivia the Pig." Carrie edged back to allow Avery and Meredith to enter the empty space.

Carrie wore a long sundress with a pattern of lavender hyacinths splashed across the front. With her hair gently curling around her shoulders, she looked like a perfect Southern belle. Carrie belonged in Magnolia. Meredith, with her fitted T-shirt, cargo pants and boots, seemed far too nineties grunge throwback for the quaint small town, and Avery didn't know how to behave in a place where everyone knew her business.

She'd dressed in a pair of tailored viscose trousers and a silk blouse. Her rationale for the formal outfit was that she should show the people of Magnolia she was a professional. She had her life together and couldn't be swayed in her plan for the inheritance by tiny dancers or personal sob stories or anything of that ilk. But as she'd hurried to the gallery, past families and couples streaming into downtown to kick off the weekend's festival, she realized her formal clothes would only make more glaringly obvious what she already knew. She didn't belong here and her father hadn't wanted her to be a part of his life or his precious town.

The gallery lights were off, although morning sun streamed in from the oversized windows facing the street.

"You said she needed more confidence," Avery told

Meredith. "A new wardrobe can do that for people. It's a fact."

"She's. A. Dog." Meredith bent down to pet the animal, and Spot did her usual flop and roll routine.

Avery had driven over to Raleigh yesterday afternoon, needing to escape her current reality in a way she couldn't manage in Magnolia. She wasn't sure what was so comforting about the anonymity of a big-box store, but wandering the aisles of a familiar layout had calmed her more than she could have imagined. And when she'd ambled into the pet supply section, something had taken over. She'd bought Spot a pink collar studded with rhinestones and a matching leash. She'd also picked up a fuzzy gray dog bed and hadn't been able to resist grabbing a couple of the adorable doggy outfits.

In her old life, Avery shopped with as much efficiency and purpose as she did everything else. She had her groceries delivered, ordered expensive hair products and makeup from an online retailer, and shopped four times a year at the high-end shopping mall near her apartment for seasonal wardrobe updates.

Meandering through a home goods section, selecting colorful towels and washcloths to take back to her sister's apartment, was a comforting indulgence.

Maybe this explained why the children's clothing industry was booming. Shopping was a universal language of love for mothers everywhere. She'd been more excited about her purchases for a dog that wasn't even hers than she'd been last year when she'd stumbled upon a perfect Vera Wang sheath dress on sale in her size.

She'd also grabbed a pink-handled brush and a package of colorful hair ties that would be perfect for Violet. But when she'd gotten back to the guesthouse and unpacked her car, her retail therapy session made her feel weak and embarrassed. She'd shoved the brush and hair ties into a drawer in the bathroom, then put the bags with the rest of her purchases into the closet. Magnolia was a temporary stop for her, not a place to call home.

As much as her endorphins had gone into overdrive during her shopping excursion, the letdown was a real kick in the shins.

But this morning she couldn't help herself from dressing Spot in one of the outfits. The dog had stayed remarkably calm as Avery'd tugged the soft cotton over her head and popped her stubby legs through the arm-holes.

She would have sworn Spot liked wearing the thin argyle sweater.

"You gave her to me to foster. I think the outfit is good for her."

Meredith smoothed a hand over the dog's soft fur. "She's already lost weight."

"She'll be ready to be adopted in no time," Avery said, then touched her chest when it clenched painfully.

Meredith and Carrie shared a look.

"I'm not keeping the dog," Avery said, ignoring the way Spot glanced up as if Avery had hurt her feelings.

"How do you feel about bunnies?" Meredith asked.

Avery shook her head. "Like I've already got enough poop in my life."

A knock at the window had all three women turning. An older man smiled at Carrie and held up his hand, fingers spread out.

"The parade is five minutes out," Carrie reported, her voice suddenly tight. "I asked Gene to keep me updated."

"So this is really happening," Meredith said quietly. "I've been to the Summer Fair Parade every year of my life, and now it feels like we're the spectacle."

"Is your dad going to be here?" Carrie asked, crossing her arms over her chest.

Meredith shook her head. "He went to his hunting cabin near Asheville. It was bad enough that he knew the truth for so many years and had to keep up appearances in town. The fact that everyone knows that my mom cheated on him is scraping at an old wound."

"What do Erik and Theo think about all this?" Carrie glanced toward Avery. "Those are Meredith's brothers."

"Erik wants Dad to move down to Charleston. He says it will be easier to leave the past behind if he gets out of Magnolia." She gave a soft, humorless laugh. "I'm sure he doesn't mean that Dad should leave me behind but…"

"It's not your fault," Carrie said. "The thing that we have to remember is we aren't to blame for this situation."

"But some of us are a living reminder of being hurt," Meredith countered.

Avery stepped closer to her youngest sister, feeling a strangely reassuring kinship at their shared feelings of being outsiders. "We're going to be the center of attention around here today."

"This sucks," Meredith whispered.

"That pretty much sums it up." Avery ran a hand through her hair, wishing she had a hair tie to hold it back. She typically wore it in a tight ponytail at work, when she wanted to be taken seriously. How would the people in Magnolia react to her? She'd met plenty of them since she'd arrived, but today was different. An image of Gray's gentle green eyes flitted through her mind. Would he be there today? He'd mentioned something about a fire truck in the parade. It was silly to take comfort in the presence of a man she barely knew, but she couldn't seem to ignore the spark that flamed to life when they were together.

"Everyone has known about the three of us for a few weeks now. People know Meredith and they've seen Avery around town." Carrie's smile was purposefully bright. "Maybe it won't be as bad as we think."

Meredith snorted but when she would have argued, Carrie held up a hand. "Or maybe we walk out there with our heads held high," she continued. "And screw anyone who wants to judge us for the mistakes Dad made."

"I like the sound of that," Avery said with a choked laugh. Just when she thought she had Carrie pegged as the dutiful daughter, willfully blind to the sins of their father, the other woman surprised her.

"I can deal with giving the one-finger salute to the Nosy Nellies around here," Meredith said, holding up a middle finger toward the bank of windows along the front of the gallery.

Carrie quickly stepped in front of the smaller woman. "It's a metaphorical salute," she said. "Remember, this is still your home."

Meredith turned to Avery. "Are you interested in actually flashing that manicured middle finger at the town today?"

"Hmm…" Avery tapped her chin as if considering the question. "Not today. But thanks for offering."

"Chicken," Meredith mumbled under her breath.

"It's a farm theme to make my cow dog feel more secure." She picked up Spot and straightened the animal's sweater. "It's all about her socialization."

Carrie and Meredith both burst out laughing, and that was how they walked out of the gallery. The three of them laughed and smiled as if they were in on the kind of private joke only sisters could share.

CHAPTER NINE

WITHIN FIVE MINUTES, Avery craved a hot bath, a stiff drink and a pound of chocolate in equal measure. Not that anyone watching would have guessed at her anxiety. She'd always been a master at keeping her feelings hidden. Even when Tony's wife had been hurling insults at her in the lobby of her office and Avery had felt as though she was dying of humiliation and shame on the inside, she'd managed to remain outwardly calm.

Mayor Malcolm had insisted the three of them join him on the podium, where he'd honor Niall Reed as part of his opening remarks for Summer Fair. That meant they were at once part of the action and somewhat removed from the throng of people who'd gathered at the center of town.

"Take a flippin' breath and try to smile," Meredith muttered, nudging Avery's shoulder. "This is a small-town parade, not the prelude to a firing squad."

"I'm breathing," Avery countered, the fact that she wasn't fooling her half sister disconcerting. "It's part of the automatic nervous system. People breathe without conscious effort."

Carrie placed a gentle hand on Avery's arm. "You could try to enjoy the morning."

"Are you having fun?" Avery looked around at the crowd, many of whom alternated between watching the parade action and studying the sisters. Avery felt a sudden kinship with the goldfish who'd been her third-grade class pet. They were on display with nowhere to hide.

"Summer Fair weekend was one of my favorites growing up," Carrie answered.

"She and Niall used to ride on one of the convertibles," Meredith explained, "like the royal family waving to their subjects."

"You were part of it, too." Carrie looked around Avery to shoot Meredith an abrupt glare. "I remember your 4-H group on your horses. You were always laughing and having fun while I was stuck with the adults."

"You loved the attention." Meredith's tone was at once accusatory and doubtful, like she wasn't sure if her recollection could be trusted.

"I wanted friends," Carrie said simply.

Before either Meredith or Avery could answer, one of the town council members leaned forward. "It isn't the same without your father," she said, managing to focus on Carrie while she ignored Avery and Meredith. "He was the heart of this town."

Avery felt the shift in Carrie, as if the words had landed like a blow. She still couldn't understand the intricacies of Carrie's complicated relationship with their father but was coming to believe that her own feelings of bitterness and Meredith's anger might be the easier emotions to unravel.

"The community is the heart of this town," Avery answered, earning a subtle glare from the aging Southern belle. "I'm an outsider and even I can tell that Magnolia doesn't need to rely on one person to keep it vibrant. It's probably time you realize that, as well."

A chorus of gasps from around the covered platform greeted her words, as if she'd made some blasphemous outburst. She and her two sisters stood there, living proof of Niall's fallibility as a man and still she was subject to the subtle canonization of his character in this town.

"Outsider, indeed," the woman mumbled.

"Well said," Malcolm told Avery with a wink before turning to the woman. "Not another word, Karen. Watch the parade. Here comes the high school marching band. Their take on the Black Eyed Peas is the bomb."

"Breathe," Meredith whispered and Avery gave a soft laugh.

"Thanks for the reminder."

Carrie linked her arm with Avery's. "Thanks for the quick comeback with Karen. She had a thing for Dad back in the day."

Avery took a cue from Carrie and linked her arm with Meredith's. They might have plenty of differences among themselves, but in front of the town, solidarity with her sisters gave her a measure of comfort and courage she couldn't explain.

Following the mayor's order, she focused her attention on the parade. She'd watched plenty of them on television as a kid, but this was the first she'd seen in person. Of course, it didn't have the grandeur of the giant pop-culture characters bobbing along crowded city streets, but she couldn't deny the enthusiasm of the participants.

She hummed along with the high school band, waved to a cluster of marching veterans and clapped for a multitude of floats. A large group of dancers from Josie's School of Dance went by, twirling and leaping their hearts out, but she didn't see Violet among the girls. Strange because this seemed like the kind of event Gray's daughter would have loved. Spot lifted her head for a brief moment to sniff the air when the first group of horses clip-clopped by.

"She probably wants to eat the road apples," Meredith said with an eye roll.

"What are road apples?" Avery asked, then groaned. "Eww." She made a face at the dog, who'd tossed a baleful look over her shoulder. "She eats poop?"

"Horse poop," Meredith confirmed. "Lots of dogs do."

"That's disgusting."

"Horse poop is filled with enzymes and partially digested proteins," Meredith explained. "In the grand scheme of things—"

"Save the equine husbandry lesson for later, ladies," Carrie interrupted.

For some reason, the quiet rebuke sparked a fit of giggles in Avery. She'd gone from the big city to a local parade, jamming to a high school band's blaring trumpet section while debating the merits of horse poop. Meredith must have understood the absurdity of the moment because she joined in the laughter, and even Carrie flashed a reluctant smile as she shook her head.

"We're going to get in trouble," Carrie told them in a hushed tone.

"We're grown women," Avery argued but made certain not to meet the disapproving stares of the town council members. Still grinning, she refocused her attention on the parade, her gaze drawn to a pair of amused green eyes.

A slow shiver rolled down her spine as she took in Gray Atwell perched on the running board of a long hook and ladder truck. He wore his dress uniform, the blue button-down shirt stretched taut across his broad chest. Her body reacted the same way it had the first time she'd seen him, only somehow it was amplified by the crowd, the other firefighters surrounding him and—God help her—the massive red truck. More laughter bubbled up in her throat and she worked to swallow it back.

"Talk about a five-alarm blaze," Meredith said under her breath.

Carrie sighed and leaned closer. "I wouldn't mind being hosed down by one of them."

Avery felt her mouth drop open as she shifted her gaze between her two sisters. "You have dirty minds," she told them before finding Gray again. He was still looking at her, one thick brow arched in question.

No way would she ever share her thoughts on this with him.

Then the fire truck had rolled past and a group of pint-sized cyclists came into view before them.

Meredith whistled softly. "Gray Atwell? That was quick work, Avs."

"I told you, don't call me Avs." She crossed her arms over her chest. "There's nothing between Gray and me. I'm staying in Carrie's apartment, so he's my landlord."

"You make it sound kinky," Meredith told her.

Avery felt color flood her cheeks. Plenty of her thoughts about Gray could be filed in the "kinky" folder, but she wasn't about to admit it.

"Enough." Carrie was back to sounding like a school-teacher disciplining her wayward students. "The parade is ending. It's time for the speech."

"Remind me why we didn't drink before this," Avery said.

"Because Meredith is a loose cannon stone-cold sober," Carrie answered immediately. "It's game over when she's drinking."

"I can control myself," Meredith argued, reaching around Avery to flick Carrie hard on the temple.

"Ow." Carrie pressed two fingers to the side of her head.

Malcolm turned to the three of them. "Ladies."

They straightened and fell silent.

Avery tried not to fidget under the weight of the stares they received from the crowed. It had been bad enough when the attention was divided between them and the parade, but now they seemed to be the only thing anyone could look at. The mayor began to speak, but apparently most people felt as though they could listen to Malcolm Grimes while their attention remained on Avery, Carrie and Meredith.

She wished she'd worn something else, an outfit that would have allowed her to blend in more. It had been easy to feel brave and confident, ready to thumb her nose at the rising crest of small-town judgment when she'd been alone in the carriage house this morning. Now she simply wanted to disappear.

These people knew Carrie and Meredith, so while her sisters were also on display, Avery couldn't help but feel as though she warranted the most interest. It reminded her of those terrible weeks between losing her job and leaving San Francisco. She'd had to return to the office to meet with Human Resources after Tony's wife had outed her publicly for the affair. Of course, no one cared about Avery's side of the story or the lies she'd been told by the man she thought she loved. Her coworkers, the people she thought were her friends, had

risen from their cubicles and come out of individual offices to line the hall, glaring at her as she walked to the
office of the HR manager.

She hadn't even questioned why the woman didn't
put a stop to the outward display of hostility. Avery wore
her guilt like a hair shirt, willing to take any anger and
animosity directed her way if it could possibly begin to
make amends for the mistakes she'd made.

But she hadn't done anything wrong in Magnolia.
No part of this situation was her doing. Of course, she
understood the locals must hate her for what she represented. Her desire to sell Niall's properties probably
didn't cast her in a positive light, either. What else could
they expect from her?

"It's curiosity," Carrie said, her lips barely moving.
"Keep smiling."

Avery wasn't sure whether to be amused or annoyed
by the way her sisters, who were still virtual strangers,
seemed to be able to read her thoughts so easily. But she
took the advice to heart and kept a smile on her face as
she listened to Malcolm give an overview of the history of Summer Fair and then transition to memorial-
izing Niall Reed.

To her surprise, the mayor offered a realistic por-
trayal of the man who'd been her father, covering both
his contributions to the town and the challenges Niall
had faced in both his professional and personal life.
She could almost see the expressions on the faces of
people in the crowd soften as Malcolm gave a high-
level account of the predicament Carrie, Meredith and
Avery had been thrust into because of the stipulations
in Niall's will.

Although she didn't like having her private business

on display for public consumption, it was necessary in a town like Magnolia for the community to understand the facts about the situation. Without that, speculation and rumors would run rampant. Avery had already been down that path. The worst of it—the thing that had almost broken her—was the gossip that she'd had a hand in Tony's son being injured. That she'd been involved in the car accident or had caused it in some way. Of course it was ridiculous, but even though she knew that in her heart, the fact that people could believe her capable of something so heinous cut her to the core.

She might not want to be Magnolia's savior, but she also wasn't keen to take up the mantle of villain for this close-knit community.

While the mayor's speech only lasted a few minutes, it felt like she was on display for hours. Finally he ended with a call to enjoy the weekend's festivities and to remember that Magnolia would continue to be a strong, vital community going forward. He was certain Niall's daughters would help solidify their father's legacy and dedication to the town.

"Not to put us on the spot or anything," Avery said into Mayor Grimes's ear when the man gave each of the sisters a hug.

"I play to win," he said with an face-splitting grin. "One of these days I'll tell you all about my illustrious football career back at UNC."

She rolled her eyes. "I'm breathless with anticipation."

The mayor threw back his head and guffawed. "I like you, Avery Reed."

"Avery Keller," she clarified.

"Uh-huh," he agreed before moving into the crowd.

"Pitting out over here." Meredith held her arms aloft and fanned herself. "I hate being on display."

"Why did we agree to that again?" Avery asked.

Carrie surveyed the crowd. "It was a show of strength. They're watching, waiting for one of us to crack."

Avery followed the other woman's gaze. Several people shot surreptitious glances in her direction. "You make it sound like a horror movie. Like we've got zombies waiting to ambush us."

"Worse," Carrie said. "Small-town gossips."

"We're all over the Magnolia Musings Instagram account."

"Did you see the front page of the *Blossom*?" Carrie turned toward them.

Avery shook her head. "What's the *Blossom*?"

"The weekly newspaper," Meredith explained.

"It's published on Fridays, and we were the headline."

"Excuse me?" Avery tried to wrap her mind around this new information. "How are we the headline?"

"A profile on each of us," Carrie said. "I didn't mention it earlier because I thought you'd freak out."

"You think?"

Meredith shrugged. "I'm not sure why Carrie and I had to be a part of it. They already know us. Everyone wants the details about your life."

Avery felt like she'd been punched. "What details?"

"Your history. Your people."

"I don't have *people*."

"Not much of a history, either." Meredith tugged on the ends of Avery's hair. "They dedicated two paragraphs to why you usually wear your hair in a ponytail. Today's style should provide a juicy follow-up piece."

"That's creepy."

"Yeah," both women said at once, then glared at each other as if irritated to agree about something.

"Mavis Bell publishes the paper," Carrie told her. "She's been running it for forty years. Usually, no one pays much attention but I heard she's doing a second printing this weekend."

"I'm going back to the carriage house," Avery said, panic fluttering in her chest. What if Mavis Bell uncovered the specifics of why she'd left San Francisco? It wasn't as if her affair and the fallout had made the news or anything. But a call to the right person would reveal too much.

"You can't leave now," Carrie told her. "People will want to meet you."

"And try to convince me not to sell the downtown buildings."

"Probably," Meredith confirmed.

"I've met plenty of people already." Just then, Spot tugged on the leash, straining to get to the steps that led off the podium, clearly ready to mingle.

"Do it for the dog," Meredith told her. "Be sure to let everyone know she'll be ready for adoption in a few weeks."

Avery didn't like the way her stomach turned at the thought of that, but she nodded. "Also that she'll come with an incredible wardrobe."

Meredith inclined her head. "Right. I'm heading over to the shelter's booth to make sure everything's under control. I'll see you two later."

"I made an appointment with a Realtor from Raleigh for next week," Avery said as Meredith started to walk away.

Both of her sisters turned to face her.

"We haven't agreed on anything yet," Carrie said tightly. "You can't decide on your own."

Meredith gestured to the crowded town square. "Interesting timing on dropping the news."

"I know." Avery bit down on her lower lip. "You're both right but we can't move forward without understanding the value of the property. It's just a meeting."

"Maybe to you," Carrie said quietly, then stalked away without another word.

Meredith pointed at Avery. "I wish you'd quit doing that."

"Doing what?"

"Making stupid decisions or comments so that I realize I'm on the same side as Carrie half the time. It's way more comfortable when I hate her."

"You don't hate her," Avery answered.

"Which is a big problem." Meredith shook her head. "We've got bowls of water for the dogs at the shelter booth. Make sure Spot doesn't get dehydrated."

Avery nodded and watched Meredith disappear into the crowd.

Why *had* she mentioned the Realtor meeting right now? Maybe she needed to remind all of them that they weren't allies in this. The mayor's speech, as innocuous as it had been, gave her all the feels. She'd always wanted to belong but had never quite found her place. Magnolia wasn't it. This small town couldn't offer her the sense of home she craved. Secrets never stayed secret in places like this, and once people found out about her past, they'd hate her and rightfully so.

She'd made mistakes and wasn't sure she'd ever stop

paying for them. How could she expect anyone else to forgive her when she couldn't forgive herself?

Spot strained against the end of the leash again, pulling her back to the present moment. Someone had dropped a chunk of donut on the ground at the bottom of the stairs, and the dog was determined to get to it. She scooped up the animal.

"No people food," she scolded gently, moving down the steps and away from the discarded pastry before lowering Spot to the ground again.

She focused on drawing air in and out of her lungs when she realized she was holding her breath again. So much for an automatic function.

A woman who looked like she might be close to Avery's age approached. "I love your outfit," she said with a disarmingly friendly smile.

Avery hadn't been on the receiving end of that kind of easy warmth recently. "Thanks." She smoothed a hand over the front of her shirt. "I think I'm overdressed, though."

"You look sophisticated," the woman told her. "Like you don't belong here."

"Oh...well..." Avery kept her smile even. The words were spoken in a lilting accent, the type she imagined Scarlett O'Hara would have had back in the day. And while Avery might agree she didn't belong in Magnolia, somehow the words still cut. "Obviously, I'm here temporarily."

"Obviously," the woman agreed. "I'm Annalise Haverford. Of the Charlotte Haverfords."

"Of course you are." Maybe Avery shouldn't have been so quick to appreciate the woman's friendliness.

Apparently there was a thin line between Southern hospitality and latent hostility.

An adorable girl with intricately curled hair ran up to the woman and hugged her leg. "This is my daughter, Margo."

"Margo," Avery repeated, eyes narrowing. Violet's kindergarten tormentor was named Margo.

"Hello," the girl said with a smile that mimicked her mother's. "Your dog is ugly."

Avery gasped and glanced down at Spot, who had flopped on her back at the girl's feet.

"She is a bit odd," Annalise confirmed. "I'm guessing she's one of Meredith's reject mutts. That one is always taking in the most hopeless strays, then trying to foist them off on people. You seem more a purebred type although…" Her tinkling laughter filled the air. "I guess looks can be deceiving."

Red splashes of fury danced in front of Avery's eyes. She bent to pick up the dog. "Spot is perfect just the way she is," she said, clutching the wriggling dog to her chest. "And any day of the week, I'll take a sweet mutt over a purebred…" She stopped and drew in a breath.

Annalise watched her, a smirk playing around the corner of her mouth, as if she relished the thought of Avery going off on her. It was difficult to believe that was possible. Why would this stranger goad her into lashing out?

A wave of affection for Violet Atwell rolled through Avery. No wonder the girl had been obsessed with braids. If precious Margo was anything like her mother…

"It was nice to meet you," she said to Annalise, taking a step away.

The woman's gaze shuttered, clearly disappointed in Avery's lack of reaction. "I'm sure we'll meet again."

Not if I can help it, Avery thought as she turned and fled through the crowd. A few people greeted her and several others tried to make eye contact, but she kept moving. Annalise's veiled slights had somehow made a crack in the wall she'd erected to barricade her emotions. Now she couldn't seem to stop the flood of feelings surging through her. Sorrow. Regret. Anger. Bitterness.

But the one that really hurt was the humiliation at where her life had ended up.

She didn't belong in Magnolia.

She didn't belong anywhere.

CHAPTER TEN

GRAY MADE HIS way through the already thick crowd gathered for Summer Fair, waving and saying a few words to friends and acquaintances without stopping for any lengthy conversations.

It wasn't exactly that he was on a mission to track down Avery...except he was determined to find her.

His gaze had locked on the elegant blonde as soon as the station's ladder truck turned the corner onto First Avenue. She'd stood between Carrie and Meredith, shoulders back and features composed, like she was some sort of ancient queen surveying the troops as they rolled by on the way to battle.

But Gray understood she was the one under siege. He'd seen glimpses of her soft underbelly and understood that vulnerability was rare and precious. Maybe he was projecting what he wanted to see, but today couldn't have been easy for her. Not for any of Niall's daughters. On display in front of the town, representing a father who'd betrayed each of them in separate ways.

Avery's distress affected him at some bone-deep level he couldn't seem to shake. It was more than the incendiary kiss they'd shared, although he wouldn't mind more of that. The connection went further than physical attraction. He *knew* her, or at least he wanted to, idiot that it made him.

He checked the animal shelter booth but didn't find her there. Carrie was deep in conversation with Josie, most likely brainstorming ways to save the downtown businesses that Niall had supported even after his circumstances changed. He admired his old friend's dedication to her late father and the town, although he understood she paid a steep price for both.

As he maneuvered past a group of teenagers huddled over their phones in the middle of the row of booths, Malcolm Grimes caught his eye. The mayor hitched his head in the direction of the alley that separated the buildings on the two main blocks of downtown.

Gray didn't bother to wonder how the older man knew he was searching for Avery. He nodded, mouthed, "Thank you," and headed for the alley.

The air felt a few degrees cooler between the buildings, the alley still shaded from the late-morning sun. He found Avery on the stairs behind the back exit to the gallery. She didn't look up as he approached, but her tiny cow dog stood and gave him a quick yip before plopping to her belly again. The dog's leash had been tied to the metal railing, although he doubted the animal would go far. She seemed to have quickly bonded to her human foster mom.

"Nice outfit," he said, almost taking a step back at the glare Avery shot him.

"I know it's inappropriate." She fisted her hands on the knees of her fancy tailored slacks. "I'm too dressy. I don't fit in. This isn't my home."

Gray held up his hands, palms out. "I was talking about Spot's sweater."

"Oh," Avery breathed, scrunching up her nose. "She likes it."

The dog wagged her stubby tail as he bent for an ear scratch. "Believe it or not, I can tell. Has she lost weight?"

Avery nodded, her features gentling in a way that made his breath hitch. "Meredith thinks so. Apparently, managing the weight loss of an overweight mutt is the only thing I'm not screwing up at this point."

"Don't forget your braiding acumen. Mind if I join you?"

She scooted over on the concrete step by way of an answer and he dropped down next to her. The muted din from the festival drifted into the quiet space, but there was still a sense of privacy, as if they were the only two people for miles.

At least that was how he felt with Avery. Close to her, the rest of the world fell away and it was easy to forget all the reasons they weren't right for each other. He spread his legs slightly so their thighs barely touched, unable to resist but also unwilling to push her for more. Not with how fragile she seemed at the moment.

"I met Margo and her sweet-tea-sippin' mother."

"Violet's nemesis," Gray muttered.

"Monday morning your kid is going to school with the best damn braids anyone has ever seen. It's going to be like the Oscars of kindergarten braids."

"So you and Annalise hit it off?"

She laughed. "Instant besties."

"Not all the women around here are like that."

"I bet some of them are worse."

He scratched his chin, considering that. He didn't pay a lot of attention to the way women interacted with each other. Stacy had accused him of not paying much attention at all. "Probably, but you're from the city and

I've been on the receiving end of your attitude. I bet you can throw back anything they dish out."

Her shoulders rose and fell as she sighed. "Annalise got to me. Or she was the straw that broke this camel's back. The morning—being on display and listening to all that about Niall—it's a lot to handle. I'm not sure I was ready for it."

"You look beautiful," he told her, tracing one finger along the seam of her slacks.

"I feel ridiculous in these clothes. They aren't appropriate for a summer festival and now it seems like I'm trying too hard."

"Yeah," he agreed. "You should take them off."

She laughed again, only this time it sounded real, which made him ridiculously happy.

"You don't even like me."

"I don't have to like you to want to see you naked."

That comment earned him an elbow to the ribs.

"Kidding," he amended quickly. "I like you. From what I've heard, everyone who's met you so far likes you."

She blinked, long lashes fluttering against her delicate skin. "Really? Never mind. I don't care. It makes me sound pathetic if I care."

"Caring isn't pathetic," he told her, needing her to believe it for both their sakes. Gray knew the downfall of his marriage had been caring too damn much. He'd spent more than his fair share of time feeling pitiful as a result.

"Do you care what people think of you?" she asked without looking at him.

He leaned in closer. "I care what you think."

The corners of her lips curved as she turned, almost tentatively pressing her mouth to his.

Based on her reaction to their first kiss, he let her lead. The last thing he wanted to do was spook her, even if the maddeningly slow place made him ten kinds of crazy. She explored him as if she had all the time in the world, nipping at his bottom lip.

When she pulled back, he remained still, hoping that the desire in her eyes meant she wasn't already having second thoughts.

"Another mistake?" he asked softly.

She shook her head but said, "I don't want to want you."

"And yet?"

"I do."

"I'm glad." He reached out and tucked a loose strand of hair behind her ear.

"What's next?" She glanced around as if she expected a bed to appear in the middle of the empty alley.

He chuckled. "Are you in a hurry?"

"Maybe."

"I'm not." He slanted his head and claimed her mouth. He wanted to reassure her but at the same time he couldn't help deepening the kiss.

They broke apart when Spot let out a series of yapping barks.

A couple of kids chased a ball into the mouth of the alley. They didn't notice Avery and Gray, but still the spell had been broken.

"I should go," she told him.

"Are you meeting up with your sisters at the festival?"

"My sisters," she repeated. "It's strange to hear them

referred to that way out loud. I should head home." She cleared her throat. "Back to the carriage house."

"Without spending any time at Summer Fair?"

She shrugged. "It feels weird walking around by myself. Like I should be carrying a sign that says Outsider."

"Come with me," he urged gently.

"Where's Violet?"

Gray felt his shoulders go stiff and forced himself to relax. "She's with her mom in Raleigh until tomorrow. I asked Stacy to bring her for the parade, but she refused."

"That sucks," Avery said simply.

"It does indeed. It also means I've got no one to hang out with today."

"You must have a million friends. You grew up here and you work for the fire department. Firefighters always have tons of buddies."

"Is that some kind of rule?"

She grinned and, once again, his heart lurched. "That's how they make it seem in all the TV shows. The department is one big, happy family."

"Mostly true, but a lot of them have their own families. At least the ones that will be at the festival this early."

"The single men on the prowl come out at night?"

"I'm not sure I'd phrase it like that."

"You're single."

"I have Violet, so I don't date."

"Is *that* a rule?"

"Only for me."

"You're a good dad, Gray."

"I try." Her words fluttered through him like butterfly wings. "I'll bring Violet down tomorrow after Stacy drops her off. Today, I'd like to show you around. Fairs and festivals are the cornerstone of small-town life. You need an appropriate tour guide to really get the most out of your experience."

"Lead on, Mr. Magnolia," she said, straightening from the step. The dog got to its feet as well when Avery untied the leash. "Could our first stop be Meredith's booth? Spot might be thirsty." She patted the dog's smooth head. "Do you need a drink, pretty girl?"

"Sure," he agreed, somewhat dazed at the contradictions of Avery Keller and how enamored they made him. He'd assumed by her polished appearance that she was like his ex-wife, but this woman constantly surprised him with her heart and the way she cared, even when she didn't want to.

He followed her toward the noise of Summer Fair, reminding himself to keep his thoughts on the moment and nothing more.

FOUR HOURS LATER, Avery was hot, sticky and her cheeks hurt from smiling so much. Really smiling, not the forced push of muscles that had become her go-to in most social situations.

Her earlier wariness felt like an overreaction now, a conditioned response that had more to do with her past than the present in Magnolia. Or perhaps the fun she'd had today was a result of Gray. As she'd guessed, he seemed to be friends with almost everyone in town. His acceptance of her smoothed things over in a way Avery could have never accomplished on her own. Even when she was with Carrie and Meredith, people remained suspicious of her motives. She was the interloper who wanted to abandon the town to strangers.

Gray simply didn't allow that to be an issue. He introduced her as his friend, an odd term given their short, combustible history together. No one contradicted his assessment, and Avery slowly slid into the role, finding it fit like a comfortable pair of slippers. She might think he was hot as all get-out. Her body practically hummed with appreciation when the fabric of his T-shirt pulled tight over his chest, but she still managed to relax around him. And Avery typically wasn't great at relaxing.

"One more try," he told her as she turned from the glass milk jugs positioned in front of a backdrop painted to look like a snowy mountain scene. They'd been playing arcade games on the fair's midway for the past half hour. Gray had easily won three prizes in a row at the ring toss. Spot seemed as excited as Avery at the new stuffed animals, but Avery wanted to win something for herself, caught up in the adrenaline of Gray's victory.

"It's hopeless," she said with a sigh. "I have no skill."

Gray put another dollar on the counter and the high school kid working the booth placed four more plastic rings in front of Avery. "You just need to get the right motion."

She stifled a laugh and glanced up at him. "Clearly you're an expert."

"As a matter of fact…" He gave her an exaggerated wink. "Face forward."

She turned toward the back of the booth, where the milk jugs had been lined up in neat rows. The object of the game was to flip the ring over a bottle's neck. A group of preteen boys played next to her, cheering and egging each other on as their plastic rings clattered to the ground. So far only one of them had managed to place three of the four rings over the necks of the bottles in a single turn in order to win a prize. One athletically inclined looking boy and Gray. He'd won at every game she'd challenged him to, and his easy confidence was both appealing and annoying as hell.

He grabbed the four rings in one large hand and stepped closer to her. His front pressed against her back. The scent of his soap and minty gum enveloped her and her body heated for a reason that had nothing to do with the heat and humidity of the day.

"You can't possibly think this is going to help me concentrate," she said, her voice unnaturally husky.

He chuckled into her ear. "It's all in the wrist action."

"So says the master," she murmured.

"Focus," he whispered, which felt impossible with his warm breath tickling her neck.

He dropped a ring into her hand, then encircled her wrist with two fingers. "Stay loose and make the toss gentle."

Avery was too busy trying to keep her knees from buckling to worry about anything else at the moment. He showed her the motion he wanted her to mimic. Sparks zipped along her skin at the feel of his calloused hand covering hers.

"Now, toss," he said.

She released the first ring and it arced through the air with far more grace than her previous tries. To her utter surprise, it landed on one of the milk jugs in the center, slipping over the bottle's neck as if there'd been no question of the outcome.

"I did it." She started to turn, but Gray held her fast.

"One down," he said. "Two more to go."

He stayed at her back for the second toss, which

clinked against the rim of a bottle but still slid into place.

The third toss landed between two bottles, but when Gray pressed the final ring into her palm, Avery was determined to make it count.

"I've got this," she murmured, more to herself than him. Gray pulled away slightly, and her body immediately wanted to protest. Instead she closed her eyes and visualized the motion of the ring soaring toward its target, then opened them again and tossed it into the air.

She held her breath for the seconds it took the ring to drop onto the neck of the third bottle. "That's three," she said, pumping her fists in the air.

"Nice, lady," the teenager working the booth told her as the pack of boys groaned and gave each other grief about being beaten by a chick. "Pick your prize."

"The bear," she said. Her grin widened as he handed her the stuffed animal with the bow tied around its neck.

She turned to Gray, only to find him huddled with the boys. There were four of them, each with his eyes cast to the ground. After a moment, Gray nodded and the boys approached her.

"Good job with your toss," the tallest said. "And not because you're a chic—" He paused when one of his buddies smacked him on the arm. "Because you're a lady."

"Yeah," another boy agreed, adjusting the bill of his baseball cap. "It was just good."

"Thanks," she said as Spot trundled forward to sniff the row of grungy sneakers.

"Can I pet your dog?" baseball cap boy asked.

Avery opened her mouth to explain that Spot didn't belong to her, then simply said, "Spot's a girl and she'd love to be petted."

The boys crouched down for the flop and roll routine while Gray winked at her. "Nice teddy bear."

"It's for you," she told him.

He blinked. "You won me a bear?"

"You can give it to Violet." She gestured to the three stuffed animals he'd won over the course of the morning, all of which he'd handed to her. "I've got plenty."

As the boys finished loving on Spot and wandered off, she stepped closer to Gray. His cheeks were suddenly tinged with pink.

"Are you blushing?"

He grabbed the stuffed bear from her outstretched hand. "I don't blush."

"Except you are." She picked up the prizes he'd given her. "It's cute."

"Firefighters are manly and hot," he countered, sounding affronted. "Not cute."

"You're cute," she said with a laugh.

"Supporting the local economy," Malcolm Grimes said as he stepped into their path. "Just what I like to see at Summer Fair."

"Hey, Mal." Gray shook the mayor's hand. "Another success on your hands."

"I try." Mal lifted the straw hat from his bald head and waved it like a fan in front of his face. "I must admit I'm looking forward to things cooling off when the sun goes down later."

"I'll be back in my air-conditioned apartment by

then," Avery told him. "Preferably on the couch with a glass of wine."

"But you'll be back for the fireworks tomorrow?" Mal arched a thick brow. "You know, one of your father's most popular paintings depicted the town's annual fireworks display."

"I'm familiar with it." Irritation pricked at the bubble of happiness that had surrounded her during her time with Gray. When she'd first received the letter revealing her father's identity, she'd spent a hazy night with a bottle of Grey Goose, trolling the internet for information on Niall. She'd scrolled through pages that displayed the images of his most prominent works. Had there been a fireworks scene among the hoards of mawkish paintings? Maybe. "I'll try to make it back," she said, knowing she sounded noncommittal. "I've got… There are… I'll try."

"Busy schedule?" Mal asked, his tone laced with amusement. She had a feeling she wasn't fooling the mayor for one moment.

"Did Lucas talk to you about the chili cook-off he's planning for Labor Day? We'd love to have Mayor Mal there as a celebrity judge."

"I'm always available for a good cause." Malcolm looked over Avery's shoulder. "Betsy Perkins and Norma Hall are arguing about how much sugar to put in the sweet tea. I've got to go."

"Mayor and mediator," Gray said with a laugh. "Your work is never done."

"True enough." Mal tipped his hat. "There's a band tomorrow night, too," he told Avery. "If you're here, save me a place on your dance card."

"I will."

She turned to Gray when Malcolm moved past them. "Thanks for the change of subject. It's still strange that people think I should be so honored to be Niall Reed's daughter."

"He's a big deal in Magnolia."

"You think?" she asked, deadpan.

He waved the stuffed animal she'd given him in front of her. "Watch the sarcasm, woman. Or my attack bear will get you."

Suddenly, Spot leapt from the ground, growling and nipping at the toy's fluffy feet.

Avery laughed. "Looks like I've got my own guard dog. Sic 'em, Spot."

"Finally Grayson Atwell has met his match," a deep voice said from behind her.

Avery looked over her shoulder to see a couple approaching, the man in the same blue button-down and dark pants that Gray wore. The woman had long auburn hair and beautiful olive-toned skin. She was petite other than her adorably rounded belly, clearly signaling the third trimester of pregnancy.

Spot continued to bark, so Avery scooped her up to soothe her. She assumed the man referred to the dog, although his assessing gaze traveled between Avery and Gray.

"Not funny as usual," Gray said, smiling broadly. "Avery, these are my friends Lucas and Jennie Michaels. Lucas has no sense of humor but he's a damn fine firefighter. Jennie is his far better half."

"More like my better three quarters now," Lucas

said. Avery laughed when his wife gave him a play-ful shove.

"Don't make pregnancy jokes," she told him. "Or you'll force me to agree with Gray about your humor."

"You know it makes me happy to have more of you to love." Lucas wrapped his arms around Jennie, who let out a squeak of protest.

"More of me to love," she muttered before smiling at Avery. "Did he just say that out loud?"

"Unfortunately," Avery confirmed. "I'm Avery Keller. I'm…" She glanced at Gray.

"Oh, honey." Jennie extracted herself from her hus-band's embrace. "We know who you are." She gave Avery a tight hug. "I'm sorry your dad was a piece of crap."

Lucas laughed. "Jen. Boundaries."

The apparently feisty brunette waved away her husband's concern. "I'm pregnant. I get a pass on boundaries due to hormones." She squeezed Avery's shoulders. "I was also raised by a single mom, so I get deadbeat dads, although yours was one for the ages."

Avery felt Gray shift closer, as if he wasn't sure how she'd respond to Jennie's blunt words. "Truer words were never spoken," she said, nodding. She would have taken Jennie's honesty over the artificial kindness she'd received from Annalise Haverford.

"It's nice to meet you," Lucas said, tugging his wife back a few steps and offering his hand to Avery. "Your dog is cute."

"Thanks." Avery shook his hand, unable to help no-ticing how handsome Gray's friend was. Lucas was an inch or so shorter than Gray and had dark blond hair cut short. His features were ruggedly handsome, with dark eyes and a strong jaw. He looked like a man whose alter ego could have been a comic-book superhero, but his smile remained so friendly and open that his attractiveness almost took a back seat. "She's not really my dog, though. I'm just fostering her for a few weeks and then she'll go up for adoption."

"Really?" Jennie reached out a hand for Spot to sniff, and the dog's pink tongue darted out for an approving lick. "My grandma's golden retriever died last year, and she's been wanting to get a smaller dog. She doesn't get around as well these days."

"Oh…" Avery's stomach twisted. "Spot has a bit of a weight problem so might be a better fit for someone active. I mean—"

"We could take her," Jennie interjected without missing a beat. "I'll be at home more once the baby is born."

"A baby and a new dog?" Lucas laughed. "I'm blaming that idea on pregnancy hormones, too."

Avery gripped Spot a little tighter, ignoring the dog's wiggling. "She's not ready for a permanent home yet," she told the couple. "There's time to decide."

"You look great, Jen." Gray stepped forward, once again managing to change the subject when he knew it was difficult for her. "How are you feeling?"

Jennie patted her belly. "Like I'm brewing up a baby orca instead of a little girl."

Gray threw back his head and laughed. "I hope she has your personality."

"Fighting words," Lucas muttered but Avery could tell he was deeply in love with his wife. He dropped a kiss on Jennie's head. "Just joking, sweetheart. I hope our daughter has your spirit and your beauty."

"And your sleep habits," Jennie told him with a wink, then turned to Avery and Gray. "We're heading over to the funnel cake stand. I do love eating for two. Some of the other wives reserved tables near the bandstand. Want to join us?"

"I need to head out," Gray answered before Avery had a chance to say anything. "I told Avery I'd give her a ride home."

They said their goodbyes, with Jennie entering her number into Avery's cell phone and insisting that they get together another time.

"Fire station friends are really like family?" Avery and Gray curved off the main path of pedestrian traffic and walked across a less crowded section of the park. "I knew that's how it was in the movies…"

"Lucas and I go way back. He and Jennie have been through a lot together. I like seeing him this happy."

"You don't have to give me a ride anywhere," Avery said, suddenly feeling self-conscious, like she'd inadvertently inserted herself into a tableau where she didn't belong. As easy as it was to hang out with Gray, she was still an outsider here. There were probably way more Annalises in this town than Jennies, and either way Magnolia was a temporary stop.

"Actually…" Gray ran a hand through his hair. "I'm the one who's without a car. I walked to the fire station this morning. If it's a problem, I can walk back to the—"

"I'll give you a ride." Avery suddenly didn't want to be alone. Even if she could capture a few more minutes with Gray, she'd take it. "It's the least I can do to thank you for this day. I had a great time."

"Me, too," he said, his hand brushing hers as they walked.

Butterflies flitted along Avery's skin. She had it bad for this man and had a feeling that could only lead to trouble for them both.

CHAPTER ELEVEN

GRAY PAUSED IN the act of chopping vegetables to watch Avery emerge from the guest cottage and walk across the lawn toward his back door. Spot trotted along next to her, and she grinned as the dog made to chase a squirrel, then retreated behind her when the squirrel charged instead of running.

He'd invited her for dinner, both because he hated being alone on nights Violet stayed with her mom and also for the simple pleasure of Avery's full-of-contradictions company. He enjoyed her far too much.

It didn't mean anything, he reminded himself. She was safe, in Magnolia temporarily and happy to wear that fact like a neon sign. The connection he felt could be chalked up to physical attraction, or so he wanted to believe.

There was no denying her appeal. Tonight she wore a pair of loose-fitting jeans that hung low on her slim hips and a thin tank top that skimmed her body. She'd pulled her hair back, although loose tendrils escaped to frame her face. The sun waned, and it had cooled off measurably from earlier. But the humidity remained high enough to keep the air sticky. As much as he liked to eat on the back patio, he'd set two places at the kitchen table, grateful for the central air he'd installed in the house when he bought it after the divorce.

She glanced toward his kitchen window at that moment, like he'd drawn her gaze to him with the force of his need. He could almost feel her breath hitch as she lifted a tentative hand to wave.

At least he wasn't the only one oddly nervous about tonight.

"That's quite a brave guard cow you've got," he said with a grin as he opened the back door.

"Did you see the cojones on that squirrel?" Avery asked as she followed Spot up the stairs. "It was traumatic even for me."

Gray chuckled. "No cute clothes tonight?"

Her blue eyes widened for a second before she relaxed again. "You're talking about Spot."

He stepped back to let her into the kitchen. "Yes, but you look beautiful as always if you were interested in a compliment."

"I'm not."

"Liar."

She shot him a glare that made him laugh again.

"All those women lusting after you at the parade has gone to your head."

"I could care less about 'all those' women." He pulled two wineglasses from the cabinet. "White or red?"

"White, please. What about your ex-wife?"

He paused, his fingers tightening on the refrigerator door handle. He didn't want to talk about Stacy. His failed marriage was a subject that even his closest friends didn't bother to bring up at this point.

"What about her?" He made sure his tone stayed neutral.

"Do you still love her?"

"Wow. I haven't even poured the wine, and already we're going heavy."

"I'm sorry." Avery bit down on her lower lip, pink coloring her cheeks. "It's none of my business. Forget I asked."

"Don't worry about it." He drew in a breath, surprised to find his stomach wasn't clenching at the thought of discussing the demise of his marriage. "We wanted different things." He uncorked the wine and poured the gold liquid into the two glasses. "Or more specifically, she wanted something different. Someone who wasn't me."

"I find that hard to believe," she said with a laugh.

He handed her the glass of wine, arching a brow in question.

"First…" She took a long drink, then held up her free hand, one finger at time. "You've got the whole hot firefighter thing going for you. That's sexy as hell for lots of women."

"Any women you care to mention by name?"

"All the women, probably. I mean, you're kind of sexy firefighter calendar material."

He choked out a laugh and studied his wineglass.

"You were on a calendar?"

"Years ago when I joined the department in Raleigh," he admitted, feeling almost sheepish. He usually didn't give much thought to the way he looked. Hell, he'd been staring at his own reflection in the mirror for nearly three decades. As far as he was concerned, there was nothing special about it.

But Avery's grin did funny things to his insides.

"What month were you?"

"April." He rolled his eyes. "I needed the money and it was a painless couple of hours."

"Do you have a copy?"

"Uh, no. And even if I did I'd burn it before I showed it to you."

"I'm going to track it down," she threatened with a giggle.

"Can we stop talking about this? Let's discuss your romantic history."

She shook her head. "I haven't even gotten to number two on the list of reasons your ex-wife was a fool to let you go."

"I'm sure I can live without hearing it."

"You're an amazing father."

Four little words but they hit him with the force of a bullet. He placed his wineglass on the counter when he realized his hand was shaking. "I'm lucky I've got a good kid. Violet is—"

"A handful," Avery said. "Don't bother denying it. It's going to serve her well one day, but right now she needs a lot of parenting. You make it look effortless, like you love every minute of it."

He blew out a breath, love for his daughter filling him like a ray of sunshine. "I do. She's without a doubt the best thing that's ever happened to me. I hate the times when she's with her mom." He cringed at how that sounded. "I don't hate her being with Stacy. I hate that she's *not* with me."

"I get it." Avery reached out and squeezed his hand. The touch was awkward, and he guessed she wished they hadn't gone down this serious path. "She knows you love her whether she's here or with her mom. I know that without a doubt."

"Yeah." He picked up his glass and took a slow sip. "Enough about my complicated history. Tell me about all the hearts you've broken."

The shift in her energy was subtle but undeniable. It was as if a curtain drew down over her features, hiding the woman he knew behind the perfectly polished disdain he'd witnessed that first day at the gas station.

"No broken hearts in my wake," she said, taking a step away from him. "Not much history to speak of. Was the house remodeled when you moved in or did you do the work yourself?"

The change in topic was obvious, but he didn't call her out on it. The end of his marriage had practically destroyed him, and if it wasn't for Violet things might have been worse. He had a feeling whatever had happened to Avery was more recent. She seemed raw and… vulnerable.

"How do you like your steak?" he asked instead, opening the fridge again and pulling out the tenderloin he'd been marinating.

"Medium," she said. "And my love life is really nothing. I fell in love with the wrong guy. He didn't care about me, and I learned a lesson about giving away my heart."

"It wasn't easy to share that."

She shook her head, traced a finger along the rim of her wineglass. "Not a big deal. We're friends, right?"

"I like the sound of that." He took a pair of tongs from the drawer. "Still a little shocked, but I like how it sounds. Now I'm going to grill you the best piece of meat you've ever had."

"Don't get me started on your meat," she said with a laugh.

He wanted to lean in and kiss her but let himself out onto the back patio instead. If she wanted to define what was between them as friendship, who was he to argue? And if their friendship turned out to be the kind that included benefits, he wouldn't complain.

Avery might not be his type, but he liked her. He also liked that her stay in Magnolia wasn't permanent. That would ensure that he kept things casual between them, even if his too-soft heart got in the way.

"THIS WAS THE most normal evening I've had in ages," Avery said as she finished drying the final pot Gray handed to her.

Gray chuckled. "*Normal* isn't exactly a ringing endorsement."

There'd been so much laughter as she helped him prep dinner, then during the meal and even after as they worked together to clean the cozy kitchen.

"I'm a big fan of normal." She took the final sip of wine from her glass but shook her head when Gray held out the bottle to offer her a refill. This was her third glass and between the intimate quiet of the house, Gray's innate sexiness and the way the alcohol loosened her inhibitions, she knew she needed to stop. Of course, she could still make it back to the guest cottage with no problem. She was buzzed but not drunk. The problem was she didn't want to leave.

Spot let out a soft snore from where she'd fallen asleep under the kitchen table. Even her foster dog felt at home here.

"What did normal life look like before Magnolia?" Gray asked gently.

She clenched her fists tight and thought about how

to answer. They'd spent the past couple of hours talking and laughing but she'd still managed to share very little about herself. It was easy to ask questions about life in Magnolia, and Gray seemed happy to share the history of the area. It was so different here than where Avery had grown up, and not just the dichotomy between a small town and the big city.

In San Francisco, she'd been anonymous. Yes, she'd had friends at work and remained as close as she could manage with her mother. But no one had really known her business—at least until her life had imploded.

Magnolia was all about roots and ties to the community, how long a person had lived in town and what brought them to the area in the first place. It was somewhat gratifying to know that although she might garner an extreme amount of interest because of her father, no one could escape the small-town microscope, at least according to Gray.

"I worked a lot," she told him. "I was in risk management for a big finance company, Pierce and Chambers."

Gray whistled under his breath. "Big-time."

She nodded and wondered that she didn't feel any pang of longing for her former life. "Sometimes I traveled but it was mainly long hours in the office."

"But you loved it?" he prompted, as if he couldn't imagine why someone would devote themselves to a career that didn't mean something to them.

"I liked the paycheck," she admitted. "I was good at the job. But it wasn't a vocation. Not like what you do." She could see the question in his gaze and figured she'd offer an answer before he could ask too much. "I was ready for a change, and then the letter came about Niall. It felt like a sign."

She held her breath, gauging his reaction to her explanation. It was a version of what she'd told Carrie and Meredith and not exactly a lie. But somehow it felt as though she was deceiving him. This man had been cheated on by his ex-wife and it had hurt him badly. His daughter was the most important thing in his life.

How would he feel about her if he knew the full truth of the destruction she'd caused her ex's family? She might have been an unwitting accomplice to the betrayal, but she should have known better. She hurt innocent people, and she never wanted to be in that position again.

Not if she could help it.

But she also didn't want to destroy whatever this was blossoming between them. Not yet. She'd called him a friend, and she meant it. Avery felt comfortable with Gray in a way that she didn't with most people.

Maybe it was because she knew nothing could ever really happen between them. Nothing serious anyway. There was a lot at stake and too much either of them could lose.

Although, after today, the thought of leaving Magnolia held little appeal. How was that possible? Heatstroke? Desperation? Probably some pathetic mix of the two.

"Fresh starts are good," he said, placing the two empty wineglasses in the sink.

"Just because I'm a lightweight doesn't mean you can't have another glass."

"I don't need anything else," he said with a smile, then held up a finger. "Except dessert."

"You made dessert, too?" She grinned. "I hope you have that in your dating profile."

"Not exactly homemade," he admitted. "But I have pudding cups, packaged cookies or an ice-cream sandwich to offer you."

"Ice cream," she said without hesitation. "It still counts in your favor that you have something in the fridge besides beer and stale Chinese."

"I'm a dad," he said with a shrug. "There's some kind of parenting rule about a well-stocked kitchen."

"I didn't know that." She took the package he handed her from the freezer, shocked when it didn't completely melt from the heat of their fingers brushing. "My mom wasn't much of a cook, but she hired a meal service to stock the pantry with healthy food every week."

"No dessert from a box?"

She shook her head. "I thought if I had anything with processed sugar, my teeth would immediately rot and fall out."

"Gullible," he teased.

"No doubt." She laughed. "It didn't help that once I snuck down to the market around the corner, bought a huge bag of chocolate and ate the entire thing in one sitting. Of course, I got sick, a fact of which my mom reminded me whenever I begged for junk food."

"I can't imagine you begging for anything," he told her, leading her through the kitchen toward the family room connected to it.

Her cheeks heated as she thought about begging Tony's wife to forgive her for the part she'd played in destroying their family. Not that she thought she deserved any sort of absolution.

"I don't make it a habit," she said, lowering herself to the sofa. He took a seat next to her, a polite distance away but still close enough that she could almost feel the thrum of attraction pulsing between them.

"That sounds like a challenge."

"Hardly." She unwrapped the ice-cream sandwich and bit into it, the cold on her teeth sending a shiver through her. She pointed it toward him. "You'll remember *I* kissed *you* today."

"How could I forget?"

"Which makes me not much of a challenge."

He leaned forward, as if he were sharing a secret with her. "You didn't see me complaining."

"So we're friends who kiss?"

"That might be the best kind."

She laughed. "Does that go for your buddies at the station? I'm open-minded—"

"Just you," he interrupted with a sexy half smile that had her heart stuttering.

The kick in her heart was accompanied by a healthy dose of fear. She liked Gray. Based on her previous experience, that could easily lead to disaster.

"I don't know if I can do this." She gestured between the two of them, figuring he had to be as aware of the pull as she was.

"We don't have to do anything," he said gently, and didn't his willingness to give her the reins just make her want to launch herself into his arms?

"Do you like movies?" she asked, needing to change the subject to something less charged.

She took another bite of ice cream as he glanced toward the television. "I can't remember the last time I watched something that didn't involve talking snowmen. By the time Violet goes to bed and I get the house in order, I'm normally beat. Most nights I don't have her I'm at work. I'd taken today off because I thought Stacy would change her mind."

"We could watch something tonight," she suggested, then felt stupid for assuming he'd want to spend the whole evening with her. He'd helped her feel more comfortable at the fair and then made her dinner tonight. Maybe this had been his way of repaying her for helping with Violet's braids.

"How do you feel about Clark Gable?" He popped the last bite of his ice cream into his mouth and grabbed the remote from the coffee table.

"Is that a trick question?"

"I used to watch a ton of black-and-white movies when I was a kid. Are you up for something old-school?"

"Sure," she agreed. "My mom loved classic movies, too. *It Happened One Night* was her favorite. But if you'd rather enjoy a rare night on your own, I understand."

"You saved me from myself today." As the television blinked to life, he moved closer, not so they were touching but enough that only inches separated them. "I put on a good face—or at least I try—but I would have moped around all damn morning feeling sorry for myself. Instead, it was a great day."

Sparks danced along Avery's spine like she was a teenage girl wishing her guy crush would pull her in to cuddle. As if everything with Gray was new and fresh and unspoiled by the complication of real life.

"Let's go with *It Happened One Night*. You can't beat Gable and Colbert."

As the actors appeared on-screen, Avery settled in, trying to tamp down her awareness of Gray. Slowly, she relaxed again, her body recalibrating to deal with his nearness. At least she no longer felt as though she might spontaneously combust. In fact, she simply felt happy—able to put aside her worries and enjoy an ideal end to a perfect day.

CHAPTER TWELVE

SEVERAL HOURS LATER, Avery opened her eyes and her vision adjusted to the darkened room. It took a few moments to realize where she was. She sat up with a stifled gasp. The last thing she remembered was the tender moment of Clark Gable tucking in Claudette Colbert as they resorted to spending the night in a hayfield.

And she'd fallen asleep, ever the romantic at heart. She'd missed the end and the trumpet and the walls of Jericho coming down—all the good stuff.

She would have expected Gray to wake her, but instead it appeared he'd covered her with a blanket and arranged a pillow behind her head.

Embarrassment washed over her as she wiped the drool from the corner of her mouth, and then she stilled. As her gaze focused on the shadows, she noticed her handsome firefighter asleep in the chair across from the sofa, his head tipped back, feet propped on a leather ottoman. Not only had he tucked her in tightly, but he'd stayed, almost as if he were watching over her.

The thought made tears prick the backs of her eyes. She put aside the blanket, unsure how to deal with the emotions surging through her. She liked it here in Magnolia, even though she knew her stay couldn't be permanent. There was no future for her in a sleepy Southern town, and definitely not with a sexy single dad.

He couldn't be *her* firefighter. She'd already learned the difficult lesson that she could destroy people without even trying. There was no way she'd take that risk in Magnolia. Less than a month in town and the people here were already too important to her.

With the knowledge that she couldn't stay came a particular kind of freedom. There was little risk to something inherently temporary, at least as far as Avery was concerned.

She stood slowly, pulse pounding, and moved toward Gray. Suddenly her reliance on a fleeting arrangement seemed naive. Of course she was risking something in wanting this man.

Rejection, for one, followed quickly by the potential for heartbreak.

But she couldn't resist, not in the intimate stillness of the quiet house. Not with desire pumping a staccato tempo through her veins.

His eyes opened when her leg brushed against his. Before he could react or she could come to her senses, she leaned in and kissed him.

He tasted like vanilla and sleep. The stubble shadowing his jaw scratched her cheek, goose bumps prickling her skin.

"Is this a dream?" he asked, his voice husky.

"If you need it to be," she answered.

Before she could pull back, he tugged her closer, lifting her hips so that she climbed onto the chair, straddling him with her knees pushed into the soft cushions.

He kissed her deep and slow, claiming her mouth as if she were the most precious thing in the world to him. Tonight's kiss was a revelation, and her body practically melted as heat licked along her spine. After minutes—

or maybe hours—he broke their embrace, cupping her face in his strong, calloused hands.

"This is real," he said, his gaze intent on hers. "I don't want either of us to forget that."

Real. Avery turned the word over in her desire-drugged mind, a puzzle she couldn't quite solve. Nothing in her life seemed real at the moment but she understood what he meant.

So close to Gray she felt grounded, held firm not just by his embrace but by their surprising bond. She'd felt untethered in her life, but this man was like a lighthouse in a storm, solid and true. Somehow she understood deep in her bones that he had the power to guide her home.

"Tonight," she said, then swallowed when the word came out rougher than she wanted it to. "Tonight doesn't have to mean anything." She didn't believe the words but spoke them with conviction, needing to convince them both. "It won't change us."

Although he didn't offer her a smile, the corners of his eyes crinkled in a way that told her he was amused by her rationalization. "So it's just physical?"

"Right."

He moved his hands, tracing a finger along the edge of her jaw as he studied her. "I can live with that."

Avery blew out a breath.

Gray chuckled, the sound doing wicked things to her insides. "Did you think I'd say no?"

"It crossed my mind."

"Then you should stop thinking so hard," he told her and like she weighed nothing, he rose from the chair, lifting her into his arms.

She wound her legs around his hips, reveling in the

heat and strength of him. He walked them through the dark house and up the stairs, anticipation and need pooling in Avery's belly.

It wasn't as if she were an inexperienced girl, but like everything with this man, the sensations he made her feel were new. She felt special in his arms, and the sensation of it both thrilled and terrified her.

"I can hear you thinking." The words rumbled low against her ear.

"I'm thinking about you naked," she replied, gratified when he paused for the briefest instant.

"I like the sound of that." He turned into a bedroom at the end of the upstairs hallway and released her.

She started to stumble a step, her knees already weak, but he drew her close, kissing her like he could spend all night with his arms around her.

His hands grazed under her shirt, the touch sparking a wildfire of need along her skin.

"More." She wasn't certain whether the word was a plea or a command, but Gray was quick to respond.

He drew her shirt over her head and tossed it to the side, then did the same with his own.

From the way his muscles bunched under his clothes, she knew he had a great body. But a whimper escaped her throat seeing him like this.

"You're beautiful," he told her and she laughed softly. "Ditto."

"Also quite the wordsmith."

"You kind of leave me speechless."

He flashed a wide grin. "Ditto."

They came together again, the short hair of his chest tickling her skin. His tongue traced the seam of her lips, and she sucked it into her mouth, eliciting a soft groan from him that shocked and delighted her. Then he trailed kisses along her jaw, down her neck and across her collarbone. He cupped her breasts, thumbs flicking over her puckered nipples through the fabric of her satin bra.

And when his mouth covered one stiff peak, she moaned, running her fingers through his hair. He undid her jeans with one hand and she quickly pushed them down over her hips. Need built inside her, and as much as she wanted to savor the feelings, she was also impatient for all of him.

She backed up until her legs hit the bed, then reached behind her to pull down the sheets and comforter. Gray watched her, his chest rising and falling in sharp breaths, eyes dark and dilated with need.

The way he looked at her gave Avery the confidence to reach behind her and unclasp her bra. The straps fell away from her shoulders and then the strip of fabric dropped to the floor. She hooked her thumbs into the waistband of her panties and discarded those as well, smiling at the muttered curse that greeted her when she straightened.

"You make me wish I were a poet," he said. "I'd write sonnets in praise of your body."

She crooked a finger at him. "I'm sure you can find another way to express your admiration."

"*Admiration* doesn't begin to cover it," he said, shucking off his shorts and boxers in one quick motion. The sight of him took her breath away but she forced herself to keep her gaze level. *"Reverence. Worship. Praise."*

"Let's go with *worship*," she said with a laugh. The sound died in her throat as he reached for her again.

"Let me worship you, Avery." He spoke the words

against her mouth, and she nodded her assent, suddenly unable to speak because all she could do was focus on drawing breath in and out of her lungs.

With the kind of care that made tears spring to her eyes, he lowered her to the bed. His big body covered hers, fitting to her in just the right way. She could spend all night with him exploring her curves, and he seemed just as willing to make the most of their time together. As he claimed her mouth again, his hand pressed lower, and she instinctively opened for him. His fingers traced along her thigh, finding her hot center and she heard his moan of pleasure at finding her ready for him.

It only took minutes for him to bring her to the edge and then suddenly she was falling over, her body splintering into a million shards of light. How was it possible to feel both energized and boneless at the same time? All Avery knew as she ran her palms over the planes of his hard chest was that she'd never experienced anything like it. And she wanted more.

As if reading her mind, he reached over and pulled a condom from the nightstand drawer.

"Let me." She took the packet, opened it and rolled it over his length, his low groan making her feel powerful beyond measure.

He positioned himself between her legs but didn't move. Instead he studied her face like he was memorizing her features.

The scrutiny was almost too much, and she let out a nervous laugh. "Are you waiting for an invitation?"

One corner of his mouth kicked up. "As a matter of fact…" He dropped a soft kiss on the tip of her nose. "No second thoughts?"

Second, third and fourth, she thought, but none that

she was going to mention right now. She'd deal with the doubts and fears on her own time. Right now was about them. Together.

"I want you," she said, placing her palm against his rough cheek. "Please, Gray."

She couldn't name the emotions that darkened his gaze at her words, or maybe she was too afraid that naming them would overwhelm her.

But it didn't matter, because he entered her and coherent thought drained from her as pleasure took over. She lifted her head so she could kiss him again, afraid at what her own eyes might reveal at the moment.

The rhythm he set started slow but built in speed like he could sense the need pouring through her. It was as if she couldn't tell where she left off and Gray began. The feeling was heady and, just as she'd hoped, the outside world fell away. All she knew was blissful pleasure and the man who shared it with her.

He whispered sweet words against her skin but it barely mattered what he said because he managed to communicate everything with his body. Every touch... every kiss. She would have never believed any man could make her feel so much, but she did with Gray. And when the release washed over her once again, he was right there with her. Joined in a way that went deeper than this physical connection.

It was as if he'd written himself on her soul.

In that moment, everything changed.

GRAY LAY IN his bed hours later, Avery's perfect body curved against him like a missing piece. Nothing had changed, he told himself over and over, as if repeating the lie would somehow make it more believable.

He'd only gone on one or two dates after his divorce and they never amounted to more than a casual diversion. Hell, most of the time he was too exhausted to think about anything but catching up on sleep if he had a night to himself.

Tonight with Avery had...changed nothing.

Damn.

If only he could convince his body and heart of that.

His heart.

The thought of giving his heart away to a woman like Avery, or at least the woman she'd been before she came to Magnolia, felt like a bucket of cold water splashed over his head.

Why the hell couldn't he fall for an uncomplicated woman, someone who'd appreciate his simple world and the things that made him happy? He ignored the fact that he'd had the best time with Avery doing ordinary activities—from the hours at Summer Fair to an unfussy dinner to falling asleep in front of the television. Although Avery had at first reminded him of Stacy with her tailored clothes and polished good looks, his ex-wife wouldn't have dreamed of going to bed without her intricate beauty routine. And there was no way she would have shared a hot dog and grilled corn with him the way Avery had in town today.

All in all, it had been perfect.

Maybe that was what scared him the most—the thought that the whole experience had really just been a perfect illusion.

Avery was leaving town once they settled Niall's estate. Sooner if she could manage it. She'd made no secret of her unwillingness to stay, even though as far as he could tell she had no life to return to in California. That should be a red flag, as well. Despite their time together, he still knew very little about the details of her life before she'd appeared in Magnolia.

He could google her, of course. He didn't depend on technology or social media, but he still understood how to use it. But that wasn't how he wanted to learn about her. There was something in her past she was unwilling to share, and he wanted her to trust him enough to confide in him without him snooping.

Or maybe he could stop acting like such an idiot and find a way to enjoy a night of mind-blowing sex. She was staying in town for at least a few more weeks, so nothing said they couldn't continue to enjoy each other, no strings attached.

Any man would consider himself lucky to have a woman like Avery warming his bed. The trouble for Gray was he didn't know how to turn off the part of himself that wanted more.

He sighed and she shifted closer. For a woman who was maddeningly prickly when awake, she was a Velcro sleeper. Another aspect to the riddle of Avery Keller, and another part of her he found hard to resist.

"I can hear you thinking." She repeated his words from earlier, spreading her fingers across his chest.

His heartbeat stuttered at the feel of her smooth fingertips.

"Then you should distract me," he suggested, curling his hand over her hip.

She lifted onto her elbow, studying him for a weighted moment. He wondered if she'd question him and how he'd answer. Then she kissed him, and he let the worries disappear, burned off like morning fog under the heat from the sun's rays.

This time they took it slow, a tangle of limbs and murmured promises. He could spend hours discovering how Avery liked to be touched, giving her the same kind of pleasure he felt when they were together. When they were both panting with need, he sheathed himself and entered her in one long thrust. She groaned and pressed closer, like she wanted more. He wanted everything, greedy for her in a way that should have scared him. But with her body quivering underneath his, all he could concentrate on was this moment.

Then there was the moment they both came apart, utter bliss with Avery crying out his name as he let himself go. Nothing had ever felt so damn good and he had a suspicion nothing would again. Arms wrapped tight around her, he drifted off to sleep, mind blissfully empty while his heart was unexpectedly full.

CHAPTER THIRTEEN

THE FOLLOWING TUESDAY MORNING, Avery waited until Gray's truck was gone from the driveway before walking out into the bright September sunshine. It was the third day in a row she'd avoided him, and shame at her cowardice once again overrode her desire to talk to him and explain her behavior.

How could she explain something she didn't understand?

After the amazing night they'd spent together on Saturday, she'd awoke Sunday morning with terror pounding in her chest. She had no business starting something with a single father, even if they'd agreed to keep it casual. Especially when nothing about her time in Magnolia felt casual.

She'd left his bed quietly, retrieving her clothes from around the room while he slept. Early-morning light filtered through the curtains, and she hadn't been able to stop herself from admiring him for a few heady seconds. He slept on his stomach, the sheet covering him from the waist down. His skin appeared almost golden, like he was some kind of bronzed warrior, which didn't feel too far from the truth.

Grayson Atwell was a good man. Far better than she deserved.

She hadn't bothered with a note. For heaven's sake, he was her landlord, only a backyard separating them.

Another reason she shouldn't have let things go so far. It was one thing to say that sex wouldn't change anything between them. Quite another to accept the outright lie.

She'd spent the rest of the morning holed up in the carriage house, surreptitiously peeking out the windows trying to glimpse signs of life from the rambling Victorian. Had she expected him to come after her? To beg her to return to his arms or tell her how much she suddenly meant to him.

Of course not.

Then a sleek Mercedes had pulled into the driveway, Violet bouncing from the back seat and skipping toward the house. Gray had met his daughter on the back porch. He'd swung her into his arms and hugged her tight. Maybe his gaze had tracked to the carriage house, but only for an instant. Avery hadn't been able to read the expression in his green eyes, and she could only imagine what he thought of her when she'd basically run away.

His ex-wife had emerged from the black sedan, all long limbs and glossy hair. Avery's stomach plummeted to her toes. The ex looked like someone she would have called a friend back in California. She was way too overdressed for a lazy weekend morning. Her slim-fitting dress grazed her knees and the understated heels she wore accentuated her toned legs. In so many ways, Stacy reminded Avery of herself.

She didn't like what that said about her.

Huddled at the corner of the window, spying on the three of them, the sharp ache that speared through

Avery's gut almost had her doubled over in pain. She'd been a shy kid and a socially awkward teen, never sure how to engage in the easy camaraderie or even the manipulative backstabbing that seemed to come so easy to most girls. She'd looked the part of a confident, refined woman, but it had been an act. She'd managed to convince herself she was happier alone, content with superficial connections to coworkers and social acquaintances. Her relationship with Tony started as an office friendship.

Both of them were driven, spending long evenings dedicated to projects when most of the staff left to enjoy their lives. Slowly, they'd grown close and Avery had forgotten to be uneasy. They had so much in common. She'd also believed him when he said his marriage was on the rocks. He'd gone so far as to claim that they'd legally separated and explained his move into his own apartment downtown, which was where he'd taken Avery after one particularly late night of work.

All of it had been a lie, and her gullibility had ruined her life.

So she watched the body language between Gray and his ex-wife with the intensity of a detective, looking for any clue that they weren't as finished as he'd led her to believe. Of course his story was plausible. He'd given her no reason to doubt him, but she couldn't help it.

Stacy had crossed her arms over her chest as she stood at the bottom of the stairs leading to the kitchen door. One hip jutted out in obvious impatience. Gray lowered his daughter to the ground, and she disappeared into the house. Once they were alone, it was clear an argument ensued. Gray ran a hand through his hair. His full mouth—the mouth that had done all manner of

wicked things to Avery the night before—had thinned
in obvious irritation. His ex shook her head, then spun
on her heel, throwing up her hands as she stalked to her
car and backed out the driveway.

He'd stood there a few seconds longer, then lifted
his head to stare at the carriage house. Although Avery
knew she was hidden behind the curtain, she swore he
could see her. Or at least sense her there. It made her
feel like a voyeur, witnessing a private interchange that
hadn't been meant for anyone else.

She'd at least gotten clarity that there was, indeed,
nothing more between Gray and his ex. But that didn't
inspire her to return to Summer Fair, even after both
Carrie and Meredith texted her. She knew Malcolm
wanted her at the fireworks. Her sisters expected her
to show. Gray would be there with Violet, and Avery
couldn't force herself to join any of them.

Violet had knocked on her door Monday morning,
and she'd braided the girl's hair. She'd taken more time
than she needed, a secret part of her hoping Gray might
stop by, even though she couldn't bring herself to seek
him out.

The kindergartner hadn't come over before school
today, and Avery wondered if Gray had purposely kept
her away.

"You don't need to hide out. I'll leave you alone if
that's what you want."

Avery whirled, dropping her keys on the ground.

Gray moved forward and then bent to retrieve them.
He handed them to her, and she couldn't help but notice
that he was careful not to touch her.

Disappointment filled her, followed closely by irritation at herself. She didn't get to have it both ways,

and she'd made up her mind that being with Gray was a mistake.

Anything that felt so good had to be bad for her.

"I'm not hiding," she lied. "I've been busy."

He breathed out a laugh. "Your nose is growing."

Without thinking, she touched a finger to the tip of it, then shook her head. "That's silly."

"Did I do something wrong?" he asked. The flash of vulnerability in his eyes made her heart clench. It had never been her intention to hurt him.

"I think we both know you did everything right. Several times."

"And yet…"

She sighed. "I'm not good at casual, Gray. I'm tightly strung and too intense for it."

He arched a brow. "Does that mean you want more?"

Yes, she wanted to answer. Even now the thought of being with him again made her weak in the knees. She could imagine pressing against him or better yet—taking his hand and leading him to her bed in the small cottage.

That would be a far more enjoyable use of her time than what she had planned for the morning.

"We've already agreed there can't be more."

"You also said we were friends." He glanced over his shoulder toward his house, then back to her. "Friends don't spend days ghosting each other."

"I didn't ghost you," she argued. "You could have reached out to me."

"Avery." He took a step closer and she caught the scent of laundry soap and mint. Heat pooled low in her belly. Spearmint gum was an aphrodisiac. A testament to how much this man affected her. He was dangerous to her control, but she wasn't about to admit that. "Don't play games."

"I'm not trying to," she said, hating the catch in her voice. She offered him a smile. "I don't know what I'm doing. No part of my life is stable and I'm not sure I can take on one more thing."

"I'm something you'd have to *take on*?"

"You know what I mean."

"It's quickly becoming clear."

"We can be friends," she offered. "But anything else is a mistake."

"I don't like it when you use that word."

"Yeah." She swallowed. "I'm sorry, Gray. You're great and so is Violet. I don't want to mess things up any more than I have already. Obviously, some fundamental part of me is broken."

He gave her the little half smile that drove her wild. "I hope I'm around to see what happens when you put yourself back together."

She sucked in a shuddery breath. The fact that he could still be so kind in this moment was too much.

"Thanks." She moved around him and down the driveway.

He didn't follow, not that she'd expected him to.

Her car was parked on the street, and she unlocked the door with shaking fingers. She drove the already familiar route toward downtown, pulling into an angled space around the corner from the bakery where she and the Realtor she'd contacted were meeting.

She'd asked both Meredith and Carrie to join her but saw neither of them as she walked into the quiet shop. She didn't understand it. Meredith wanted nothing to do with Niall's legacy and Carrie had already given up so much for her father.

It would be easier for all of them to sell. Why not unburden themselves of the complicated history they hadn't chosen to dictate their futures?

She forced a smile as she approached the table where the Realtor waited for her. Jacob Martin stood and held out a hand. "You must be Avery. It's great to meet you. I'm excited about the opportunity to help you."

"Me, too," she answered even though her stomach twisted. "I'm going to order a coffee."

"I've got a double espresso." Jacob held up his cup. "Need lots of energy for this project."

"Right. I'll be back in a minute." She turned for the counter, pressing a hand to her cheek.

Several people greeted her as she made her way to the register. They seemed genuinely friendly, which remained a revelation.

"Dirty chai?" the high schooler behind the counter asked. "With a shot of vanilla?"

"You remember my order?"

The freckled redhead grinned. "You're kind of famous around here and you've got the best clothes. It makes you memorable."

Avery glanced down at her simple drop-waist denim dress. It had always been a favorite of hers, although there was nothing notable about it. She'd never been described as memorable. Her superpower was blending in, at least in her former life. In Magnolia, she was unique, and not just because of her connection to the famous Niall Reed.

"Thank you for that," she said, offering the barista

a genuine smile. "I'd love a slice of banana bread along with it."

"You bet." The girl rang her up. "Can I ask if there are any special websites where you shop? I mean, I know it's probably super exclusive and expensive stuff, but…"

"Let me think about that." Most of her clothes came from high-end stores, but she figured she could find some places that sold more affordable styles and make recommendations. It was too bad Magnolia didn't have any cute clothing stores.

She paid, and the girl handed her a small brown bag with her bread and she moved to the end of the counter to wait for her drink. As she did, she studied the bakery's charming interior. The space was painted a sunny yellow with white trim around the windows and black café tables and shelves lining the far wall.

A shop like this—with the quality of products and personal service—would have been standing room only in her old neighborhood. She truly didn't understand Magnolia's dependence on her father. This place was special and not just because of Niall.

Downtown exuded a kind of picture-postcard charm. In addition to the dance school, hardware store and bookshop housed in the buildings she now owned, the other side of the street boasted a florist and an Italian restaurant and deli, complete with an awning-covered patio out front. Last weekend's festival seemed to bring crowds into town. If they could capitalize on that, then maybe the economy could be reinvigorated.

She shook her head as she carried her tea and food to the table. Magnolia wasn't hers to fix.

"Are your sisters joining us?" Jacob asked as she sat

across from him. He looked to be about ten years older than her with dark hair slicked back from his round face. He wore a dark suit and sported a gold pinky ring, making him look more out of place than she felt. His office was in a neighboring town, and she'd chosen him precisely because he had no ties to Magnolia.

Avery glanced at the door once more. "Not today." She plastered on a reassuring smile. "You and I will come up with a plan, and I'll coordinate with them."

He passed three folders toward her, frowning. "It would be easier if all three of you are in agreement with how to handle the properties."

"Understood." She traced a finger over his logo splashed in bold letters on the front of the folder. "Tell me about our prospects and how quickly you can make it happen."

"Someone woke up on the wrong side of the fire pole again today."

Gray flipped Lucas the one-fingered salute as they checked the equipment on one of the station's trucks the following Sunday. Ever since talking to Avery last week, Gray had indeed been in a crap-tastic mood. He'd held it together for Violet, but otherwise a black cloud hovered over him, refusing to budge.

It should be easy to put Avery out of his mind. They'd spent exactly one fantastic night together, and he wasn't some green boy who couldn't separate emotions from sex.

Only he couldn't seem to manage it with this particular woman.

It didn't help that every morning his daughter skipped over to the carriage house for her daily dose of braids. She'd come home yesterday excited that Avery had bought pink ribbons to weave through her hair.

She wanted nothing to do with Gray but had somehow managed to charm his plucky daughter. Whoever came up with the phrase "the way to a man's heart is through his stomach" had never met a single dad.

The crazy part was he hadn't even realized something was missing from his life until Avery had blown into it. Now he pined after her smile and her sass. His life hadn't felt lonely, but now the bed was too big and he realized he wanted someone to talk to, even if that talk was trading playful jabs back and forth.

He knew she'd met with a Realtor after their argument. That fact proved this was for the best. Her time in Magnolia was temporary. To remind himself of that, he'd spent a painful hour watching tutorials online about braiding when he couldn't fall asleep last night. He needed to be ready when he was back on call, which was bound to happen sooner than later.

"It's the hot chick in your guesthouse, right?" Lucas wiggled his eyebrows. "I could tell you had it bad when we saw you with her at Summer Fair. Even Jennie noticed, and very little besides food holds her attention these days."

"Don't call her a chick," Gray practically growled.

Lucas's wide grin told Gray that he'd used the term just to get a rise out of him. "You like her."

"It doesn't matter." Gray finished checking the ladder truck's gauges. "She's here temporarily and if she convinces Carrie and Meredith to sell to some shady developer, it will change everything."

"Magnolia doesn't need change."

"It's coming," Gray said, scrubbing a hand over his face. "Whether we like it or not."

"Also, you avoided answering the question. Do you have a thing for Avery Keller?"

"Who doesn't?" Sam Anderson, one of the newest recruits from the training academy, entered the bay from the break room. "She's hot."

Gray muttered a curse under his breath.

"I like how she always looks like she should be walking through the lobby of some fancy hotel." Sam nodded. "She's something different."

Lucas shook his head. "Which would appeal to you since you've been here three months and slept your way through most of the single women in town."

"I'm guaranteed to please," Sam said with a laugh.

"Put that on a business card," Lucas told him.

"Think Avery Keller would like it? I could—"

Before the other man could finish his sentence, Gray had grabbed him and shoved him up against the side of the truck. "You'll do nothing with Avery," he said through clenched teeth. "Not even look at her."

Sam held up his hands. "I didn't realize she was yours."

The idea of that was like a right hook to the jaw, but Gray shook his head. "She's not mine. We're friends. You'll treat her with respect."

"Sure, man." The young firefighter straightened his uniform shirt when Gray released him. "I've got a line on a sweet nurse from Winthrop. We've just scratched the surface of what I can offer the ladies around the region. Next week I'm meeting a woman I've been DMing over in Raleigh." He held up his hand, ticking off potential conquests on his fingers. "I'm kind of full up at the moment, and your girl looks like she'd be high-maintenance in the end. I don't do complicated."

Gray gaped as Sam disappeared around the back corner of the truck. "Were we ever like that?" He turned to Lucas. "Please tell me we were never like that."

"Nope," Lucas confirmed. "You're too soft to be a player, and I've been hung up on Jennie since fourth grade."

"I'm not soft."

"Like a damn marshmallow."

Gray opened his mouth to argue, then snapped it shut again and slammed shut the ladder truck's side door with more force than necessary. Was that why Avery had cut him off before they'd really begun? He could talk a big game about keeping things casual, but that wasn't what he did.

"She's not mine," he mumbled when Lucas continued to study him.

"But you want her to be."

"It's better this way."

"Man, no." Lucas shook his head. "I told myself that line for years with Jen. Even believed it for a while. That never made it the truth."

"You two are different." Gray waved a hand in the air. "You're, like, destiny or something. Avery is just another woman who's wrong for me and out of my league on all the levels."

"So, right up your alley?"

Gray was about to tell his friend exactly where he could shove his sense of humor when the dispatcher's voice came over the loudspeaker, calling the company out to a house fire. The main alarm sounded and the crew rushed toward the engine. After donning their gear, Lucas climbed into the driver's side and Gray got in next to him, all thoughts of joking set aside as he hit the siren knob and the truck headed out.

"It's the Davidson farm," Gray muttered as they turned the corner onto the county highway leading out of town. "What's Mason gotten himself into this time?"

This wasn't the only call they'd had to the thirty-acre property on the outskirts of town. Mason Davidson was pushing ninety, a third-generation local to Magnolia. His wife had died two years prior, and since then he'd called the station directly at least a half dozen times, most of them for noncrisis issues that he deemed urgent. But it was the first report of a fire they'd received and Gray hated to think the older man had a true emergency.

He cursed as they drew closer to the property. Even from the two-lane road that bordered the fields, he could see dark clouds of smoke wafting up from the old farmhouse. No flames were visible against the blue sky, but where there was smoke...

"Are you ready?" Lucas asked as he turned into the driveway.

Gray nodded, adrenaline pumping through him. "We've got this."

CHAPTER FOURTEEN

AVERY KNEW THE moment Gray woke up, and her heart practically skipped a relieved beat.

"What the hell..." he muttered, glancing around the hospital room with wide eyes that quickly narrowed.

"You're fine," she told him, jumping up from the chair where she'd been camped out for the past hour. "You were unconscious when they brought you in, but a full recovery is expected. A few of the guys from the station were in the waiting room earlier. I told Lucas I'd call when you woke up. If you want your friends here..."

He blinked at her, looking angry as a grizzly bear separated from his stash of salmon. "Violet," he whispered, his voice hoarse.

"Home with her grandma." She stepped forward, suddenly shy at the intimacy of this moment. "I can call and ask your mom to bring her here if you want." She glanced at her watch. "She's probably not asleep yet."

"I'm going home," he said, yanking at the tube giving him extra oxygen.

"Gray, wait." Avery placed a hand on his arm. "You've got to calm down."

He stilled, staring at her pale hand on his sun-kissed skin like she was a poisonous spider perched on him. "I need to get home to my kid. I don't want her to see me in the hospital."

"Okay," she agreed, not sure how to soothe him. "But you have to be discharged first. They'll want to examine—"

"I'm fine," he said, the words sounding almost like a snarl.

"You had a bad accident." She lifted her hand to his forehead, tracing the bandage that covered the skin above his left eye. "Do you remember?"

"Yeah." He closed his eyes for a brief moment. "The first floor gave way and my mask got dislodged in the fall. The basement was filled with smoke, and I was wedged under a heavy floorboard. Couldn't breathe. Why are you here, Avery?" His gaze zeroed in on her again.

"I saw your mom and Violet at the house. Your daughter told me you'd been in an accident."

"That doesn't answer the question."

"We're friends."

"Huh." She wasn't sure whether that one syllable conveyed agreement or disbelief. In truth, she shouldn't be here. She'd spent the past few days maintaining her distance, trying to convince herself she didn't care as much as she did. But the thought of Gray injured impacted her at a deep level. She'd needed to see him—to see for herself that he was okay. How many kinds of a fool did that make her?

He sat up straighter, wincing when he tried to pull in a deep breath. "What do you know about my injuries?"

She swallowed. "Should I get the doctor or nurse?" When she would have taken a step back, he encircled her wrist with his big hand. God, he had the best hands.

"Tell me."

"You were brought in with thermal burns to your airway and possible chemical damage to your trachea. They did a brain scan and chest X-ray. No other traumatic injuries were found. Carbon monoxide poisoning was a concern but they ruled it out."

"The timing is terrible."

"I guess the timing's never good for almost dying."

He rolled his eyes. "I didn't almost die. But I had planned to serve Stacy with papers filing for sole custody."

"Oh, Gray." Avery turned her hand so she could link their fingers together. As much as she wished she could remain immune to this man, she couldn't stop her feelings. "I know how badly you want that. This doesn't have to stop you."

"I'm a firefighter. My work is inherently dangerous. At any moment, I could be injured or worse. Today was a routine call to a structural fire that got out of hand. No judge is going to grant me sole custody."

"You can't give up. Talk to your attorney. Talk to Stacy."

He shrugged, sinking back against the pillows. "I need to go home."

"Then let's get you out of here," she said, squeezing his fingers.

"I want to go now."

"That's clear." She released him and took a step back. "But we're going to do this the right way. Yes, your job is dangerous but otherwise you live above reproach." She pointed a finger at him. "Don't start making stupid decisions now."

"Get me out of here," he whispered, suddenly sounding exhausted. "Please."

The *please* undid her. She'd only known him a short time but in every situation, he'd been totally capable. Even when he'd claimed otherwise. Right now she could see the weight of his responsibilities and the pressure of single parenting, like they were a millstone around his neck.

She hurried out of the room, bypassing the nurses' station to push through the door of the doctors' lounge. She ignored the calls of protest she heard behind her.

Three men sat around a table, each of them hunched over individual laptops.

"Which one of you is Grayson Atwell's doctor?"

A man with sandy-blond hair and friendly brown eyes raised his hand as if a teacher had called on him. He looked like he should be catching waves on a Southern Californian beach instead of in a community hospital. She wasn't sure whether that should put her at ease or make her more anxious.

"He needs discharge papers." She gave the doctor her best commanding stare. "Right now."

The other two looked at Gray's doctor, vaguely amused expressions on both their faces.

The man flipped closed his laptop and straightened from the table. "I'm Brodie Jepsen," he said as he approached her. "What's your relationship with Grayson?"

"W-we're friends," she stammered, refusing to take a step back despite the man looming over her. She was on a mission and wasn't going to be deterred from it. "I'm Avery Keller."

He frowned. "Friends?"

"Just friends," she clarified and thought she saw his expression soften slightly. "But his daughter is at home, and he wants to see her. Can you please help?"

"You understand there's a discharge process?"

She nodded. "I'm also guessing that you can fast-track it."

"If I choose to," he agreed.

"Well then…"

"Let's go see how the patient is doing, and I'll make my decision."

They walked down the hall together and entered the room, only to find Gray in a standoff with one of the nurses.

"Dr. Jepsen," she said, throwing out her arms. "Please tell this patient to stop being a stubborn pain in my butt."

Gray rolled his eyes. "I can't understand it when you use that complicated medical jargon, Julie."

"I take it the two of you know each other," the doctor said, folding his arms across his chest.

"We dated in high school," Gray muttered.

"He was smarter back then," the nurse added, earning a laugh from the doctor.

Something that felt strangely like jealousy slithered along Avery's spine. Stupid of her. Clearly Gray and the spunky nurse were only friends now, even if they'd once been close.

"I need to go home," Gray announced to the room in general.

"Understood." Brodie moved forward. "Avery is quite the advocate for you."

Gray's gaze moved to her as if the words the doctor spoke didn't make sense.

"Are you his ride?" Julie asked. "Or should I call—"

"I can take him."

Brodie turned to face her. "But you're *just* friends?"

"Yes," she agreed slowly, glancing up at Gray when he made a noise low in his throat.

What was that about?

The doctor nodded. "Julie will check your vitals one more time, Gray. If everything's good, she'll go over the discharge instructions. But only if you promise that you'll call or come in if anything changes. I have an inhaler prescribed but you were lucky your injuries were superficial given the nature of the fall. We'll have you out of here as soon as possible."

"Now would be even better." Gray ran a hand through his hair. "I always read Violet her bedtime story. She sleeps better with a routine."

Avery pressed two fingers to her chest. There went that melting sensation again.

"What time does she go to bed?" Julie asked gently.

"Eight," Gray answered.

The nurse put a hand on his shoulder. "You'll make it."

"Thanks, Juls."

And the melting abruptly stopped.

"Have you lived in Magnolia all your life?" Brodie asked Avery as Julie spoke to Gray.

Avery choked back a laugh. Was it possible she'd met the one person in this town who didn't know her history? "I'm new," she said. "I'm only here for a few weeks visiting family."

"Got it." He leaned in: "Any chance you'd like to have dinner while you're in town?"

"Doc, do I schedule my follow-up with you?" Gray called from the other side of the room.

"You can see your regular doctor for that," Brodie

answered without taking his eyes from Avery. "There's a great little Italian place out near the beach."

"What if I don't have a regular doctor?"

"I'll refer you," Brodie said, his voice tight.

Avery shot Gray a glare over the doctor's shoulder, then lifted her gaze to Brodie's. "Thank you, but it's not a good time right now. My life is a bit on overload." Not to mention, she couldn't imagine being with anyone but Gray.

"If you change your mind, you know where to find me."

As promised, the discharge process went quickly. On the way out of the hospital, Avery called Carrie to explain the situation. There wasn't anything she expected of her sister at this point. She'd already talked to Meredith earlier to ask for help with Spot. But somehow Carrie's gentle voice soothed her. She retrieved her car from the parking lot and pulled up to the main entrance. Julie helped Gray out of the wheelchair and he tried to hide his wince as he coughed.

Avery adjusted the vents when she climbed back in so they blew in his direction.

"I'm fine," he mumbled.

"You look like death warmed over." His skin was pasty and wan, lines of pain bracketed the corners of his mouth. "Did they give you a prescription for pain meds in addition to the inhaler?"

"Yes, but I won't take them." He gave a sharp shake of his head as she pulled out. "I need to be lucid for Violet."

"Gray, come on. You were in a serious accident. There are people who can help while you're recovering. You don't need to do this alone."

"What people? I'm not calling Stacy. She'll find a way to use this against me, and we're already fighting enough."

"Your mom," Avery suggested, hating the desperation in his tone. She didn't want to see him like this. "Your friends."

"Yeah," he whispered. "But I don't need anyone."

"You don't *want* to need anyone," she corrected. "There's a difference."

He grunted a response, then closed his eyes. They drove the rest of the way to his house in silence. The hospital was on the other side of town, but it was still less than twenty minutes until she pulled into his driveway.

Before she'd even gotten around to open the passenger door, Violet came flying from the house. She was dressed in a blue polka-dot nightgown, her long hair loose.

"Daddy!" she yelled as she ran toward the car.

Avery tried not to gape as she glanced at Gray. The sure and steady father she'd come to know had replaced the exhausted man from the car ride. He grinned at his daughter, holding out his arms but remaining in the front seat. Avery understood the pain hadn't subsided but admired him all the more for the brave face he put on for Violet.

"Are you okay?" the girl asked as she nestled into him. She placed a small hand on the bandage that covered his forehead, much as Avery had done in the hospital. "Gram said you breathed in all the smoke."

"Just a little." He wrapped an arm around her, and Avery could imagine what it took for him to handle this moment with such composure. "You can make me a get-well card."

"With a purple marker," she told him.

"My favorite color."

Avery smiled at that, then startled when a throat cleared behind her.

"I'm fine, Mom." Gray lifted his gaze as Lila Atwell stepped forward.

"You always are," Lila said. She placed a firm hand on Avery's arm. "Thank you for staying with him. I can manage it from here."

Slap down, Avery thought. She'd been coming home from a walk with Spot when Gray's mother had arrived with Violet. The girl had immediately tumbled out of the car to greet Spot. She'd announced to Avery that her daddy had gotten hurt and Avery hadn't given a second thought to offering her help.

It had been obvious then that Lila didn't want to accept. She'd looked Avery up and down as if she were three-day-old fish. But if the past few weeks had taught Avery one thing, it was that she could continue functioning in the face of any level of judgment.

Which was why she smiled and nodded as if in agreement even as she moved around Lila.

"Your daddy is going to be moving slowly for a bit," she told Violet. "I bet it would help if you held his hand on the way to the house."

Lila sniffed. "I can handle things. This doesn't concern you."

Avery froze. She'd become more immune to censure, but not entirely oblivious to rejection.

"Mom." Irritation laced Gray's tone.

"So you managed to rescue my sister," a voice called into the awkward silence. "But not yourself?"

Avery drew in a shaky breath as Meredith and Carrie emerged from the carriage house. She never would have imagined taking comfort at the sight of two virtual strangers, but somehow her half sisters no longer felt that way to her.

Gray chuckled. "How many women does it take to get one gimpy man from a car to the house?"

"We don't need help," his mother insisted.

If they heard the protest, Carrie and Meredith ignored it. They simply joined the group, and their presence gave Avery the confidence she needed to take control again.

She instructed Meredith to get the folder with the discharge papers and prescriptions from the back seat while she helped Gray out of the front seat. Carrie stood a few feet away, ready if he needed additional help, and Violet took his hand. Avery avoided eye contact with his mother, gratified when he whispered "Thank you" against her ear as she supported him.

They were almost to the house when his mother spoke behind them. "If you don't need me, I suppose I should go home. I need to get dinner started and let out the dogs."

Avery saw Gray's shoulders stiffen. He'd been through enough today without having to deal with attitude from anyone, even his mom. She didn't understand Lila's animosity. As he eased himself away from her, Carrie reached out and squeezed her arm, another bit of unexpected comfort.

"I appreciate you coming over." He walked slowly toward his mother. "I'm going to be fine."

Lila stepped forward and wrapped her arms around him. Emotion pulled at Avery's heart. As much as Gray was a grown man, he was still this woman's son and his job wouldn't stop being dangerous.

"Your injuries will heal," Lila said, cupping his face in her delicate hands. "I'm worried about the rest of you."

"Thanks, Mom. I'll call you later," he said, then looked over his shoulder. "Vi, give your gram a hug goodbye."

"Bye, Gram." The girl hugged her grandma as instructed.

He moved slowly toward the house as his mother walked down the driveway, nodding at Carrie and offering Meredith a friendly wave but not looking back toward Avery. What had she done to earn this woman's ire?

"Come on," Violet urged, grabbing her hand. "Daddy's gonna need you."

Oh, no, Avery wanted to protest. He wouldn't need her. Suddenly, she wanted to call back his mother.

"We should go, too," Carrie said. "I'll pick up the prescriptions and drop it back off."

"I can't do this," Avery whispered urgently.

Meredith sniffed. "Seriously, how many women does it take to deal with one injured man?"

"I need you," Avery blurted. It was one thing to have stayed with him at the hospital but this moment felt more intimate than she was prepared to handle on her own. She felt color rush to her cheeks. "I mean—"

"We'll stay," Carrie said, and even Meredith nodded without hesitation.

Violet's hand felt soft in hers, but also steady. For a woman who had sworn off getting involved with anyone, Avery found herself entangled in these people's lives in a way she couldn't have imagined.

Gray paused at the back door, looking over his shoulder. His gaze found hers. He looked exhausted, in pain and vaguely unsure of what to do next.

"Violet, will you open the door for your daddy?" She turned to her sisters. "Thank you."

"You're not alone," Carrie told her, and they walked toward the back of the house together.

GRAY GRITTED HIS teeth against the pain in his chest hours later. He'd heard Avery send her sisters to the pharmacy to pick up his prescriptions, and the inhaler and orange pill bottle sat on the coffee table, mocking him. He'd taken a dose of over-the-counter pain medicine when he'd first arrived home and had no intention of adding narcotics to the mix, no matter how much he hurt.

He hurt like hell.

"Do you need anything?"

He glanced over to find Avery on the chair across from him, concern shining in her blue eyes. The evening had been surreal, with the three Reed sisters fussing over him like a trio of hens.

He should feel guilty for sending away his own mother but couldn't manage it. She'd made her disapproval for his work clear from the moment he'd joined the fire department. He could only imagine how this day would spur her on.

Violet had clearly loved having the three older women in the house. While he'd sat on the sofa trying to ignore the burning each time he drew in a breath, they'd painted his daughter's nails, given her a facial and then baked a batch of chocolate-chip cookies with ingredients he hadn't even known were in his cupboards.

After a dinner of delivery pizza, Carrie and Meredith had left. At some point, Avery's chubby dog had joined the party, and Gray had snuck the animal a bite of crust, earning an amused scolding from Avery.

He should have given Avery permission to leave, as well. She'd already done way too much to help him. More than he imagined she wanted to in any case. But he liked having her close.

Tomorrow he'd blame the injury for his weakness. Right now, he simply sighed with relief at not being alone.

"Where's Violet?" he asked, surprised to see the sky beyond the windows had turned dark.

"She went to bed about forty-five minutes ago. I took care of it because it seemed more important that you sleep."

He shook his head. "Nothing is more important than her."

"Yes," she agreed, her tone soft. "But you'll do her more good recovered than if you push things. Most people with your injuries would still be in the hospital."

"I'm—"

"Fine," she interrupted. "I know." She stood and moved around the coffee table, plucking up the pill bottle as she did. "Can I get you a glass of water to take one?"

"I told you I'm not taking drugs. The pain is temporary."

"Stubborn," she muttered as she lowered herself next

to him on the sofa but returned the pain meds to the coffee table. "It hurts like hell, right?"

"Only when I breathe."

"Can I do anything?" She reached out and traced her fingers over his furrowed brow. The touch was cool and soft and immediately he relaxed.

"That works," he told her.

"Were you scared?" She continued to run her fingers across his skin, and it was like he'd been given a dose of the best pain meds known to man. The pressure inside his chest unfurled. He concentrated on the pleasure of her fingers on him, trying not to embarrass himself by moaning out loud.

"The floor collapse happened too fast," he said honestly. "But in the moments after, before I lost consciousness, I was terrified. Not for myself but for Violet. I'd never purposely do anything to cause her pain."

"She's okay," Avery promised. "You're here and that's what counts. Kids are more resilient than we think."

"I'm not sure if that's true or if I'm just giving her fodder for the therapist's couch when she gets older."

"Trust me." Avery laughed. "She'll be okay. She's tough. Probably gets that from you."

"Thank you for being here today."

Her fingers stilled and he wished he hadn't spoken. More than anything, he didn't want her to stop touching him right now.

"Why did you send your mother away?"

Slight adjustment to his previous thought. More than anything, he didn't want to think about his mom.

"If I tell you, will you keep up with…" He lifted his arm and twirled a finger around his head. "All this."

She smoothed his hair from his forehead, and he sighed. "Things are complicated with my mom. My dad was a policeman. He died on the job."

"I'm sorry, Gray."

"I barely remember him. Chase is four years older so it was harder on him. Hell for my mom. We were living in Philadelphia at the time because she wanted out of the South. But she moved back to be near family and raised my brother and me on her own. It wasn't easy. We weren't easy. But she loved us and did her best. What she wanted most was for us to be safe. We were two energetic boys, and we pushed the limits all the time. Chase ended up becoming a corporate attorney. That made her happy. Nothing bad happens to lawyers on the job. Firefighters are another story."

"Bad things happen to lots of people, unfortunately." Avery traced a finger over the rim of his ear, sending a waterfall of sensation through his body. "Your job might have more inherent risk, but that's no guarantee."

"She doesn't approve of the risks I take." He wrapped his hand around her wrist, then laced his fingers with hers. As much as he enjoyed the way she was touching him, too much more of that and he'd end up making a fool of himself. "She also didn't like Stacy so I'm sure the thought of my being hurt and Stacy getting custody of Violet kills her. Hell, it kills me."

"Nothing is going to happen to you." Her brow furrowed as she studied him. "Did your mom have some involvement with Niall?"

He shook his head. "Not as far as I know."

"She looked at me like I was the enemy."

"You remind her of Stacy," he said, almost reluctantly.

He could tell by the way she tried to tug away her hand that the observation upset her. He didn't release her.

"Clearly a mark against me," she said with a bland smile.

"Also not true," he added.

"I saw her the other day when she dropped off Violet. I was watching out the window of the carriage house. Your ex-wife looks like someone I would have been friends with back in my old life."

"And now?"

Her full mouth thinned. "I'm not that person, or at least I don't want to be. I didn't even realize how much I'd grown to not like myself until I got here."

"I like you."

"You shouldn't."

"My daughter likes you. Your sisters like you." He used his thumb to draw circles on the center of her palm. "Is it possible that you sell yourself short in the likability department?"

"I spent the night with you and then freaked out." She arched a brow. "That's not likable."

He grinned. "It's probably because you were over-whelmed by the best sex of your life."

Her eyes widened a fraction before she purposely rolled them. "Don't flatter yourself."

"I know I felt that way after being with you." He brought her hand to his mouth and brushed a kiss over her knuckles. "Totally blown away."

"Oh."

He loved the color that bloomed in her cheeks. "So what next? If you don't like who you were before, why not reinvent yourself here?" He held his breath as he waited for her response. Silently prayed for her to see things his way. He didn't want to let her go. Not yet. And if she stayed, maybe he wouldn't have to.

Instead of answering, she yanked her hand out of his grasp and stood. "I should go. You probably want to shower and rest."

"I might need help bathing."

"I…um…"

"I'm joking," he told her, pushing himself up to a sitting position. "Unless you can't resist me."

"I can resist you."

"We'll see."

She reached out and playfully swatted the side of his head. "Clearly the accident did nothing to affect your ego."

"We can all be grateful."

"I'll be back in the morning," she told him. "To drive Violet to school."

"You don't need to do that." Reality came crashing back as he thought about how long a full recovery might take. He couldn't push it even if he wanted to pretend like he was fine. If he didn't give his body time to heal, he'd be of no use to anyone. "I can ask my mom to help." He also hated relying on his mother but wouldn't have much of a choice until he felt better.

"It's no problem," Avery said. "You actually saved me from falling through a floor. The least I can do is help out now. Are you sure there isn't anything else you need tonight?"

You, he wanted to tell her. How could he ask her to stay when she'd already done so much? He couldn't even explain to himself why her presence made such a difference. It all went back to the fact that he was a total idiot where women were concerned.

"Okay, then." She glanced around the darkened room, like she was as reluctant to leave as he was to have her go. She took a few steps away, then turned back to him. "Call or text if you need anything. I'll keep my phone turned on."

He gave a small nod, not trusting himself to speak. He'd probably do something really stupid like beg her to stay.

She scooped up Spot, who was blissfully snoring from her place on a blanket that had been arranged like a bed on the rug.

"Do you have a guest room?" she asked, her voice hesitant.

"Upstairs, second door on the right as you head down the hall."

"Would it be weird if I stayed there tonight? I'd feel better if—"

"Please do," he blurted, then cleared his throat. "I mean, it's not necessary but in case Violet wakes up. She usually doesn't, but I'm not exactly at my best if she needs anything and—"

"I'll stay," she whispered.

He wanted to insist she join him in his bed again, but as much as he craved her touch he'd be fairly useless at the moment.

"Thank you," he answered instead.

"Good night, Gray."

He wasn't sure why it made him so damn happy to have her here. She was seeing him at his weakest, but he couldn't have cared less. It didn't even bother him if pity led her to make the offer. He'd gotten used to being alone since his divorce, but Avery changed everything. He should head up to his bedroom but instead adjusted the sofa pillow behind his head and closed his eyes. Somehow knowing she was under the same roof made it easy to fall asleep.

CHAPTER FIFTEEN

AVERY WAS IN the kitchen braiding Violet's hair the next morning when she heard a car door slam. She was almost to the door when it burst open and she stood face-to-face with Gray's ex-wife. His narrow-eyed, angry-looking ex-wife.

"Uh-oh," she muttered.

"Hi, Mommy," Violet said but didn't move from where she sat on the stool at the island. "See my fishtail braids?" Avery had given the girl strict instructions on fidgeting or getting down from the stool until she finished braiding. Violet took her braids seriously.

"Who are you?" Stacy demanded of Avery, ignoring her daughter's greeting. "Where's Gray?"

"He's sleeping," Violet reported. "Avery had a sleepover. She doesn't like childrens but she's the best at hair."

Stacy's nostrils flared.

"Not exactly a sleepover," Avery explained. "Gray was injured in an accident and—"

"Why do you think I'm here?" Stacy asked, a steel edge to her voice.

"Honestly, I have no idea."

"You're his girlfriend?"

Avery opened her mouth to deny it, but changed her mind. This woman had cheated on Gray and broken his heart. Avery knew the kind of damage that could do. Hell, she'd been part of inflicting it. She had no sympathy for a woman who had done the scorning.

"That's not your concern," she replied.

"It is." Stacy stepped closer. "If your involvement with Gray involves my daughter."

"Put away the claws, Stace."

Avery turned to see Gray slowly making his way down the staircase. He'd showered and wore a white T-shirt and athletic shorts. His color was better than it had been yesterday and he didn't seem to be wincing with every breath. She wondered how much was feeling better and what part of the seemingly quick recovery was for his ex-wife's benefit.

"I heard you were at the hospital yesterday," Stacy said, stepping around Avery like she was a pile of dog poop. "Why didn't you call me?"

"Mommy, I got a hundred on my spelling test."

"In a minute," Stacy said, holding up a finger toward the girl.

Violet's expression turned mulish as she glared down at the granite counter.

Avery quickly slipped over to Violet. "Maybe you'd like your mommy to finish your hair?"

"You." Violet breathed out the syllable through pursed lips.

"Then we should give your parents some privacy." She wanted to be a part of this scene like she craved a root canal, which was to say not at all. She'd done nothing wrong. Gray and his wife had divorced long before Avery'd entered the picture. Not that she was really part of the picture. She'd spent the night in the guest room and woke early this morning, tiptoeing downstairs to prepare a quick breakfast for Gray and his daughter.

Instead she'd found Violet on the couch, watching television. Spot had spied the girl and scampered to her, bounding up on the couch for a few morning licks. Violet had giggled, hugging Spot to her chest before turning a serious gaze to Avery again.

"Daddy never sleeps late," the girl had told her, not questioning Avery's presence. "But he's not awake yet. I went in his room and he's breathing."

"Of course he's breathing," Avery answered. The poor girl was clearly more worried than she'd let on the previous evening when Avery had tucked her into bed. Avery had glanced up the stairs, then offered Violet a reassuring smile. "I told him to sleep in today," she lied. "What would you like for breakfast?"

"Donuts."

Avery continued down the stairs. "Does your daddy let you have donuts for breakfast?" She pointed a finger at Violet when the girl opened her mouth to answer. "If you lie, I'll know and no braids for a week."

"Only on weekends," the girl mumbled. "I have to eat fruit with it. Like that matters."

"So what about school days?"

"Healthy junk," Violet said. "Can I have toast with peanut butter?"

"What's the magic word?"

That question earned an eye roll. "Try *abracadabra*."

"Try *make your own toast*."

"Please, can I have toast?" the girl amended.

Avery smiled, ignoring the fact that she sounded like someone's mother, a fact that was comical in and of itself.

"Would you please turn off the TV and take Spot out to do her business? I'll get started on toast."

"I'm resting," Violet argued. "Thinking about school makes me tired."

Avery shrugged. "Fine but you'll wake up real quick if that dog has an accident on your leg."

"Gross." Violet hopped off the couch and headed for the back door. "You aren't fun."

"Never claimed to be," Avery had answered.

Now she wished she'd thrown good sense to the wind and taken the girl for donuts. At least they would have missed Stacy's angry arrival and the confrontation that felt inevitable with the air inside the house sparking with tension. Violet continued to stare at the countertop as if it held every bit of her attention. Yet Avery had no doubt Violet was aware of what was about to go down.

The girl might not think Avery was fun, but anything had to be better than watching her mom and dad tear into each other. Gray sent her a pleading look across the room. Yesterday he might have seemed vulnerable but no more. Despite the bandage on his forehead and the scrapes to his arm, he'd returned to the alpha male who elicited all sorts of unwanted reactions in her.

"Do you hear Spot whining?" Avery asked softly, cupping a hand over her ear.

Violet gave a sharp shake of her head.

"I do," Avery continued. "I bet she's gotten into something and made a huge mess in the carriage house. You want to check it out with me?"

Another head shake.

"I'll give you ten dollars," Avery whispered, desperate to be gone before Stacy let Gray have it.

"Violet should have been with me last night," Stacy

said, her voice pitched low. Out of the corner of her eye, Avery saw the woman jab a finger into Gray's chest. "You should have called me."

"Twenty," Violet mumbled.

Avery released a breath. "Done."

She grabbed the girl's hand and tugged her off the stool. Stacy didn't turn around, and Gray kept his attention fixed on his ex-wife like he was staring down a cobra.

"It's not a big deal," she heard him say as she ushered Violet toward the back door.

"You had her here with some too-skinny tramp."

Avery winced as she exited the house. She gulped in deep breaths of the sticky morning air. There was no reason for her to feel ashamed or guilty but the emotions flooded her anyway. She was back in California with Tony's wife confronting her. Her stomach knotted like she could feel the weight of the condemning stares of people she'd thought were her friends.

"Was that a bark?" She tried for a concerned tone, hoping to distract the girl.

"What's a tramp?" Violet asked, reaching back to touch the unfinished braid. "Oh, no. It's ruined."

"Easily fixed," Avery promised. She decided to ignore the question.

She'd been labeled much worse but somehow Stacy's coarse assessment cut her just as deep. Maybe because she'd promised herself she'd never be in that position again, and here she was in a similar predicament through no fault of her own.

No fault other than caring. She should have learned her lesson. When Avery cared, people got hurt. That didn't stop her from caring about Gray and his daughter.

She could move in with Carrie. Her father's decrepit, overstuffed house had plenty of available rooms. She'd just have to clear out layers of junk to find a potential bed. Who knew what else she'd find.

Meredith lived on a ranch at the beach outside town. She hadn't been there, but it was past time to change that. There had to be an extra bed.

She tried to come up with a plan as she toasted another piece of bread for Violet and then rebraided her silky hair. At the same time, she kept up a continual stream of conversation. No chance Violet could ask difficult questions if she couldn't get a word in.

The girl was just finishing the last bite of her cinnamon-and-sugar-sprinkled toast when a knock sounded on the door.

Avery swallowed hard as she opened it, expecting to see Gray's ex-wife on the other side, ready to claw out her eyeballs.

Gray stood there instead, his gaze giving away nothing.

"Thank you again." He ran a hand through his hair, lowering his voice. "I'm sorry this morning turned into a shit show."

"Is your wife—"

"Ex-wife," he corrected tightly but nodded. "Stacy is in the house. She's going to drive Vi to school."

Disappointment lanced through Avery. There was no reason for her to feel possessive toward the girl, but she did anyway.

"I had sugar bread," Violet reported as she appeared next to Avery.

"Cinnamon toast," Avery explained. "With just a

tiny bit of sugar added. I don't have much in the way of quick breakfast items and—"

"Don't worry about it." Gray held out a hand to his daughter. "Your hair looks nice."

"I know." She gave Avery's leg a quick hug but didn't make eye contact, almost as if she were embarrassed about the sentiment. Avery understood the feeling.

"Are you going to thank me?" she asked, tapping a finger on the top of Violet's head. "Your manners need some work, kid."

That earned a smile and her heart lurched in response.

"Thanks," Violet said with a cheeky grin. "Your breakfast making needs some work, too."

"Violet." Gray sounded both shocked and exasperated, but Avery laughed.

"Have a good day at school, Violet. Tell Margo hello from me."

Violet giggled as she slipped her hand into Gray's. He shook his head and mouthed, "I'm sorry," to Avery. She knew he was apologizing for far more than his daughter's attitude.

She shut the door behind them and leaned her forehead against it. Emotions pummeled her from all sides, clamping down on her chest. She struggled to draw in a normal breath. There was no reason to be so affected by the scene with Stacy, but she couldn't seem to get control of herself. It galled her, because she'd vowed never to lose it again. She'd left San Francisco with the intention of keeping herself out of any emotional entanglements. At this moment, the mess with her father's estate and her jumbled feelings about that seemed like the least of her worries. Not when her heart threatened to beat out of her chest.

Spot trotted over and scratched at her leg. She lifted the dog into her arms, nuzzling her soft fur. If only everything could be as simple as a dog's straightforward affection.

"YOU CAN COME out to Last Acre every morning for the rest of eternity." Meredith handed Avery a push broom later that week. "I'll put you to work, but you aren't moving in with me."

"One night," Avery pleaded softly. "You could let me stay one night."

"What's wrong with Carrie's place?" Meredith pointed to the wide planks of the beach house's front porch, and Avery dutifully began to sweep. She'd first come out to the property after Gray had been picked up by his friend Lucas the morning his ex-wife had shown up at the house.

After Stacy had driven away with Violet, he'd returned to the carriage house but she hadn't answered the door when he knocked, feeling somehow too vulnerable to handle a confrontation. The thought of contributing in any way to conflict between Gray and his ex-wife brought back all the emotions of her disastrous past in California.

Spot had barked and whimpered, and of course, he knew Avery hadn't left, but she couldn't face him.

Not when she had no way to explain her powerful reaction to Stacy's anger. The situation was totally different than what she'd previously experienced, and her rational side understood that his ex had no claim on him. That it wasn't the same as it had been with Tony.

Too bad her rational side seemed to have melted away in the heat that seemed to linger interminably, making her wonder if North Carolina would ever cool down.

She wiped a hand over her brow, then continued to sweep. At least out here a breeze blew in from the ocean so there was some relief from the scorching heat. They were well into September now, and she'd heard talk that the weather should break soon. She could only hope.

"That house is creepy," she told Meredith. "I don't know how Carrie stays there. She's made a ton of progress on cleaning things out, and I promised I'd be back to help take another load to the donation center this afternoon. But I don't want to stay where Niall lived. He wanted nothing to do with me when he was alive. I don't want to feel any attachment to him now."

Meredith cocked a brow. "I meant the carriage house."

"Oh." Avery bit down on the inside of her cheek. She hadn't told either of her sisters about Stacy, and they certainly didn't know about her past. "Nothing's wrong with it," she lied. "I thought you and I should get to know each other better." She offered what she hoped was a confident smile. "Carrie's take on all of this is pretty clear. She was Niall's real daughter and the one with the most to lose by moving on. I'm still curious about where you stand on things."

"I stand on my property," Meredith answered. "I don't give a rat's ass what happens to his house or to the buildings downtown, but I need the ranch."

Avery followed her sister's gaze toward the large fenced-in enclosure where what looked like a mini herd of dogs was milling about. Beyond that area was the barn, which she'd toured yesterday. In addition to the half-dozen rescue horses housed there, they'd visited pigs, goats and an enclosure of energetic bunnies.

"Did it seem strange at all when Niall leased you the property? You pay next to nothing for the rent. I understand why he did that downtown. Those were his neighbors. But he could have sold this property at any time and made a significant profit."

"I figured he had his reasons."

"Really? Because from what I understand—"

"I knew about his affair with my mother," Meredith blurted. She turned to Avery, arms stretched out like she expected a crucifixion. "Is that what you wanted to hear?"

Avery shook her head, too dumbfounded to speak. They stared at each other for several long minutes before Avery found her voice. "Did you know he was your father?"

"No," Meredith said, looking away again. "I never suspected that. I guess he and my mom were together off and on for years, but I thought it started after I was born." She drew in a shaky breath. "I caught them together when I was six."

"Oh, Meredith."

Her sister's chin lifted as if she refused to be cowed by the past. "I didn't even really understand what was happening, but even an innocent kid knows they shouldn't find Mommy naked in bed with a man who isn't their father."

"That's putting it mildly."

"Yeah, I guess. It was at our house in the summer. Dad had taken my brothers to a baseball tournament for the weekend, and I was supposed to be staying at my grandma's house. She only lived a few blocks from us. I'd forgotten my favorite pillow and rode my bike home to get it. I still remember the way he looked at me when he walked out. It was this strange mix of anger and affection but there was no remorse." She laughed without humor. "For all the man's sins, I don't think he ever felt a moment of shame."

"Must be nice," Avery murmured.

"My mom was as mad as I'd ever seen her. She told me I ruined everything." Another sad laugh. "Little did I know she wasn't just talking about her affair. I guess my father had always known that I wasn't his biological daughter. He'd agreed to raise me as his to avoid a scandal because he loved my mom. I wish he'd turned her away when he had the chance. Niall broke things off with her after that. One more strike against me, and it was pretty much the end of her willingness to keep up the charade of happy wife and mother. She left on Halloween night."

"Just disappeared?"

Meredith nodded. "Dad took us trick-or-treating. We got back and she was gone. She'd left a note for him but nothing for any of us."

"Have you talked to her in the years since?"

"Nope." Meredith smoothed a hand over her cheek, then looked away. "I'm not crying."

"I know."

"Last I heard, she's in Florida."

"Does finding out about Niall make you want to contact her? Don't you have questions?"

"Dozens of them," Meredith admitted quietly. "But it feels disrespectful to my dad…" She paused, cleared her throat, then continued, "Disrespectful to the dad who raised me to be curious. I shouldn't want to know. He should be enough."

"I'm not sure that's how it works." Avery put the broom aside and went to stand next to Meredith. "I bet he'd understand."

"Nope." Meredith rolled her shoulders as if she could unload some of the heavy weight that way. "He's had a hard time with all of this being public. He's a proud man, you know?"

"You said he'd gone to visit your brother. Is he still away?"

"He's back but I haven't seen him." She sighed. "He usually comes out a couple of times a week to help with the animals but…"

"He'll come around," Avery promised.

"You don't even know him."

"You're weirdly hard to resist."

That earned a smile. "I'm pretty damn adorable," her youngest sister agreed.

"If you like pet hair."

"Don't trust anyone who doesn't like animals."

A laugh bubbled up in Avery's throat.

Meredith grinned. "Firsthand experience?"

"My ex-boyfriend thought dogs were stinky and dirty. Probably cats, too, but we never made it that far."

"I bet he turned out to be a jerk."

"He turned out to be still married," Avery said, then blew out a breath. It was the first time she'd admitted that fact to anyone who hadn't already known about her relationship with Tony. She hadn't even shared the details of her breakup with her mother.

"That's rough."

"But not the worst of it." Now that she'd begun to

open up, the words poured out of her like a dam that had finally given way. "We worked together, and his wife confronted me at the office. She couldn't believe I didn't know. She was so angry."

"I can imagine." Meredith inclined her head. "You had no idea?"

"I like boundaries in relationships so the things that should have tipped me off felt like quirks at the time. They had two boys. She'd dragged them downtown with her. After telling me off, she stormed out of the building. Tony tried to stop her but she got the kids in the car and drove off. Except she hadn't buckled the younger one into his car seat. She ran a stop sign a few blocks from the office and her car was T-boned by a delivery truck."

Meredith cursed under her breath.

"The four-year-old was severely injured. He had to undergo emergency surgery and was unconscious for almost a week. They thought he wasn't going to pull through."

"But he did?"

"Yes, although as I understand it he has a long road to a full recovery." She turned to the other woman. "I almost killed him."

Meredith's small hand wrapped around Avery's upper arm. "You had no responsibility in that accident."

"I destroyed her family," Avery protested. "I drove her to that level of heartbreak."

"Would you have been with him if you'd known?"

"Of course not."

"Did you end it when you found out?"

"If I never speak to him again it will be too soon." She shrugged. "Not that my moral compass or the fallout I endured means anything to a heartbroken wife and mother."

"You said the two of you worked together?" Meredith released her arm but stayed close. "I assume that's the real reason you left your job?"

"Not just my job." Avery tried for a smile but found her mouth wouldn't move in that direction. "I lost my life."

"That doesn't seem fair." Meredith frowned.

"Unfortunately, it showed me the quality of the life I had. I was a little bit obsessed with my career. The people I thought were my friends were also my coworkers. They wanted nothing to do with me or the repercussions of the situation. Tony wasn't exactly my boss, but he was way higher up on the food chain."

"He cheated." Meredith threw up her hands. "How could anyone take his side?"

It was a question that had plagued Avery in the weeks after discovering Tony's duplicity. "I think it's partly the age-old double standard. And partly he had an injured kid in the hospital. He also made it clear that I'd seduced him. That he'd confided in me about a rocky period in his marriage and I took advantage of the situation. You can imagine how that went for me."

"Did they fire you?"

"The HR manager took pity. I think she could tell I was shell-shocked by the whole situation. She allowed me to resign and promised not to divulge the details of my termination with any potential employers."

"Your married superior cheated on his wife with you. The wife made a huge scene at your workplace. They branded you with some sort of modern-day scarlet letter."

Meredith slapped a hand on the porch rail. "It sounds like a bad made-for-TV movie."

"Without the happy ending," Avery added. "I was on my second week of couch potato-ing when I got the letter about Niall."

Meredith blew out a breath. "So this is a case of cutting yourself, then breaking your leg? Suddenly the finger doesn't hurt as badly."

"Something like that." Avery shuddered. "I know it's not the same situation, but the look on Gray's ex-wife's face when she found me with Violet brought it all back."

"Gray and that overinjected ex-wife have been divorced for a while. I heard she'd even moved on from the guy she cheated on Gray with." Meredith's focus on Avery intensified. "Did you tell him all this?"

Avery bit down on her lower lip. "I haven't told anyone."

"No one?"

"Not even my mom."

"But you told me." Meredith pointed at her own chest. "It's like we're really sisters or something."

"Yeah." Emotion bloomed in Avery's heart, delicate like the first flowers of spring. But she knew that fragility was a misnomer. This connection she had with her sister was deep and true, a crocus able to withstand the snow or wind or whatever nature threw at it and still retain its beauty.

"This is why you're avoiding Gray?" Meredith bent to pet Spot, who'd wandered up onto the porch. "Again."

"Maybe."

The dog did her usual flop and Avery finally found herself able to smile. "I think she's lost more weight."

"You've got a way with her," Meredith said. "Don't change the subject. You should talk to Gray."

"He was so hurt by Stacy's cheating. How can I admit to him that I'd caused that much pain to someone?"

"You're missing a key point," Meredith argued. "He was hurt by his *ex-wife*. She betrayed him, not the man she fooled around with."

"Do you truly believe that? Do you think he harbors no anger toward the guy?"

Meredith straightened. "You have a point, but as I understand it, he knew the dude. That makes a difference."

"A small one."

A crashing sound came from the barn, followed by a cacophony of bleating and then barking from the dog herd, which had gathered at the fence.

"Stupid goat," Meredith muttered. "Frank must have gotten out of his stall again. He's determined to get into the oats every chance he can find."

Avery picked up the broom again. "Good luck with that."

"You're coming with me," Meredith called over her shoulder, already moving for the porch steps.

"I should hold down the fort out here." Another crash reverberated in the quiet of the morning.

"I need you."

Those three words were like a shot directly to Avery's gut, just as they had been when she'd been the one to say them to Meredith and Carrie. As much as she'd become accustomed to not needing anyone or being needed in return, she hadn't realized how lonely that made her life until she came to Magnolia.

She trotted to catch up with her sister. "The property is twenty acres, right?"

"Around there." Meredith cupped her hands around her mouth. "Frank, you better stop making trouble," she called.

"It must be a huge amount of work on your own."

"A ton," Meredith said absently.

"What if we could find another location for the shelter and sell this property? The Realtor I met with, Jacob, thinks a developer might offer a decent price for the whole thing with the intention of subdividing it."

Meredith whirled on her so fast it made Avery's breath catch.

"This is my home," the petite firecracker said, tension lacing her tone. "You want to dump the gallery and that mess of a house in town, fine. I'll back you. They mean nothing to me. Less than. But don't even think about making a move for the ranch."

All Avery could do was nod in agreement. She half believed Meredith might take her to the ground if she argued. She had at least four inches on her tiny sister, but that didn't mean Meredith couldn't kick her ass.

"Got it." She held up her hands, palms out. "Although, you might rethink letting me stay here. I could help."

"You just stepped in a pile of horse poop." Meredith chuckled as Avery grimaced at her dirty sneaker. "Not sure how much help you'll be on the ranch, city girl. You're taking care of Spot, and I might bring over a few kittens for fostering. That will help."

"Kittens?" Avery swallowed and scraped the bottom of her shoe along the ground. "If I was here—"

"Work things out with Gray instead," Meredith suggested, hauling open the wide barn door. "He's a stand-up guy, Avs. Even if you don't want forever with him, be smart enough to take advantage of the now."

Avery paused as Meredith disappeared into the barn where the noise level sounded like a late-night rave gone wild. Could it be that simple? Take advantage of the now. *Live* in the now.

She'd always been a planner and a worrier, a crazy combination of ambition and anxiety. It seemed impossible to let that part of her go but things couldn't get much stranger than they already were. Why not change up the plan and see what happened?

CHAPTER SIXTEEN

"You should be at home resting."

Gray looked up from the paperwork he'd been staring at for the past half hour to see his mother standing in the doorway of the office at the fire station.

"Did Lucas pay you to say that?"

Lila chuckled as she entered the room. "No, but your friend is a smart young man."

"Which must mean I'm not?" He forced a smile but tension ricocheted down his spine. His mother had always hated his chosen profession. He knew she wished he were more like his ambitious older brother, holed up in a corner office, with a paper cut the biggest potential physical hazard on the job.

As the town's longtime librarian, his mom valued books and quiet and learning and…all the things Gray chafed against growing up. He'd taken after his father—an adrenaline junkie with a deep commitment to service but an equal devotion to action.

The kind of action that had killed his father and landed Gray in the hospital. He'd been cleared by his doctor to return to work but was relegated to desk duty. There had already been two dozen calls this week, and it tore him up to watch his crew heading out for each call while he manned the fort at the station.

Lucas had been the most vocal that Gray should take

a few personal days to recover but that might have more to do with Gray's black mood versus concern for his injuries. He was healing fine. His chest still ached, but he absolutely wouldn't stop or allow anyone to believe the accident had sidelined him.

He'd received a call from Douglas Damon the day after the accident. Gray's attorney had wished him well for a speedy recovery but also mentioned that he'd heard from Stacy's attorney asking if Gray wanted to formally amend their current custody arrangement while he recuperated. Gray had downplayed the severity of the accident, although he didn't think he was fooling the older man. Then Douglas brought up the fact that a private security company outside Raleigh might be hiring an investigator, the words nudging open a dark cavern in Gray's stomach.

He loved his job. It was more than work to him. It was his calling, and he felt honored to serve the people of Magnolia in that capacity.

But he hated to think that his devotion might also cost him a chance at more time with his daughter.

"You're intelligent." His mother slid into the chair across from the desk. "More than you give yourself credit for."

Gray waited for the backhand side of her compliment. When his mother only studied him, he blew out a breath. "You don't have to soften it, Mom. I know how you feel about the fire department and my role here. You think I'm reckless, just like Dad."

She flashed a wistful smile. "I think you care, just like he did."

"That caring got him killed."

"Yes," she admitted slowly. "But he would have been miserable doing anything else."

Just like Gray.

"I want to talk to you about your new girlfriend."

Gray felt his brows draw together. "Avery isn't my girlfriend," he said, although saying the word out loud in association with her felt strangely right. But he couldn't have a girlfriend if the woman in question continued to take such great pains to avoid him. He'd barely seen her since the accident, although every day she left some get-well gift on his back porch. Brownies, a stack of magazines, DVDs of old-school family movies, a six-pack of his favorite beer.

Her thoughtfulness touched him even as it annoyed him that she dropped off the presents at odd hours when she must know he wasn't home. He didn't know where she went when she left the carriage house early in the morning only to return after dark each night. But he wanted to, and that irritated him the most.

"I saw how you looked at her," his mother said. "You wear your heart on your sleeve, Grayson. You always have."

"She's in town temporarily," he countered, unable to deny his ridiculous infatuation with Avery. No point with his mom. She knew him too well. "Nothing will come of it."

"Didn't you say the same thing when you first met Stacy?"

"She got pregnant," he reminded his mother. "It's different."

"And this Avery—"

"Mom." He pushed away from the desk. "I'm not discussing my private life with you."

"I worry."

"You don't need to."

"Could you turn off your concern for your daughter?"

"She's five."

His mother chuckled. "Trust me, things don't change that much when a child grows up." She glanced around the office "You're a wonderful father. I know your job gives you a lot of satisfaction, and it's not my place to judge."

He counted in his head, waiting for the inevitable *but*. One…two…

"But it was difficult to watch your sorrow after the divorce. I was heartbroken for your heartbreak. I don't want that again for you."

"My heart is fine," he insisted. "Well insulated, protected by many layers of scar tissue."

"I want you to be happy."

"What if Avery Keller makes me happy?"

"I knew Niall, of course."

"Everyone in town knew Niall." He sucked in a breath. "Please don't tell me that you—"

"Slept with him?" She made a face. "No. Although, it wasn't for lack of trying on his part. He tended to be drawn to women who were alone or unhappy. That man had more than his share of demons. He had horrible boundaries and hurt a lot of people despite all the good he did for Magnolia."

He walked over to the window that looked out onto the street front. "You make him sound like a predator."

"He hurt a lot of women."

"Yeah, I think we can all agree on that." He lifted a hand to the warm glass. The sidewalk in front of the station was empty at the moment. The leaves on the big maple that shaded the building fluttered. In a few weeks, the calendar would usher in another temperate autumn in North Carolina. It was Gray's favorite time of year. He liked the change of seasons, even if it wasn't as dramatic along the coast.

He couldn't help but wonder if Avery would be there to see it.

"I'm not sure what that has to do with Avery." He turned to face his mother. "Or Carrie or Meredith for that matter. You aren't suggesting they be blamed for the literal sins of their father."

"Of course not." His mother wrung her hands together in her lap. A sure sign that he wouldn't like whatever was coming next. "But she's damaged. All those girls are."

"Christ, Mom."

"Don't swear at me." She rose and took a step toward him. "I have sympathy for her position. The three of them have a long road to healing. But my concern is you. You're in a better place now. A good place." She offered a smile, and he knew he should return it.

Instead, he simply watched her, waiting for the next blow.

"If you're lonely or you want to meet someone, there are plenty of nice women around. Women who are stable."

"You don't even know her," he said through gritted teeth.

"Neither do you," she countered.

He closed his eyes for a long moment, counted to a full ten in his head. His mother meant well, but this was why he didn't often involve her in his life. He was a grown-ass man, and she wanted to treat him like a kid.

As if sensing that she'd overstepped some invisible line, Lila came forward and gave him a hug, careful not to squeeze too hard. "If you need anything, call me. I'm here for you, Grayson." She pulled back, lifting a soft hand to his cheek. "There's a new English teacher at the high school this year," she told him. "I met her when she came into the library. Good taste in literature and very pretty. I could invite her for dinn—"

"I appreciate the thought, but no." With a sigh, he dropped a kiss on the top of his mother's head. She loved him, even if her skepticism about his capacity to manage his own life chafed. Sometimes he wished his perfect brother would make some monumental screw-up in his life. Take some of the focus off all the ways Gray seemed to stumble.

"Very well." She turned to leave, then paused and reached into her oversized purse, drawing out a plastic container and fork. "I almost forgot. Here's lunch for you."

"Thanks, Mom." He didn't bother to mention that he'd been managing his own meals for the whole of his adult life and he hadn't starved yet.

"I also dropped off a casserole to your house." She handed him the container of food. "Tuna noodle. It was your favorite as a kid."

"You're the best."

She beamed at that. "Someone left a bag with a vibrating massager on your back porch. It looked more like some kind of kinky sex toy."

Gray choked and tried to keep his expression neutral.

His mother sniffed delicately. "I threw it in the trash before Violet got ahold of it."

He wasn't going to begin to explain Avery's trail of random and thoughtful gifts. How could the woman have known that his shoulders had ached with stiffness all week long?

"The wives of some of the guys at the station have been dropping by get-well gifts," he lied. "I'm sure it was just a massager."

"Either way." She sniffed. "Enjoy the casserole."

He lowered himself back into the chair as she walked out of the office. He wasn't sure whether to laugh or cry at the state of his life. Battling his ex-wife on one side and avoiding his mother's well-intentioned interference on the other. Yet the one woman he wanted to be a part of his life was still dodging him.

Gray might not know how to handle the first two, but he wasn't going to let Avery ignore him much longer. That would be the smart thing, of course, but there was one benefit to believing his brother had gotten the brains in the family.

Gray could take impulsive action without feeling guilty. It was past time to test that theory with regards to Avery.

"I HAVE AN IDEA." Avery looked between Carrie and Malcolm, both of whom she'd arranged to meet at the gallery later that afternoon.

The mayor's bushy eyebrows lifted. "Should we be scared?"

"I'm not selling," Carrie said immediately.

"Just hear me out," Avery pleaded. "We need to do something, Carrie. You might not want to let go of your dad's properties, but none of us will benefit if the bank repossesses them."

"Our dad." Carrie crossed her arms over her chest. "He was *our* dad."

"I have a dad," Meredith chimed in from where she was sprawled on the floor of the gallery, legs propped up on the wall. "I also have twenty minutes left on my lunch break so let's get on with things."

"We have chairs," Carrie said, her tone clipped. "You don't need to be on the floor."

"I'm stretching," Meredith explained. "It relieves tension. You might want to try it. Could loosen that stick lodged in your—"

"Ladies." Malcolm held up his hands. "We're all on the same team here."

Meredith bit off a laugh. "What's it called? Team Dysfunction?"

"We're not having enough *fun* for that," Carrie added.

Oil and water would mix better than those two, Avery thought. She wasn't sure what had happened to the Meredith who'd been both vulnerable and supportive earlier that morning. Maybe she should have requested the meeting out at the beach. The property seemed to soften her youngest sister's sharp edges in a way nothing else did. But the downtown location made more sense for everyone.

Carrie was spending the morning at the gallery cataloging Niall's art. The mayor's office was only a few blocks away and Meredith had a shift at the vet clinic in town where she worked part-time.

"We need a plan to revitalize downtown." She cleared her throat and tried to ignore her tingling fingers. What if they thought her ideas were stupid? This type of plan wasn't exactly in her wheelhouse, but she truly believed she could make a difference. "Magnolia is just as historic as some other destinations along the coast. I've been researching online, and this place rivals Savannah as far as architecture and charm. Plus the beach is close enough to be a draw."

She smoothed a stray lock of hair from her face. After leaving the animal rescue this morning, she'd driven to the beach, awed by the beauty of the waves crashing along the shoreline and the endless miles of white sand and sea grass. "It feels like the beach here is one of the few undiscovered areas of the Eastern Seaboard. I can't figure out why you wouldn't have tourists flocking to the area."

Malcolm rubbed a hand along his jaw. "Niall wanted to be the focus of things. Yes, we're close to the ocean but the town never emphasized that. He thought it would dilute the appeal."

"What does that even mean?" Meredith asked, stretching her arms above her head. "How can you dilute the appeal?"

Carrie cleared her throat. "If the town could flourish without Dad, he would have lost his power to control things."

"Jackass," Meredith muttered.

"A truth universally acknowledged," Carrie said quietly.

"Was that humor?" Meredith twisted so that one leg crossed the other. She was beginning to look like some sort of circus contortionist. "Does Daddy's little princess finally see that we were the butt of his sick joke all these years?"

"I'm *not* a princess," Carrie said through clenched teeth.

Avery stepped forward, placing herself between her sisters. "As fun as it is to watch the two of you rip into each other, that's not the point of why I asked you to meet today."

Meredith arched a brow. "You have a point?"

Without thinking, Avery flipped her sister the middle finger, earning a sudden laugh from Carrie and a reluctant grin from Meredith.

"Thank god my wife gave birth to four boys," Malcolm said with a sigh. "If you three are any indication, I couldn't have survived daughters. What's the plan, Avery?"

"We need a strong business model to start." She pulled a notepad from her tote bag, the effervescence in her chest making her feel like she'd just chugged a fizzy drink. "I've done some preliminary research on strategies for redevelopment and the risks involved in various plans." She detailed what she'd read and the examples of other towns the size of Magnolia that had turned around their fortunes. "It would help to bring a marquee restaurant or store into downtown and also focus on attracting new corporate businesses into the community. We'll lease out the space connected to the gallery and convert this part of the building to a storefront."

"It's an art gallery," Carrie argued. "It's always been an art gallery."

"Filled with a bunch of half-rate paintings that no one wants." Meredith flipped onto her hands and knees, flexing her back in a traditional yoga cat-cow pose. "Artists usually have a resurgence in popularity once they die, right? Has anyone bought one of Niall's sappy scenes in years?"

"No," Carrie admitted. "But I'm working on launching an online store with his work. We may be able to attract buyers that way."

"You realize how much we owe in taxes?" Avery forced herself to say the number out loud and registered the shock on both the women's faces.

"What happened to selling?" Meredith asked, glancing up through her long eyelashes.

"I'd still like to sell." Avery hugged the notepad to her chest as if it were some kind of medieval shield. "But the fact is the properties aren't worth what we owe at this point. The Realtor said it could take time to get approval to sell from the probate court. If we can lease the space and drive up real estate in Magnolia, it would not only help the town but also put us in a better position to make money from finding a buyer down the road."

Malcolm took a step closer, his jaw set. "So you aren't doing this for Magnolia? All your talk about the town being an undiscovered gem—you don't mean any of it. It's still part of your endgame to sell and bolt."

"No one is talking about bolting," Avery insisted. Couldn't he see that her endgame would benefit his objective? "More important, no one expects or wants me to stay in Magnolia for the long haul so—"

"That's not true," Malcolm interrupted. "That tiny wannabe bovine wants you to stay." He pointed a finger toward Spot, panting softly where she was curled near Meredith. As if she could feel all eyes on her, the dog lifted her head, gaze trained adoringly toward her foster mom.

Avery's heart skipped a beat, but she forced a casual laugh. "She'll love whoever ends up feeding her on a permanent basis."

Meredith reached out and scratched the dog's floppy ears. "She's bonded with you."

"Then unbond her," Avery snapped.

"That might be easier to accomplish with a dog than with people." He gestured between the three women. "You're sisters. That's a tie that can't be broken."

The truth of those words felt like both a gift and a curse, but Avery rolled her eyes. "We didn't even know we shared DNA a month ago, and plenty of siblings are close despite miles between them."

"Yes," Malcolm agreed slowly. "But who's going to keep these two from sniping at each other if you leave?"

"You can," Avery all but shouted.

"No, ma'am." He shook his head. "My plate is already overflowing with general town craziness."

"They're adults who—"

"Can hear you talking about us," Meredith said, straightening and placing her hands on her trim hips. "Of course we can manage on our own. I've hated her for decades and we've rubbed along just fine."

Carrie drew in a sharp breath. "You hate me?"

Meredith blinked. "I mean, I used to hate you. Past tense. I don't hate you anymore."

"If you had a choice—" Carrie narrowed her eyes "—of spending time alone with me or getting punched in the face, which would you choose?"

"How hard of a punch are we talking about?" Meredith asked with a cheeky grin.

"You're the worst," Carrie muttered, then turned to Avery. "You can't leave."

"I can't stay," Avery protested weakly.

Meredith moved to stand next to Carrie. Once again, they were a study in contrasts. Carrie with her fine bone structure, loosely braided hair and flowing sundress while Meredith wore athletic tights and a ripped T-shirt that read Mother of Dogs. Her dark hair was held back in an array of colorful clips with short tendrils sticking out near her temples.

"Malcolm is right," Meredith told her. "We need to do this together. The three of us. Princess and I won't be able to agree on anything. We need you."

"Besides," Carrie added. "You've already said you need a fresh start. Why not in Magnolia?"

"I wasn't built to be a Southern belle," Avery argued. "I hated *Gone with the Wind.*"

"Frankly, my dear sister," Meredith deadpanned. "I don't give a—"

Carrie nudged Meredith to silence her. "It's your plan. You have this amazing idea for turning things around in town. You can't just throw it on the table, then cut and run."

"I'm not going to…" Avery paused, an unfamiliar bolt of satisfaction rolling through her. "You think the idea is amazing?"

Carrie nodded, then nudged Meredith again.

"Stop touching me. Yeah, it's good. Rough but good. I mean, more people coming through means more potential adopters for my babies."

"And Niall wasn't the only business owner suffering." Malcolm ran a hand over his bald head. "If we can turn things around, everyone will benefit."

"So you admit my endgame—" Avery mimicked his words, adding air quotes for good measure "—as you call it, isn't just me being selfish and looking out for my own interests?" She had no idea why she even cared what these people or anyone in this town thought about her, but she couldn't seem to turn off her emotions.

Malcolm shrugged. "Let's make sure it works."

"Does that mean you'll stay?" Meredith asked.

"And that we can forget the idea of selling?"

Avery's pulse pounded. She wanted to hate the way they looked at her expectantly but it felt good to be important to someone. "Nothing is off the table as far as I'm concerned, but we're going to try to salvage this without selling to an outsider. If we're successful, you two can buy me out."

Meredith and Carrie gave her matching frowns. "I thought you were going to stay," Meredith said.

"For now." Avery pressed a hand to her stuttering heart. "All I can promise is for now."

CHAPTER SEVENTEEN

AVERY FORCED HERSELF not to move as Gray's truck rumbled into the driveway a few nights later. She sat in one of the cushioned chairs on the patio between the two houses, enjoying the cool breeze that whispered through the white oak trees. A few of the outer leaves had just started to turn yellow, making her breath catch at nature's reminder of time passing. She'd been in Magnolia for three weeks now, longer than she ever would have imagined, but this was only the start.

What had she committed to with her sisters and Malcolm? It was difficult to say exactly, hard to know if her ideas would take root and make a difference or if the town's slow decline was too difficult to forestall. She had to believe it would work.

They'd talked through several scenarios and the mayor had already scheduled a meeting with the town council. Avery's background was in risk analysis. Ironic since she hated wagering anything in her personal life. But she could determine risk potential and find solutions to safeguard assets without blinking an eye. Magnolia was a strong bet. They'd need people and companies willing to invest in the town's future.

Enough people loved the town to find a way. It seemed strange to count herself among that group, but she couldn't deny the sense of place she felt in this community. Not that she planned to make this her forever home. She couldn't allow her mind to go there when that meant letting down the protective wall around her heart.

She jolted back from her meandering thoughts at the sound of a door slamming. Gray came around the front of his truck, pausing when he caught sight of her.

Awareness made her toes curl, but by now she'd gotten used to her visceral physical reaction to him. Maybe he hadn't noticed that she'd been keeping her distance since the accident. She'd left little gifts on his doorstep every day, unable to stop herself from offering something, even if it was a lame substitution for real connection.

For all she knew he hadn't even realized they were from her. Maybe he had a secret admirer. She could imagine plenty of women admiring Gray. And Avery had pushed him away because she wasn't willing to actually take the risk when there was so much at stake.

Stupid, stupid woman.

She lifted her hand in a lame wave as he approached, trying to act cool and nonchalant, like she hadn't been waiting for him.

"You didn't run and hide," he said when he reached her chair.

She sniffed. "I don't know what you're talking about."

One side of his mouth kicked up. "Thank you for the gifts," he said, his voice pitched low.

"Sure." She made a point to ignore the way her body reacted to his tone. The way she went hot all over despite the break in the weather that had led to tonight's cooler temperatures. "Not a big deal."

"My mom thought the massager was a sex toy."

"Oh, no." Avery felt her eyes go wide. "You didn't tell her it was from me?"

His grin widened. "I'm not discussing sex toys with my mother."

She stood up, nerves making her body feel electric. "It wasn't a sex toy."

He studied her a long moment, and she felt color rise to her cheeks. Damn the man. "I'd much rather have you than a sex toy anyway."

His voice scraped against her insides like sandpaper, leaving prickly heat in its wake. Standing had been a mistake, putting her toe to toe with him, close enough to see the flecks of gold in his eyes. His minty breath tickled her cheek. One easy sway and she'd be pressed against him. Her whole body screamed to be pressed against him.

"You're injured," she told him as if he weren't aware of the fact.

"I'm fine."

"How many times have you said that this week?"

"Enough."

"Does anyone believe you?"

"Aren't you supposed to be nice to people in recovery?"

Without thinking, she reached up and brushed a kiss across his lips. "Does that make it better?"

He hummed into her mouth. "You have no idea. But that's not where it hurts the most."

She laughed, pleasure spiraling through her at his silly flirting. "You should talk to your doctor about that."

"My doctor's more interested in you than me."

"Is it my fault I'm irresistible?"

He pulled back a few inches, his gaze intense on hers. "Are you going on a date with the doctor?"

Avery bit back a laugh. How could he think for a minute that was a possibility? Thoughts of Gray filled her mind at every turn. Although, the smart choice would be to stay away, sometimes a connection couldn't be denied.

"No," she said, deciding against a coy response or a joke to lighten the moment. She could see the vulnerability in his gaze, and she wanted him to know her heart. Just for now. "You're the only guy I want to be with."

"I noticed you didn't use the word *date*," he said, narrowing his eyes.

"Dating feels complicated. I've got a lot of complications in my life already."

"I'm a simple man." He smoothed a hand over her cheek. "We don't have to make this difficult, but I won't hide what's between us."

She swallowed at the ferocity of his words. "Okay," she answered finally. "But I need to take things slow, Gray. I wasn't planning on any of this."

"Slow works for me." He leaned in again and brushed his lips across hers, with the obvious intention to go slow.

As heat pulsed through her body, she leaned into him. He deepened the kiss, pressing his open palm to the back of her neck like he wanted her with the same ferocity she felt. Emotion and need rose like a wave inside her. After a few minutes, she tore away, trying to gain control but understanding it was probably a losing battle.

Gray took her hand and drew her toward the house. "I have a feeling we'll work even better inside."

"Where's Violet?" she asked. No way would she take the chance on the girl finding the two of them together.

Gray's fingers tightened on hers. "She's staying with my mom tonight. I might have overdone things at work."

Avery tugged them to a stop. "What does that mean?" She spread her fingers across his chest. "Are you having trouble breathing? Do you need to see a doctor? To rest? To lie down?"

He flashed a sheepish grin. "I'm fine. A little worn-out is all. My mom wanted to take Violet to a movie anyway, so it made sense that she'd spend the night, too. Of your choices, I'll take 'lie down.'" His slow wink made her heart clench and other parts of her body break out in a happy dance. "Preferably with you on top of me."

"I should go home."

"You are home."

She gestured to the carriage house, ignoring the deep feeling of satisfaction that zipped through her at the thought of this being her home. "We both know what I mean."

"I do," he conceded. "But I don't like it. Stay with me. If it makes you feel better, slow might be the only speed I have going at the moment." He paused, then added, "I don't want to be alone tonight."

"Yeah," she breathed without thinking. That was the heart of it for her, as well. Being alone had felt normal in her old life. Magnolia made her want more.

And wanting more meant wanting Gray.

"I can take care of you," she offered, then blushed at the silly offer. "I know you don't need it. You don't need *me*. But I want to help you."

"I'd love to accept." His voice grew serious. "Based on our recent history, I'm afraid that means you'll push me away on the other end of whatever happens tonight. Don't push me away, Avery."

"I'm sorry." She pressed her lips together, unsure of how to explain all of her doubts and how they manifested. "I have trouble trusting things that make me happy."

"I make you happy?"

"You do." Her stomach did flip-flops at the admission. The last man she'd let in had almost broken her. Certainly her heart had suffered some significant damage. Gray was nothing like her ex-boyfriend, but that scared her even more. Her feelings had the potential to leave her emotionally eviscerated. She knew the likelihood of system breakdowns and losses better than most people, which was why she kept her heart closely guarded and probably the reason she'd gotten involved with Tony. His rigid boundaries felt safe to her. She'd thought they were alike in all the ways that counted. Of course, the truth had turned out to be both different and devastating.

Gray wasn't simple but her feelings for him were straightforward. That didn't make them any less terrifying.

"You're getting that look in your eyes," he said. "The one that tells me you're thinking about lacing up your running shoes. And we haven't even done anything yet."

"I'm thinking about it." She blew out a breath. "I'm trying something new here that involves letting myself feel what I'm feeling instead of pushing it away."

"And you feel like bolting?"

"I feel scared of the possibility of being hurt. Of not being enough or wanting too much or how my heart is going to break when it's over between us."

"You maybe want to give us a chance to start before you end things."

She held on to the idea, twirling it in her mind like a kaleidoscope with the two of them as the reflecting surfaces tilting toward each other. If she kept her focus on the darkness, that was what she saw. But when she lifted her inner gaze to the light, the world in front of her exploded in colors and shapes, falling over each other as the patterns changed and repeated.

"I think I'd like to try that," she said softly.

"Good." He wrapped his arms around her waist and pulled her in for a gentle hug. "I'd like it, too."

They stood together for several moments and the intimacy of the moment, surrounded by birdsong and the rustle of the evening breeze felt more intense than anything she'd experienced. Yes, her heart might break at the end of this but she understood it could also be worth the risk.

Then her stomach growled. Not a cute little rumble but an obnoxious bellow. The kind a teenage boy would be proud to claim.

Gray chuckled and released her. "You need food."

"I was too nervous to eat," she said with a nod. "I was afraid you wouldn't want anything to do with me after what a coward I've been this week."

He held one finger to her lips. "You aren't a coward, and we've established that you're entitled to your feelings, in whatever form they take. But we should think about dinner." He tapped his free hand to the scrape on his forehead. "Luckily for you, not everyone in a small town brings get-well gifts in the form of sex toys. Most deliver casseroles." He wiggled his eyebrows. "And blueberry cobbler."

"I love cobbler." Like the flutter of butterfly wings the realization flitted across her heart that she might also love this man. She immediately rejected it. Feelings were one thing but falling in love in the span of a few weeks... Well, that would just be madness.

Stick to casserole and cobbler, she reminded herself. The present moment. Everything else would work itself out.

At least that was what she hoped.

GRAY KNOCKED ON the front door of his ex-wife's condo in a posh section of Raleigh a week later. He hadn't planned to have this conversation with her but his time with Avery had given him a new perspective on his future.

True to her word, she hadn't run away again. He knew there were moments when she wanted to. Her gaze would shutter and her shoulders grow stiff. She had the nervous habit of tugging her bottom lip between her teeth in worry, an adorable tell he'd come to recognize.

She still wouldn't reveal much about her past or why she struggled with emotional intimacy, but he was a patient man. And she stayed. He tried to give her the space she needed, to allow her to set the pace.

It was easy to include her in his and Violet's routine. She'd only spent the night with him that first night when his daughter had been at her grandma's. He'd been exhausted enough that he'd fallen asleep shortly after dinner but had woken in the middle of the night to find Avery curled against him, still in her T-shirt and jeans.

The idea that she hadn't left even though he'd been pathetic company warmed his heart more than he cared to admit. He'd taken great pleasure in peeling off her clothes, ignoring her protests that he needed more rest. He needed her and had relished proving that she was the best medicine he could imagine.

As amazing as being with her again had been, he enjoyed the small moments when they were hanging out just as much. Violet had warmed to her and loved taking care of Spot. She still enjoyed giving Avery sass, and Avery seemed to love responding in kind. He didn't exactly understand the dynamic of their relationship but it worked for the two of them, so he wasn't going to question it.

Now that she'd opened herself to the possibility, Avery was quickly becoming part of the Magnolia community. Her motives for helping to chart Magnolia's future remained unclear. A few of the old-timers seemed to believe she and her sisters were besmirching Niall's name by minimizing his ongoing impact in town. Gray could see, like many others, that their initial efforts at reinvigorating the downtown business district offered Magnolia its best chance at revitalization.

He wanted it to work, not just for the community, but so that Avery could see she belonged there. She insisted they keep their burgeoning relationship quiet in town. She had no problem being seen with him and had even offered to take Violet to her dance class. That was as much as she was willing to give, and he couldn't find it in himself to push her for more. Not when it meant he could drive her away instead. Maybe he was being stupid. It wouldn't be the first time. And he knew Violet's attachment to Avery could lead to issues if things didn't work out.

For all of Gray's pragmatism at the fire station, he was both an optimist and a romantic at heart. Avery fit with him on a soul-deep level and he couldn't stop himself from believing that would be enough to see them through whatever came next.

Stacy opened the door and immediately stepped outside, shutting it behind her.

"Aw, hell," Gray muttered under his breath. "You're not alone."

"You should have called first," she said with a sniff.

"It will only take a minute."

"Where's Violet?" She looked around him toward his truck parked at the curb.

"She's at a birthday party."

"So then why are you here?"

"I want full custody," he blurted. His attorney would go apoplectic when he found out Gray had gone directly to Stacy with the request. But the truth was it would be a long shot to have a modification ruling in their favor without her agreement. Stacy was neglectful but not in a way that would persuade a judge. Gray knew how charming his ex-wife could be when she wanted to be. His accident had also reminded him she'd have a reason to fight his petition if she chose to go that route. He'd loved her once and still believed that she'd loved him in her own way.

Certainly he could convince her to see his side on this. It would benefit Violet most of all.

"Absolutely not," she said in a hiss of breath. "Have you lost your mind? She's my daughter." She dabbed at the corners of her eyes. "I'm her mother."

"I know," he said gently.

"This is about that woman," she said, her gaze turning obstinate. "The hoochie you're shacking up with."

Gray felt his blood turn cold. "Stace, don't do this."

"You don't get to have it all." She spit out the words like poison. "All I hear about lately is that woman and her braiding and her dog." The emotion from moments earlier had disappeared like a puff of smoke, vaporizing so fast he wondered if he'd imagined it. Or maybe it had just been manufactured, like her affection for him through most of their relationship. She'd suck him in when she needed something, then freeze him out when he didn't live up to her arbitrary standards.

"Avery isn't living with me, and she cares about Violet." He kept his tone measured. Stacy loved to push him for a reaction, and he wouldn't give her the satisfaction of it. Too much was on the line.

"I thought you'd sworn off dating." She pointed a finger at him. "You love telling me how Violet's your priority."

"That hasn't changed." He blew out a breath. How had this conversation gotten off track so quickly? He should have expected it with his ex-wife. Stacy was a master at manipulation, and when things didn't go her way, she'd argue circles around him.

"I can't believe you'd suggest that I give you full custody of our daughter."

"Come on, Stacy." He ran a hand through his hair. "You know this is best."

"Tell me all about your whacked out logic for this."

"I wouldn't call it that," he said through gritted teeth. "I've thought about this. I'm not trying to push you out of her life. I'd never do that. But she needs stability."

"You think I don't give that to her?" Stacy's tone had turned pouty.

"I think you have a lot going on. Your practice is growing so your hours are crazy and you travel a ton to speaking engagements and conferences. More times than not you can't take her on your scheduled days. I know you don't mean it as a rejection, but it hurts her just the same."

"Do you want alimony?" Her eyes widened. "Is that your intent? You know how hard I've worked. We agreed in the divorce that the sweat equity and support you gave me in building the practice wouldn't factor going forward. It's mine, Gray."

"Of course," he agreed, pulling in a deep breath. He had to keep a hold on his temper and patience. He wouldn't get anywhere by blowing up. "I don't want to take anything from you."

"You want my daughter."

"She stays with me almost all the time. Nothing about the current arrangement will change other than making it formal."

"But then I won't have options. What happens if I want more time?"

"I'll give you as much time with her as you want. We'll work it out. But she needs more consistency, Stace. No more of you missing scheduled nights or weekends with her."

"I can't help my schedule," she muttered. "It's not my fault that things get out of hand sometimes. I still love her."

"I never said you didn't." He shook his head. "Consider the request, please. If we can work this out on our own, Violet benefits. The outcome will be better if we agree before my attorney files a motion."

"You won't win in court."

"I won't give up," he countered softly. He couldn't. Not when so much was at stake.

They both shifted their attention to the front door as it opened. A man stood there—shirtless—glaring at Gray. "Everything okay, babe?" he asked Stacy.

"Give me a minute," she told him.

"Your smoothie is waiting."

"A minute," she repeated. With an eye roll, he closed the door.

"New boyfriend?" Gray lifted a brow. "Nice chest."

"Shut up. I have to go to a conference this week in San Diego. I'll think about your little bomb and we can talk next week."

Gray started to nod in agreement, then paused. "Wait. This week? How long have you known? Violet has her dance recital this coming Saturday. She expects both of us to be there."

"Video it for me," Stacy said, waving her hand. "Don't give me a hard time. I'm a single mom. Things are going to come up. I told you about this weeks ago."

He set his jaw but kept his mouth shut. She hadn't mentioned a trip and had to know how important the recital was to their daughter.

Finally, he asked, "Does Violet know?"

"I haven't had a chance to mention it. You can tell her." Stacy wagged a finger at him. "You better not throw me under the bus. She certainly isn't going to get into a private college on your paltry salary. I'm doing all of this for her."

"Think about custody, Stacy." He forced an encouraging smile. "I promise it doesn't have to change anything."

She gave a reluctant nod. "I'll call you next week. My smoothie is melting."

"Sure," he agreed. "Have fun in California." He walked away, his gut burning at the thought of relaying this news to his daughter. Violet might act tougher than most girls her age, but he knew how it hurt when Stacy didn't make her a priority. He also understood that he'd try to cover for his ex. Anything to keep her receptive to his plan. She had to agree to modify custody. Gray would do whatever he had to if she'd only say yes.

CHAPTER EIGHTEEN

"I DON'T BELONG HERE."

Avery pressed herself against the side of the building, heart racing. The heat of the bricks only made her sweat harder, which added to her panic at the thought of walking into the dance studio with Gray.

"I'll admit," Gray said, glancing behind him, "it's a little unorthodox to be hiding in an alley. We don't see that a lot in Magnolia. Especially when—"

"Hey, Gray," someone called from the street. "Everything okay?"

Avery wanted the ground to swallow her whole.

"Sure, Bubba," Gray shouted back. He shifted so he blocked her from view of anyone passing by. "Be there in a minute."

A puff of hysterical laughter burst through her lips. "Bubba," she murmured, then glanced up at Gray through her lashes. "Is that really his name?"

He nodded. "Bubba Roshek. His family has lived around here for as long as anyone can remember. He runs the car dealership out on Route Five. Gave me a great deal on the truck."

"Do you remember I called you Bubba that first morning at the gas station?"

"Yeah." He ran a hand over his jaw. "I didn't *reckon* you'd confused me for the real Bubba. Not sure if you got a good look but he might be as wide as he is tall. Hairy, too."

"What am I doing, Gray?" She held her hands fisted at her sides, anxiety coursing through her like a riptide, threatening to pull her under.

He reached out and laced his fingers with hers. He lifted her hand to his mouth and brushed a feather-light kiss across her knuckles. She'd spent the past few days with Carrie working on clearing out the garage at Niall's house. Her normally manicured fingernails had seen better days. Tiny cuts dotted her fingers from her battle with one of the three foster kittens Meredith had foisted on her.

Oh, yes. Avery Reed had gone from corporate finance risk manager to manual laborer sweating her butt off as she cleared out her dad's hoard only to return home to her cats and an overweight mutt. She felt like the poster child for a premature midlife crisis.

"I thought you were coming with me to Violet's recital?" He checked his watch. "The performance starts in ten minutes. My mom is saving seats for us."

"Your ex-wife should be here," Avery told him.

"Agreed, but she isn't. You don't have to do this, either, if it's too uncomfortable. Violet—"

"Stop." She shook her head. "Stop letting people off the hook so easily. I told Violet I'd be there, and I will." She blew out a breath. "As soon as the need to puke passes."

He smiled but she could see the hurt in his eyes. Of course he didn't want to hear that he let people— women—take advantage of him. No man wanted to believe that. But she'd heard him make excuses for his ex with Violet. Avery could tell the little girl hadn't bought what he was selling, but she'd taken the news like a champ. Or like a kid who was used to being put on the back burner by her mother.

Avery could relate. Only she hadn't had a father like Gray to soften the blow when her mother missed important events in her life because she'd been busy at work.

"Why the sudden wave of nausea? You've been getting more involved with the revitalization plan every day. It won't be a surprise for people to see you out in the community."

"That's the problem." Avery tugged one hand out of his grasp and pressed it to her stomach. "Now there are expectations."

"Such as…"

"Like I'm supposed to care about this place," she blurted, then wished she could take back the careless words as Gray took a step back.

"Ouch," he whispered.

"I didn't mean it like that," she quickly amended. "I do care. I care so much it scares me to pieces."

"Is this about the running shoes?" he asked, his gaze gentling.

As embarrassing as it felt to admit how vulnerable her feelings made her, the alternative of him thinking she was coldhearted… Well, that was even worse.

"We're making great progress on the plans for downtown. But I can see the way people look at me now. Like I'm some kind of small-town savior."

"No one is going to put pressure on you in that way."

"Carrie, Malcolm and I were meeting yesterday at the gallery to discuss a new online marketing campaign. Joe from the diner delivered lunch and homemade brownies that his eighty-year-old mom made. He's also behind on his mortgage payments and told us that if he loses the business, his wife will leave him and his oldest son will have to drop out of college." She drew in a shaky breath. "How's that for pressure?"

"Wow."

"Right? I want to see Violet dance. That little ankle biter has wound her sassy self around my heart. But I'm afraid for people to depend on me. I'll let them down. I'll let her down." *And you*, she added silently. Most of all, she didn't want to hurt Gray.

"You're complicating this," he told her, taking several steps toward the alley's entrance and holding out a hand. "Just watch the recital today, and you can deal with saving Magnolia tomorrow."

She studied him, looking for a reason to argue. It couldn't possibly be as simple as he made it sound. She'd never done that. She analyzed risk and then made the most prudent decision she could.

Magnolia challenged everything she knew about herself. Everything that gave her life meaning. On the flip side, she'd never felt as alive as she did in this town.

Particularly with this man.

She straightened from the wall, ignoring that the fabric of her shirt stuck to her back. Nerves didn't matter. Violet had asked her to come to the recital, and Avery wouldn't allow her own cowardice to be the reason she disappointed the girl.

Ignoring the shaking in her knees, she stepped toward Gray. "*Simple* is my middle name," she said, kissing him quickly. She swatted his hand away when he tried to pull her close. "Which is why I'm not walking into the dance studio holding your hand. No reason to give people more incentive to talk about me."

He dropped another kiss on the top of her head and then they walked toward the sunlit sidewalk together. "It might distract them. You could go from being the town savior to my sweet honey-bun."

"Or they could talk," she said with an eye roll, "when I throat punch you for that sassy mouth."

He leaned closer. "You love my sassy mouth."

"In your dreams," Avery said, shocked she was able to get out the words without choking on them. Because her immediate thought had been *I love you*.

She truly had fallen in love with Gray Atwell.

So much for analyzing risk and making a sensible decision.

GRAY COULDN'T BELIEVE how much better it felt to walk into Josie's dance studio with Avery next to him. He'd gotten so used to handling things on his own. There was no point in wasting time thinking negative thoughts about his ex-wife.

She'd given him Violet, and for that he'd always be grateful.

But he wanted something for himself.

Someone.

Avery, specifically.

He understood how much it took for her to be there with him. She didn't want to be a part of the community, but she fit with Magnolia. She fit with his life.

She needed time to get used to the idea. He had to believe if he let her take the lead, she'd be willing to give so much.

Her significance in people's lives went well beyond him. She was the glue that held together the fragile bond between Niall's daughters. The fact that she was an outsider and had no background with either Carrie or Meredith, or an agenda of her own definitely calmed the waters.

She smoothed parts of him, as well. Rough spots he hadn't even realized he'd developed like scar tissue over his battered heart.

Avery wouldn't hold his hand as they entered, but her fingers grazed his arm as if she needed to ground herself with his presence. He waved to several parents, then found their seats next to his mom.

"You were almost late," she said with a humph, then looked around him to Avery. "I didn't realize you were a ballet fan."

"I own this building," Avery said without missing a beat. "I like to support my tenants, and of course, I want to see Violet." She flashed a smile so sweet it made his teeth hurt. "I did her hair for the recital."

"How nice of you," his mother said, then leaned toward Gray. "Call me next time."

"It's fine, Mom." He patted her arm. "The performance is starting."

He'd told his mother that Avery was coming, so he did his best to ignore the tension radiating from her. He understood her desire to protect him, but Avery made him happy. She made Violet happy.

Gray hadn't given a thought to his future beyond raising his daughter since the divorce. But now he could see much more.

The performance began with Violet's class taking the stage in their pink leotards and matching tights.

Violet twirled and kicked across the dance floor, and his heart swelled with pride. At the end, she returned to center stage with the other girls for their bow. She gave him a little wave and smiled at her grandmother.

When her gaze landed on Avery, she scrunched up her nose and tugged on one braid, reminding Gray of the performance Josie had staged to show Avery the importance of the dance studio.

He glanced at Avery from the corner of his eye. She subtly stuck out her tongue, then winked, earning a wide grin from Violet.

"You have a funny way of bonding with her."

"I told you I don't like kids," Avery muttered with an eye roll. "I treat her like a person, not a little girl."

"You have no desire for kids of your own?" he asked, then immediately regretted the question. What the hell was he thinking putting her on the spot in the middle of a dance recital?

So much for letting her set the pace. He wouldn't blame her if she went screaming from the building in response.

"Hypothetical question, of course," he added. Maybe if he played it off she wouldn't notice. Damn. It wasn't as if he were imagining Violet with a younger sibling who had blue eyes and golden-blond hair. Except...

"I wasn't cut out to be a mom," Avery answered, keeping her gaze trained on the dancers taking their curtain call. "Obviously, my mother didn't expect to get pregnant from her fling with Niall. She never really warmed to motherhood the way most women do. I take after her." She bit down on her lip. "Look at me with Violet. I'm not a good influence."

"You do okay," he said because she couldn't handle anything more. He knew she'd get anxious at the thought of how important she'd become to his daughter.

Maybe he'd made a horrible mistake by letting her into their lives. Even if she wanted to believe they were keeping things casual, he could see the magnitude of her influence. But it went both ways. She was setting down roots in Magnolia. Like the spindly trails of ivy over a brick facade, the town was winding itself around her. She might think the vines were delicate, but he knew the strength of them. The power of this community.

She turned to look at him, as if she expected more of an argument. He wouldn't give it to her. She needed to find her own way to what he already knew. Gray was not only patient, but determined. He'd learned it the hard way. He'd met with Douglas yesterday to develop a custody modification petition for Stacy to sign and take to the court. As he'd expected, his attorney hadn't been pleased that Gray had gone to his ex-wife on his own, but he didn't regret it.

He believed she'd agree.

He couldn't allow himself to consider any other alternative.

Just like he wouldn't let the worry take hold that Avery might break his heart. It wasn't naivete. It was optimism.

When the dancers had taken their final bow, he opened his arms and Violet ran forward to hug him. She smelled like berry shampoo and little girl. He breathed deeply, wanting to savor this perfect moment. He'd worked hard to give her a good life. Wouldn't it be amazing if they both got what they needed in the process?

She hugged her grandma, then turned to Avery.

"Where's Spot?" she demanded.

"At home." Avery shrugged. "She had gas this morning because someone gave her a piece of cinnamon toast. I didn't want her stinking up the place."

Violet's bony hip jutted out. "It was half a piece because she was still hungry."

"Whatevs," Avery answered.

Gray heard his mother's gasp but only smiled. He was used to this snarky banter and knew both his daughter and Avery relished their unique bond.

"You did pretty good out there," Avery said. "You flubbed a few steps but you kept going. That's what makes a real professional."

Lila stepped forward. "My granddaughter was perfect," she said, her voice tight. "If you can't—"

"No, Gram." Violet tugged on her grandma's hand. "I messed up, just like Avery said. But I found my place again. Miss Josie says if you fall seven times you have to get up eight." She squinted as if she were working out the math of that statement in her head. "That means you can't stop trying even if you aren't perfect yet."

His mother's eyes widened. "You're perfect to me," she said, gently squeezing Violet's fingers.

"Who wants cake and punch?" Gray asked.

"Me," Violet shouted and pulled her grandmother toward the crowd gathered at the reception table at the far side of the studio.

"I should go check on Spot," Avery said, glancing around.

"You're nervous again."

"What if people talk to me?"

He chuckled. "You're capable of carrying on a conversation. I've watched you do it."

"I'm not ready to answer questions about what's happening with Niall's estate or what it means for the future."

"Even if I ask them?"

Her mouth opened to form a small O. Although he knew the basic gist of the work she was doing with her sisters, they hadn't yet discussed the implications for her prospects in town.

She swallowed and nodded. "I thought we agreed to stay in the moment."

"Yes, but I can be in the moment and still plan for the future." He took a step closer, ignoring the people who filed by them on their way to the reception. "I love you, Avery. You have to know—"

She flapped her fingers in front of her face like she'd just eaten a hot pepper. "You can't say that," she whispered fiercely. "Not here. Not now." She shook her head. "Just no."

"Okay," he said, needing to make this better. He knew she wasn't ready, but once again, had led with his heart instead of his brain.

Stupid, stupid heart.

"I didn't mean it."

"You didn't?" Her eyes flashed and he realized he was digging himself deeper at a frantic pace.

"No... I mean yes." He ran a hand over his face. "I meant it but didn't mean to say it here. Now." He glanced over his shoulder. "Want some punch?"

"Punch," she repeated.

"And a cupcake." He nodded. "The bakery makes a special recipe for Josie. You should try them. They're the best." *Oh, shut up, you idiot.* He was babbling like a madman.

"I'm going to go," Avery said slowly. "Please explain to Violet that I needed to check on Spot. She should stop by the carriage house when you get home. I have a gift for her. A little something to congratulate her for the performance."

"You didn't have to—"

"Have her stop by." She took a step back, away from him. He felt the distance like it was the Grand Canyon that separated them. "By herself," she clarified. "It's a girl thing. And I…I need a little time."

"Avery."

"It's fine, Gray."

It was anything but fine yet all he could do was nod and watch her walk away.

CHAPTER NINETEEN

"HE OFFERED YOU PUNCH?" Carrie smothered a laugh.

Meredith didn't bother to hide her loud cackle. "As in... 'I love you... Want some watered-down punch?'"

Avery dropped her head to her hands, elbows perched on the dining room table in Niall's run-down antebellum home later that night. "Something like that, only way more awkward."

"You should have taken a cupcake for the road," Meredith advised, her expression solemn. "Sunnyside Bakery makes the best. Everyone agrees."

"She can buy her own cupcakes." Carrie placed a mug of tea in front of both Avery and Meredith and then slid into a chair at the head of the table. "We can all buy as many cupcakes as we want. No one needs a man to buy them a cupcake."

Meredith and Avery shared a look. "As much as I appreciate the girl-power sentiment," Meredith told Carrie, "sometimes a cupcake is just a cupcake. You're reading too much into it."

"I don't think so."

"Besides," Avery couldn't help but add, "Josie provided the cupcakes. Gray just offered one to me."

Meredith tapped her palm on the glossy wood. "We're getting off topic here. Grayson Atwell, one of the finest male specimens Magnolia has to offer, is in love with our Avs."

"Stop calling me Avs," Avery protested automatically but there was no heat in the words. She liked that Meredith said the annoying nickname with affection. Both of her sisters were taking a sisterly amount of interest in this new development with Gray.

Carrie had asked them to meet at the house to sort through several boxes of photographs and mementos she didn't want to tackle on her own.

After leaving the recital, Avery waited for Violet to come knocking on her door, which the young girl did as soon as she arrived home. Avery had bought an antique brass kaleidoscope that seemed perfect for Gray's daughter, then found herself uncharacteristically nervous about how Violet would react to the gift.

Turned out there'd been no reason to worry.

"It reminded me of you," she'd told the girl as Violet unwrapped the carefully packaged box. "It's colorful and ever changing and kind of a pain in the butt to get to move the right way."

Violet had turned the apparatus over in her hands, then walked to the window to hold it up to the light.

Wait for it, Avery told herself, grinning when Violet sucked in a sharp breath. Avery knew a rainbow of colors exploded when the light hit the lens as the barrel turned.

The girl stood at the window for several minutes, and emotion spilled through Avery. Gray had said he loved her, and she loved him right back, just as she loved his daughter.

But that didn't stop her fears from trying to claw

their way out of the box where she'd locked them up tight. What if she hurt them? What if she was left with another broken heart?

What if she never wanted to leave Magnolia?

Could she truly make a life in this town?

"It's okay," Violet had said when she finally turned around. "I mean, thank you and stuff. I didn't ask you to come to my recital so you'd buy me something."

"I know." Avery moved forward until she could tug on the girl's braid. "I wanted to, and you were really great in the routine."

"I gotta practice pirouetting," Violet said, staring at the kaleidoscope. "My turns suck."

"You probably shouldn't say *suck* in kindergarten." Avery grinned. "We all have stuff to work on. It's what makes us human."

"Daddy's gonna love this." Violet took a step toward the door. "We're having noodles for dinner. Wanna come over?"

"Another time," Avery had said brightly. "Tonight I'm having dinner with my sisters."

"I'm gonna have a sister," Violet reported, causing Avery's breath to catch in her throat.

"You are?"

"If Mommy or Daddy ever get married to someone else. They'll have a baby, and it won't be a brother. I don't want a brother." The girl nodded as she opened the door. "See ya, Spot." Violet bent to pet the little dog, then turned to Avery. "Thanks again. It's better than okay."

"Yeah," Avery had agreed and given the girl a hug that felt both awkward and somehow perfect between the two of them. As Violet returned to her house, Avery had been grateful for the plans with her sisters because the thought of spending the whole evening alone held no appeal.

Now she turned her attention back to Carrie and Meredith, curling her hands around the mug of tea, hoping the warmth would seep into her soul. "He asked me about having kids," she blurted.

"Good lord," Meredith muttered. "The man is hot but he has no game."

Carrie sipped her tea, then placed the mug on the table and straightened. "Are you saying Gray asked you to have his baby?"

"Did Niall keep anything stronger than tea around here?" Meredith demanded.

"Oh, yes." Carrie stood. "Good idea, Mer-Bear."

Meredith growled under her breath. "I know you didn't just call me that."

Avery almost chuckled at how innocent Carrie appeared. "You gave nicknames to both of us," she said sweetly. "I figured you'd want one, too."

"Not Mer-Bear." Meredith's chin tipped up. "You can call me Queen."

"Doubtful," Carrie murmured. "Let's not get off topic again. We were at the part in the story where Gray begged Avery to have his baby."

"That's not exactly what happened." Avery shook her head. "He simply asked if I ever wanted kids. Hypothetically."

"That isn't a hypothetical question," Carrie called. She'd walked into the kitchen and returned a moment later with a bottle of scotch and three shot glasses on a tray. "It's a prelude to getting down on one knee."

"Oooh." Meredith rubbed her palms together, then took the bottle of liquor, opened the top and poured amber liquid into the three glasses. "That's so romantic."

Avery's mouth went dry as she scrambled to gain control of her thoughts around Gray. "We were waiting for a dance recital to start." She pressed a hand to her chest. "It wasn't romantic. It was awkward. There was certainly no talk of a ring."

"I bet he'll go with something vintage." Meredith placed a glass in front of Avery. "Maybe pear shaped?"

"Are you crazy?" Avery downed the shot, hissing as the whiskey burned her throat. "Having a conversation with the two of you is worse than trying to corral those foster kittens. You're supposed to help me figure out how to deal with this." She thumped her glass on the table, and Meredith filled it. "He said he loved me." She threw back the shot, grateful for the burn now that she was prepared. Easier to feel pain in her throat than in the vicinity of her heart.

"Do you love him?" Carrie took her seat again.

"Let's toast to love," Meredith said, holding up her glass. Carrie clinked hers and then both women trained their gazes on Avery.

"Heaven help me, I *do* love him," Avery whispered.

All three women tossed back the liquor. Avery wasn't a regular drinker. She liked control too much. But she welcomed the warmth in her belly and the way it spread through her arms and legs. Her head felt hazy, as if whiskey had blurred the sharp corners on all her problems.

"Isn't that a good thing?" Meredith poured another

shot for herself, then tipped the bottle in Avery's direction.

"No more for me." She shook her head. "I didn't come here to fall in love. Or to get involved with a man. When I drove past Magnolia's water tower that first morning, I assumed it would be a onetime thing. I thought I was going to sign some documents, hopefully get a little money to restart my life and then actually restart my life." A drop of liquor slid down the edge of the shot glass. She ran a finger across the rim. "It's all too much, too soon."

"You are starting over," Carrie pointed out, her voice gentle.

"The plan wasn't to stay," Avery argued, the words bouncing off the walls of the dining room. Now that they'd cleaned out most of the house, she could understand how grand it might have been in Niall's heyday. A crystal chandelier hung above the table, tiny pinpoints of light sparkling. The walls were papered in a heavy brocade print. The color had faded to a dingy beige, but the quality of what it must have been remained obvious. Niall had been a powerful force back in the day, cosmopolitan and intriguing in his eccentricity.

Of course he'd held court over this small town. In a place like New York City, he would have blended in, another charismatic artist in a sea of big-city talent. In Magnolia, he was a unicorn.

"I wish he were here," she whispered, more to herself than to either of her sisters.

"Gray?" Meredith pulled her phone from the back pocket of her jeans. "Are you ready to profess your love? Want me to call him?"

"Our father," Avery corrected, and Meredith placed the phone on the table with a sigh.

"Him," she muttered. "All of this goes back to him."

"He would have loved that part," Carrie said with a sad laugh. "He reveled in being the center of attention. The depression hit hard once his commercial success faded. He couldn't understand why people weren't interested in him anymore. That's why this town remained so important, and he wrecked his own finances to save face."

"Most people didn't like him despite how they act." Meredith kept her gaze trained on the table as she spoke, like she was revealing some kind of terrible secret and didn't want to see their reaction to the news.

Avery was shocked. "What do you mean? People around here idolized him. We all heard the mayor's speech at Summer Fair. I've lost count of the number of stories I've heard about his largesse."

"Memories often turn the past into a halcyon version of reality." Carrie hefted a box onto the table. "Meredith's right. Dad was an insufferable ass for most of his life. He could be charming when he needed to, and he never let anyone forget what they owed him. Most of the town owed him in some way."

Meredith grabbed the bottle of scotch and drank directly from it, not bothering with a glass. She leveled a look at Avery. "How many times have you heard someone say 'bless his heart' when talking about Niall?"

"A few I guess." Avery scrunched up her nose as she considered the conversations she'd had with regards to her biological father. "Actually, most of them. I figured it was some Southern way of expressing sympathy."

"Sympathy for what an ass he was," Meredith clarified.

Carrie giggled, then motioned for Meredith to hand her the whiskey. She wiped the opening with the end of her sleeve, then took a drink.

"Do you think I have cooties?" Meredith demanded.

Carrie looked genuinely surprised. "Of course not. I've spent too many hours cleaning out this house. I'm overly sensitive to germs." She pushed the whiskey toward Avery. "Bless your heart," she explained, "or bless his heart in this case, can mean several different things. It was probably meant as an insult to Dad without coming out and smearing his name. Did you hear anyone use 'God love him'?"

Avery nodded as she tipped the bottle toward her lips. "Plenty."

"Huh." Carrie shrugged. "People around here must have hated him. I never realized."

"Because you were his little princess," Meredith reminded her.

"Awww…" Carrie's smile was saccharine sweet. "Mer-Bear. I love it when you say that."

"Fine." Meredith's mouth pursed. "I'll leave off calling you princess as long as I don't have to hear that ridiculous nickname again."

"Agreed." Carrie's cornflower blue gaze met Avery's. "Do you want more help on the Gray issue or should we start with the boxes?"

More help? Avery pressed her lips together to keep from laughing. Her sisters had talked in circles without offering one piece of concrete advice. The last thing she needed was more help, although she realized she felt less anxious than she had when she'd first arrived.

Hard to say whether that could be attributed to the sisterly support or the alcohol.

"Boxes," she answered.

Carrie rose from the chair, swaying ever so slightly. "I found most of the contents in the desk drawers in Dad's office. I started to go through it, but there were personal letters and photographs." Her knuckles grew white as her fingers clenched the box's lid. "I couldn't manage it on my own."

"Why not just throw it all away?" Meredith asked, eyeing the box like it contained a den of venomous snakes.

"I don't know," Carrie admitted. "I thought maybe something in here would offer a clue as to why he made the choices he did. Don't you all wonder?"

"Of course," Avery answered at the same time Meredith bit off, "Nope."

"That's a lie," Carrie said. "I know you care more than you'll admit."

"Whatever," Meredith mumbled, leaning over to reach for the box. "If we aren't going to dissect Avery's love life, let's get on with this. I have horses to feed later."

"You said your dad was taking care of them tonight." Carrie lifted an eyebrow in challenge when Meredith rolled her eyes.

Instead of arguing or admitting to the lie, Meredith flipped off the lid to the cardboard banker's box and pulled out a stack of papers.

"What is all this?" Avery grabbed a few off the top, her breath hissing out as she recognized a familiar face in the photos tucked between scribbled notes and random receipts.

"Mom," she whispered.

Both Carrie and Meredith stared at her. "Your mom is in one of the photos?"

She nodded, unable to manage a cognizant thought with the riot of emotions tumbling through her. "She was young." She held out the photo after staring at it for several long seconds. "In San Francisco with Niall."

Her mother looked carefree in a way Avery didn't recognize. She wore a paisley-patterned sundress with her hair piled high on her head. Niall's arm was draped around her shoulders, both casual and possessive, and her mother smiled at the camera with so much joy it was physically painful to see.

"This must have been when they met." Carrie took the photo, then passed it to Meredith. "Didn't your mom tell you it was a one-night stand?"

Avery nodded. "But they look too familiar for that. I didn't ask her for details even after learning about Niall. She doesn't like to talk about it. I think she considers a surprise pregnancy one of the few true failures of her life."

"Of course she doesn't think that," Carrie said, her voice sharper than Avery would have expected. "She got you from it. No matter what else, that's a blessing."

"Right," Avery agreed, because what was the alternative? Saying out loud that her very existence was a mistake?

"Wait." Meredith shuffled through the papers in front of her. "Here they are again. Niall has a mustache in this photo."

"That's impossible." Avery snatched the photo from her sister. "My mom only knew him for a night…or a weekend…or…"

"They had a longer relationship than she's told you?" Meredith kept digging. "Most of the stuff is junk. Old receipts or notes that I can't even read because his penmanship is horrible."

"It always was," Carrie murmured. "He started dictating his correspondence to me when I was in high school. He refused to use a computer. Everything had to be in longhand."

"I don't know about that," Meredith countered. "Here's a typed note signed by Niall and addressed to someone named Melissa."

Avery swallowed. "That's my mom."

"He tells her he's glad she plays soccer," Meredith said. "The letter thanks her for the photograph. He says, 'She has my mother's eyes.'"

"He's talking about me." Avery felt like her brain was going to explode, and it wasn't from the alcohol. "I played soccer one season when I was eight. My mom gave him updates about me."

Meredith gathered up the rest of the papers and photographs, then shoved them back into the box and slammed the lid on top. "I can't do this," she said, her frantic gaze darting between Avery and Meredith. She looked like some sort of wild animal, scared and cornered.

"It's okay," Avery said in the same tone she used when she'd been trying to lure the foster kittens out of their crate the first night they'd stayed with her.

"It's not. I don't want to know this stuff." Meredith pushed back from the table. "What if there are pictures of my mom in there? Or letters to her? I can't read about her being unfaithful to my dad." She dragged in a shaky breath. "My real dad. How could I even look him in the eye if I knew—"

Carrie yanked the box off the table. "I'll burn it all," she promised, then put an arm around Meredith. Avery came to her other side. "None of it matters. It doesn't change anything. You did nothing wrong."

"Then why do I feel so guilty and responsible?" Meredith let out a sound that was somewhere between a sob and a growl.

"We're in this together," Avery reminded her. Reminded them all.

"At least you get great sex as a distraction," Carrie said.

Meredith laughed at that and looked up at the two of them. "Yeah. I haven't had great sex in…" She shuddered. "Oh, crap. I can't even remember."

"It's been almost a decade for me," Carrie said.

Avery took a step back. "Are you joking? You haven't had sex in ten years?"

"I've had sex," her sister clarified. "But nowhere near great sex."

"It was Dylan Scott." Meredith pushed her chair away from the table and stood. "Back in high school, right?"

"The summer after," Carrie confirmed.

"Who's Dylan?" Avery reached around Meredith to pick up the liquor bottle again. This night was so off the rails. Holding tight to her buzz might be the only thing to get her through.

"He was the baddest of the bad boys."

She smiled at Meredith's overdramatic tone. "You sound like a movie trailer announcer."

"It was like the nineties version of *Rebel Without a Cause* or *Grease* or something."

"It wasn't like *Grease*." Carrie sniffed. "No one sang on the bleachers. That's silly."

"Maybe it was more *Saved by the Bell*," Avery suggested with a laugh.

"Dylan Scott was cuter than Zack Morris. Magnolia had a drive-in back in the day." Meredith turned to Carrie. "I bet you lost your V card at the drive-in, right?"

Carrie threw up her hands. "How do you even know about Dylan and me? He would have been five years ahead of you in school."

"My brother Theo ran in that same popular group. All the girls knew Dylan. He was hot like Gray, only hotter because he was so wild." She leaned in. "He drove a motorcycle."

"Motorcycles are dangerous," Avery said automatically. It was something her mother had drilled into her for as long as she could remember. Not that it wasn't true, but it struck her that she'd been raised to live in fear. Fear of adventure. Fear of risk. She'd always played it safe, and look at where that had gotten her. Her ex had been perfect on paper: successful, driven and undemanding. Also married, but clearly from the photos she'd seen tonight, wedding vows didn't mean much to her mom.

"Dangerous but fun," Carrie said with a wistful smile.

"What happened with you two anyway?" Meredith asked.

"It doesn't matter." Carrie crossed her arms over her chest. "I don't know how we got off on this subject."

Avery flashed a grin. "Better discussing your love life than mine."

"I don't have a love life. It was high school. I barely remember him."

Meredith chuckled. "You remember the great sex."

"You two are the worst."

"She's the worst." Meredith pointed at Avery. "I'm not sure I've ever had great sex with anyone but myself."

Carrie gave her a funny look. "You can't have sex with yourself."

"Have you never been invited to one of Julie Martindale's 'toys for women' parties?" Meredith asked.

Avery gulped back her shocked gasp. "The loan officer at the bank?"

"I thought she was selling kitchen gadgets," Carrie said, her already big eyes widening further.

"She's got something cooking, but it's not a salad spinner." Meredith's words were slightly slurred, her gaze unfocused.

Avery checked the scotch. Only about an inch remained in the bottle, and it had been half-full at the start.

"We're drunk," she announced.

"That one got the brains in the family," Meredith said in a stage whisper.

Carrie dissolved into a fit of giggles. "I need a glass of water and then we're going to watch some reality television. You both need time to sober up. No one is driving until morning."

"Lemme text my dad," Meredith said. Avery was shocked she offered no protests.

They must be really far gone if Meredith was willing to do what Carrie said without a fight.

She hadn't wanted to spend the night in Niall's house, but somehow at the moment it didn't seem so bad. An impromptu slumber party with her sisters felt like just what she needed to help her leave the ghosts of the past right where they belonged.

CHAPTER TWENTY

GRAY OPENED HIS EYES, surprised to find his bedroom still bathed in darkness. He slept soundly unless something specific woke him.

His first thought was Violet, and he sat up, squinting toward his open door as his eyes adjusted to the shadows.

Then his gaze switched to the window as a small rock smacked against the glass. He padded over, leaning forward to look down.

A rush of adrenaline radiated through his body.

Avery stood in his backyard, the pale moonlight glinting off her hair. It gave her a fay quality, Titania come to life on his lawn. Blame his sleep-addled mind for that bit of whimsy. He unhooked the latch and slid open the window. The air had cooled from the heat of the day, although it still was warmer than his air-conditioned house. Crickets chirped from the trees that bordered the property and he breathed in the earthy scent of the night, the moment strangely erotic.

She waved. "Are you awake?" she called in a loud whisper.

"Unless this is a dream."

"I need to talk to you."

"How about I come down there?"

"'Kay." She nodded, toeing the grass with one bare

foot. "I love you, too," she blurted, lifting her gaze to him before lowering it toward the ground again.

That woke him fully.

"Give me ten seconds," he said, ducking back into his room. He grabbed a T-shirt from a hook on the door and pulled it over his head as he navigated the hallway and stairs in the dark. He didn't want to take the chance of waking Violet.

By the time he got to the kitchen door, his heart hammered in his chest. Not from exertion but as a re-action to Avery's words. He breathed a sigh of relief when he walked outside to find her still standing on the lawn. A part of him had expected her to disappear in the short time it took him to get to her. Or he feared he'd been dreaming.

"Say that again," he said as he approached her.

She bit down on her lip, and he stifled a groan. "I love you."

"Again."

Her lips curved into a small smile. "You heard me."

"Please." He stood in front of her now, so close he could see the flutter of eyelashes against her skin as she slowly blinked. "I want to hear it again."

She leaned in, wound her arms around his neck. "I love you."

"I love you, too." He whispered the words against her mouth, then kissed her, relishing the feel of her body relaxing into his. "You taste like gum and whiskey," he told her a moment later.

"The gum is fresh, and the whiskey is old. I got a little drunk tonight with my sisters."

"Are you still a little drunk?" His heart thumped cau-tiously. He didn't want her words to be alcohol fueled.

She shook her head. "I don't think so." She checked her watch. "I fell asleep at Carrie's so it's been hours since I had a drink. Although, I walked here just in case." Her brow furrowed, as if she were concentrating hard. "I don't feel drunk. Not like earlier. We did shots. Not the best choice I've made recently."

"Was there an occasion?"

"I told them you offered me a glass of punch."

"You talked about me with your sisters?" He rested his forehead against hers. "I can't decide if that's good or bad."

"They like you."

"And you love me?" He lifted his head.

"I do."

Those two little words walloped him with the strength of a hurricane.

"Does this mean you're hanging up the running shoes for good?"

"That's the plan." She scrunched up her nose. "But just be warned, I'm thinking about taking up kickboxing."

He threw back his head and laughed. "I'll remember that." Lacing their fingers together, he took a step toward the house. "Want to come upstairs so I can show you how happy this makes me?"

"I'm kind of a hot mess right now." She tugged at the hem of the thin hoodie she wore. "Tonight was an emotional roller coaster."

"Hot messes are my favorite kind." He glanced over his shoulder. "Violet's upstairs so I need to go in, but it's going to kill me to have you in the carriage house tonight."

She gave him a slow, sexy smile. "We can't have that."

"Nope," he agreed, and let out a quiet exhale when she followed him to the house without another word.

AVERY STOOD IN line at the Sunnyside Bakery later that week, deciding between a bear claw and a frosted scone. She'd gone to her first Zumba class at the Magnolia community center that morning, so maybe she'd order both.

As she talked to Mary Ellen Winkler, who owned the bakery, someone tapped on her shoulder. She turned to see the Realtor she'd met with weeks ago, Jacob Martin, frowning at her.

"Oh, hey." She offered a rueful smile. "I've been meaning to call you."

"I left five messages," he said, impatience lacing his tone. "It's important, Avery."

Her stomach did a tiny flip. Something about his demeanor made her edgy, which was part of the reason she hadn't called him back. Of course she'd gotten the messages. He'd sounded excited in the first one and then subsequently more urgent in each of the others. He hadn't left any details, but she had a feeling whatever he wanted to tell her would complicate things in a way she'd like to avoid at the moment.

She'd made the decision, at least in her mind, to stay in Magnolia. The biggest step had been admitting her feelings to Gray. After the disaster that had marked the end of her previous relationship, she hadn't been looking for love.

It found her just the same.

She didn't want to examine her feelings too closely, afraid the intensity of them would overwhelm her. The sense of home she felt in Magnolia couldn't be denied. So much of that had to do with Gray, but she'd also come to feel like she belonged in the tight-knit community.

She and Malcolm were close to finalizing a deal with the state's tourism board to have Magnolia featured as one of the must-see destinations for visitors to the state for the fall and holiday seasons. They'd decided to focus on the road-less-traveled charm of the town, capitalizing on the desire for offbeat adventurers to discover the next hot tourism spot.

If they could increase tourism by 20 percent over the fall and holiday seasons, it would help local businesses to stay in the black for the fiscal year. The chamber of commerce had agreed it would invest any additional revenue into a full-blown marketing campaign for the following summer season.

She had a plan for attracting new shops to downtown and was in talks with several potential restaurant owners. She still needed to convince Carrie to open up the gallery as a painting studio, offering classes and hosting parties with Carrie as the main instructor. They needed money and she was hustling to think of any way to get it. But she could imagine it…everything…her future…a life she never thought existed for her but now felt like the most natural fit.

As expected, not everyone supported her new path in life. The tense phone call she'd had with her mother was a perfect example. Melissa apparently hadn't appreciated the text Avery sent with the photos of her and Niall.

"Why are you doing this?" her mother had demanded when Avery accepted her call.

Avery tried to explain that she needed to understand her past to move forward, but her mom hadn't seemed convinced.

"The part I don't understand," her mother had said, impatience clear in every syllable, "is why you aren't moving on. If you don't want to come back to San Francisco that's your choice. But some tiny dot on the North Carolina map isn't for you, sweetheart. I raised you to want more."

"I *want* to be happy," Avery answered without thinking, only to be met with silence on the other end of the line.

Her mother had hung up shortly after. Maybe she was so far removed from a time when she'd felt happy that she'd lost sight of its value. But Avery had seen it in her mother's young eyes in the photo with Niall. She'd been happy, if only for a short period.

"I got an extra," she said, holding up the brown bag as she led him to a table. "Would you like some?"

"I have an offer on the downtown buildings," he said instead of answering.

Avery gripped the edges of the ladder-back chair she'd just slipped into. "You told me it would take months or possibly years." She swallowed against the emotions bubbling up in her throat. "That a buyer for the downtown property was a long shot at best, and that selling the ranch would be the smarter option."

He leaned forward. "Has your sister agreed to put it on the market?"

"Careful, Jacob." She raised a brow. "You're drooling at the prospect."

"I'm not denying I want the listing." He shrugged. "Any real estate agent would. That land is a virtual gold mine. We could subdivide—"

Avery turned when a throat cleared behind her. Shae, the high schooler who worked part-time for Meredith stood behind her. "Hey, Shae. Shouldn't you be in school?" She felt her cheeks grow warm. "It's nice to see you, of course, but—"

"I have a free period and it's open campus for seniors," the girl said, frowning between the Realtor and Avery. "Is Meredith selling the rescue?"

Several people at tables nearby turned to look at them. Shae didn't have much of an inside voice. "No," Avery said, trying for a convincing smile. Then she looked at Jacob. "No," she repeated with more force before returning her gaze to Shae. "You know how much the animals mean to Meredith."

The girl nodded but didn't look convinced. "It's a good job, too. Meredith gives me time off when I have a big test or during final-exam week."

"She appreciates everything you do."

"Yeah." Shae hugged her arms across her middle. "I just wanted to see how Spot and the kittens were doing."

"We're in the middle of a meeting," Jacob told the girl, his impatience clear.

Avery stared at the man, trying to remember what she'd liked about him when they first met. Probably the fact that she'd been desperate to unload her inheritance and he'd seemed like her best chance to make that happen.

"The kittens are growing every day." Avery smiled

at Shae, hoping the girl didn't associate her with the brusque Realtor. "While Spot is shrinking."

Jacob tapped his pen on the table—*tap, tap, tap*—some sort of Realtor Morse code that clearly conveyed his annoyance without him having to say a thing.

The girl offered a nod and a shaky smile, then said goodbye and turned away.

"That was rude." Avery's gaze snapped to Jacob's.

He threw up his hands, as if confused by her reaction. "We're in the middle of a legit meeting."

"That isn't how things are done in a small town," she insisted. "You should know that."

"Sorry," he mumbled. "It feels like I've been trying to track you down forever." He pushed a shiny black folder toward her. "You won't get a better offer than this, but the buyer wants an answer by the end of the month so you'll have to get the attorney on board. As the executor, he's the one with the actual legal authority to sell while the estate is in probate."

She pressed a hand to her chest. "I can't make something happen that quickly. Douglas will never agree to it and my sisters would be furious. Besides, things have changed since we last spoke."

I've changed, she added silently.

"You haven't looked at the offer." He tapped that damn pen on the folder again. "At least look before you give me an outright no."

Heart thumping in her chest, Avery opened the folder. She drew out the top sheet of paper, her gaze scanning the paragraphs for—

She gasped.

"That's more than the list price we discussed," she

said, glancing back up at Jacob, who now wore a smug smile.

"Twenty percent more," he confirmed. "I don't know much about the people behind the holding company that made the offer. Some big-time restaurateurs. But they've got money, which is the important part."

This was Avery's way out. Her fresh start. A solution to her financial precariousness and a way to cover the expenses for Niall's home and set up Meredith so that the taxes on the ranch could be paid. Never in a million years would she have imagined this as an option, and certainly not this soon. But here it was. Hers for the taking, if only she could convince everyone else. The question was, did she want it?

"They've actually expressed interest in your dad's ranch, as well."

She frowned, her gaze sharpening on Jacob. "The ranch isn't for sale. How would they even know about it?"

"I guess one of the principals in the company has some ties to the area, and he's looking for a big home if he moves back here. I don't know the details, and I don't really care." He leaned forward. "I need this commission, and you've already told me how important the sale is for you. You can't change your mind. This is right for both of us, Avery."

"You don't know me," she whispered even though he was only repeating her words back to her.

"I know you're not a fit for Magnolia." He gave a wary glance toward the half-eaten bear claw. "How often did you indulge in carbs before you got here?"

Avery paused in the act of lifting a bite of pastry to

her mouth, shocked at his boldness. "What does that have to do with anything?"

"We barely know each other," he continued, "and I can already tell you're losing your edge. People like you need challenge. This town can't offer it to you." He placed two fingers on the folder and did his tapping routine again. "This will give you the new start you told me you want. I understand the allure of the slow pace in the South—for all I know you suddenly fancy yourself some kind of modern-day Scarlett O'Hara. But I don't believe it."

"I don't fancy myself anything." She clenched her fists and dug her nails into the fleshy centers of her palms. Just the other night she'd curled up with a Margaret Mitchell tome and fallen asleep within five minutes. Not that she'd admit that to anyone. Her lack of appreciation for the queen of all Southern belles felt like some kind of inherent flaw.

"This isn't about me, despite the commission and the notoriety of the sale. This is about you." He paused, drew in a breath as if sensing her mounting anxiety and homing in on her weakness. "It's about the community. Think of what it will do for Magnolia to have your father's downtown properties owned by a company that wants to invest in the town. I've heard you're working with the mayor on tourism plans. If you care about this place, you'll make it happen. For Magnolia."

"I'll…I'll think about." She straightened from the table, grasping the folder so hard it almost bent in half. Her chair scraped on the wooden floor, and she stumbled as it caught on a raised edge.

"They want an answer," he called to her as she hurried away. "You know this is the right decision."

She burst into the bright sunshine of the morning, an all too familiar knot in her stomach, afraid that nothing would ever be right in her life again.

GRAY RUBBED HIS sweaty palms against his pant legs as he sat in the waiting room of Stacy's office.

"She wants you to try the Voss," Tammy told him, handing him a bottle.

"Sure," he agreed. Now was not the time to argue. Not when Stacy had texted and asked him to meet her, explaining that she wanted to discuss his proposal. If his ex-wife wanted him to drink special water, he wasn't about to complain.

The door to the inner offices opened and Stacy appeared. "Thanks for waiting, Gray."

"Thanks for the water," he said, holding up the bottle as he stood.

She nodded at Tammy in approval. "I'm glad you're enjoying it. Please follow me."

"Okay." He tried to ignore the tightening in his gut. Something about her friendliness put him on edge. It had been a long time since Stacy had smiled at him in the way she was now. Maybe she'd had a great conference or finally saw the logic of his plan for sole custody. She had to understand that he still wanted to be partners in raising their daughter, but Violet needed the stability he could give her.

He and Avery could give her.

His shoulders relaxed slightly as he remembered he wasn't alone anymore. Someone had his back.

"How are things?" Stacy asked as he followed her into her office, closing the door behind him.

"Good."

"Your injury?"

"Fine." He shrugged. "It was minor."

"Your job is dangerous," she said, taking a seat behind the gilded desk he'd helped her design when she'd planned her office space.

"I'm careful, Stace. You know that."

Her glossy lips pursed. "Perhaps not as careful as one might expect with your choice in girlfriends."

"What are you talking about?" He resisted the urge to bristle.

"I don't think I want a woman like Avery Keller near my daughter. She certainly isn't the kind of influence that can benefit Violet."

"Avery is great with Violet. She's worked hard to connect with her." Anger pounded through him. Now he understood Stacy's smile. She was like a hyena, a sinister predator circling for the kill.

"What do you know about her life before she arrived in Magnolia?"

He opened his mouth to answer, then paused. What did he know? That she grew up in San Francisco and had left her job before making the cross-country drive. She was an only child and had a close but often strained relationship with her mother. Sure he wanted to know more but figured it would come in time. She was dealing with a lot of change. Although she'd told him she loved him, he didn't want to push. To potentially push her away.

"Enough. Don't play games. If you have something to

say, spit it out. Avery is a part of my life and she's good for Violet. Nothing you can tell me will change that."

"Maybe." She clicked one manicured nail against the lacquered desktop. "Did you know the son of her ex-boyfriend ended up in the hospital and she was responsible?"

Gray swallowed but didn't respond.

Apparently, he didn't need to because Stacy continued, "Her boyfriend was also her superior and the former coworker I spoke to says she seduced him. A married man."

Disbelief flooded him. Avery wouldn't do that. He knew her last relationship had ended badly but surely the details weren't this sordid.

"Stop, Stacy. Whatever you think you know, I don't want to hear it."

She flipped open the laptop on the desk, hit a few buttons, then turned the computer toward him. "I tracked down someone close to the man's wife. They were married at the time Avery was with him. These are photos of their son in the hospital with injuries he sustained in the car accident."

Bile rose in his throat, his gaze riveted to the photos of a dark-haired boy only a few years older than Violet. The child's head was bandaged and both his right arm and leg casted. He didn't want to look. He couldn't believe the Avery he knew was capable of causing injury to an innocent boy. But none of the myriad of rationales racing through his mind explained why she wouldn't have told him about her past. She knew what Stacy's betrayal had cost him, the damage caused by the destruction of his marriage.

"Tell me how," he whispered, his mind reeling at the memory of Avery evading questions about her past. "How did she cause it?"

His ex slammed shut the laptop. "You can ask her. Or don't." She gave him a pointed look. "The details don't matter. That woman isn't fit to be part of my daughter's life. You have to see that." She stood. "And certainly your pathetic bid for a change in our custody agreement is ridiculous in light of this."

"One has nothing to do with the other," he said, but the words sounded weak even to him.

"Of course it does." Stacy walked around the desk and strode to the door, hips swaying as if she owned the world.

Owned him anyway. Which it appeared she did at the moment.

"I might be dedicated to my career," she said in a strident tone. "Perhaps I've missed a few scheduled visitations. But I'm careful about who I let into her life."

Gray wanted to argue. Stacy didn't let Violet meet her boyfriends because she dated the type of guys who were interested in a sophisticated doctor, not a single mother with the complication of a kid who needed her.

But he didn't protest. It took enough for him to stand with his weak knees and walk toward the door with his head held high.

"I still want custody," he managed to say. "It's best for Violet."

"What about your girlfriend?" Stacy arched a brow as he moved past her.

"I'll deal with it," he promised, although he had absolutely no idea how to manage that when he could hardly catch a breath. Not when his heart had just broken in two.

CHAPTER TWENTY-ONE

AVERY SMOOTHED A hand over her hair when she heard Gray's truck rumble into the driveway later that afternoon.

"He's here," Violet said, clapping her hands.

Spot yipped and ran in an enthusiastic circle around the girl's legs. Avery couldn't help but smile. A few weeks ago the dog wouldn't have bothered to get up. Spot was now down four pounds, well on her way to a normal weight for a dog her size. It was time, she knew, to let the animal go.

She had no doubt Meredith would find a great home for Spot. The real question was whether Avery could stand to let her go.

Would it be so wrong to keep her? Could she claim this new life, dog and everything?

The conversation with the Realtor still played in her mind. She had to make a decision. If she could convince Douglas Damon to sell the property downtown and her sisters to support the idea, the money would go a long way to helping her start on a new path. But she knew how much the gallery meant to Carrie and how nervous Malcolm and the others were about losing control over the business district. She'd given them a plan for revitalization and if her path led her to remain in Magnolia, there was no reason to sell.

Stay in the moment, she told herself. Gray's mom had been with Violet after school while Gray finished his shift. But when Lila had asked Avery to stay with the girl so she could attend an author event with her book club, Avery had gladly agreed. A month ago, it would have terrified her to be responsible for a child. Now she saw it as a privilege.

"Daddy," Violet called when Gray walked into the house. "We made meat loaf. I squished my hands in it. It was super yucky."

Avery laughed as she turned from setting the table. "She washed her hands, and I hope it tastes better than it sounds." As simple as the iconic recipe was on paper, Avery remembered making meat loaf with one of her many after-school babysitters. Her mom had done little home cooking, and although Avery seemed to be following in her footsteps, she'd had a great time in the kitchen with Violet.

"Where's your grandma?" Gray asked, crouching down to hug his daughter.

He hadn't yet looked at Avery, and something about the edge in his voice made her stomach clench.

"She had to meet her book clubby friends. Me and Avery went to the grocery. I got a free cookie."

"Free cookies are awesome." He smiled at his daughter, but his shoulders remained rigid. "I need to talk to Avery for a minute, sweetheart."

Violet made a face. "Grown-up talk?"

"'Fraid so."

The little girl turned to Avery. "Can I take Spot up to my room?"

"Of course," Avery answered. "The meat loaf has

about twenty more minutes until it's ready. We've got plenty of time."

"Come on, Spotty." Violet picked up one of the dog's favorite chew toys and headed for the stairs.

Avery couldn't help the pride that swelled in her chest as the dog trotted after Violet. Spot was happy and healthier now, and Avery had accomplished that.

As Violet disappeared up the stairs, she took a step toward Gray. "What's wrong? Did something happen at the station?"

He held up a hand, as if he didn't want her to get too close.

"Tell me about Tony Monteroy," he said, finally meeting her gaze. The accusation in his tone pierced her heart.

"How do you know about Tony?"

"Stacy filled me in on the details."

"Your ex-wife went looking into my past?" Icy dread pricked along Avery's skin. "She had no right."

He gave a barely perceptible nod, as if acknowledging her distress. A stand-up guy even when he was obviously mad as hell. Avery really didn't deserve him. An interesting observation at the moment because she had the feeling she was about to lose everything.

"Why didn't you tell me yourself?" His voice held no trace of emotion, which she hated.

"I was embarrassed. Falling for the wrong guy ruined my life. I trusted him, and he lied to me just like he betrayed his wife. I didn't tell you because it was a mistake. I don't know what Stacy heard or who she talked to, but you know me. I never would have gotten involved with Tony if I'd understood he was still married. His son..." She choked back a sob at the thought of the little boy who'd been hurt. "I feel terrible for what happened to that boy, but his accident wasn't my fault," she told Gray after a moment. Despite her guilt, she'd finally come to the realization that she didn't have to shoulder the blame.

"Stacy is going to use your history against me."

Avery sucked in a breath. Of course. Why hadn't she thought about that possibility? She might know in her heart she wasn't completely responsible for the lives that had been ruined, but that didn't change what people thought of her role in destroying a supposedly happy family.

"Will you let her?" she asked when she trusted herself to speak without her voice shaking.

Gray rubbed a hand over his jaw and looked away.

In that moment, she understood the truth and her heart splintered. She thought she'd been brokenhearted after the breakup with Tony, but that was more like an explosion of shock and pain. The deep sorrow she felt now was akin to the loss of an integral part of herself.

"Violet has to be my priority," he said finally.

Not exactly an answer to Avery's question but she got the meaning behind his words. She did not matter. Again.

"Yes," she whispered because what else could she say? He was a good man and a great father. The lack was with her.

His shoulders hitched as his gaze slammed into hers. Had he expected her to argue? To get down on her knees and beg him to give her another chance?

Oh, she wanted to beg. But she wouldn't because this was always to be the ultimate outcome of their relationship. It had been stupid for her to believe she could have something more. She simply wasn't built to be loved unconditionally.

"I should go," she told him.

Gray took a step forward as if to stop her, then shook his head. "Probably for the best."

The best for who, she wanted to scream. Certainly not her and her shattered heart. She could feel the tears tracking down her cheeks but didn't bother to wipe them away. Her eyes would dry eventually but she feared not even time would mend the physical pain that threatened to consume her.

"How bad is it?"

"She hasn't showered in three days, and I can't get her to eat more than a few bites at a time."

"Does she stink?"

"Is that really of consequence right now?"

"I'm curious."

Unwilling to listen to her sisters' incessant arguing any longer, Avery grabbed the book that sat on the nightstand next to her bed and hurled it at the cracked door. "I don't stink," she called, her voice raspy from crying.

Carrie pushed open the door and stepped into the room with a mug of tea in one hand and a paper bag in the other. "Meredith stopped by to see you," she said with false cheer. "She was worried."

"Not about you," Meredith clarified as she followed. "I wanted to make sure Spot was okay. By the way, you might not smell but you look like death warmed over."

"Spot's fine." Avery smoothed a hand over the dog's soft head. The little animal perked up, then settled back against Avery's hip. Other than to do her business a couple of times a day, she'd refused to leave Avery's side since Carrie had picked them up after the breakup with Gray.

Meredith stepped toward the bed, arms crossed over her chest. "She needs exercise."

"This place is way bigger than the carriage house and it has stairs." Avery glared at both her sisters. "She's fine. I'm fine."

"Hunky-dory," Meredith agreed with a sniff. "You remember that guy in the first *Alien* movie? The one who had the creature pop out of his chest? I bet he thought he was fine, too."

Avery flopped back against the pillow. "Go away."

"She brought you a bear claw," Carrie announced, moving to the bedside table and placing the tea and pastry bag on top.

"Only because Carrie made me. I'm mad at you."

"You're not even friends with Gray," Avery said, pressing her palms to her forehead. "Shouldn't you take my side?"

"I heard you were trying to convince Carrie to sell the ranch."

"Who told you that?" Carrie asked, her voice shocked.

"Shae saw Avery and that Realtor meeting," Meredith answered. "She overheard them talking about listing the buildings downtown and then he asked about the ranch."

"You're selling the gallery?" Carrie snatched the bag off the nightstand again. "You can't do that. Nothing has been finalized with the estate."

"I talked to Douglas," Meredith said before Avery could explain the situation. "He has the authority to sell during probate. It's more complicated but can be done."

Carrie gasped. "How could you—"

"I'm not selling," Avery shouted, sitting up. "I don't want to sell." She tossed aside the covers and climbed out of bed. "I don't want to leave Magnolia and I'd never make that decision without talking to the two of you." She threw up her hands. "Why does everyone think the worst of me?" Her voice cracked on the last word, and she hated how vulnerable it made her. Hated caring the way she did about these people and this town.

"No one thinks the worst of you." Carrie held out the bag from the bakery like a peace offering.

"I kind of did," Meredith admitted.

Avery laughed softly at that. Leave it to Meredith not to pull any punches.

"You both know about my initial meeting with Jacob Martin," she explained. "It was before I'd decided to stay in Magnolia." She unrolled the bag and ripped off a small section of pastry. "He put out some feelers and has a buyer interested in the downtown properties. I told him I wouldn't sell."

"But do you want to?" Carrie asked softly. "If you and Gray aren't together, does that change how you feel about staying?"

Avery thought about her answer as she chewed. After swallowing, she shook her head. "Gray wasn't the only reason I want to be here," she said, dropping her gaze to the floor. "Magnolia feels like home because of the two of you. I like having sisters."

"Me, too," Carrie whispered and they both looked at Meredith.

"It's not as bad as I thought it would be," she said with a shrug.

"But do you want me around?" Avery forced herself

to ask. "Look at the damage I caused back in San Francisco and now with Gray. I hurt people."

Carrie plucked the bag from her hand and took out the bear claw. She pulled it apart and handed a piece to Meredith.

"Hey," Avery protested. "That's my breakfast." Spot shoved her nose against the back of Avery's leg. "I'm not sharing with you, either," she told the pup.

Carrie took a small section for herself and gave the rest to Avery. "Sisters share," she said simply. "We've been over the situation in California. You made a big mistake in choosing the wrong man, but what happened after isn't your fault."

"Gray will come around." Meredith plopped down on the edge of the bed. "That guy is head over heels for you."

"I don't deserve him."

Carrie stalked forward and slapped at the pastry. It landed on the floor next to Avery's feet. "Enough," she yelled. "You don't deserve to be rewarded for your extended pity party."

Avery blinked.

"I would have eaten that," Meredith muttered.

Carrie pressed her fingers to her mouth, as if shocked she'd lost her temper. Avery had the feeling her sister could use more letting go. They all had something to overcome. She needed to stop mentally face punching herself for not being perfect. All the self-incrimination was doing nothing for her life.

"Tell us the truth. Do you want to sell the gallery?" Carrie asked, her voice barely above a whisper. "If the money means that much to you, I want you to have it."

"You can't be serious," Avery answered.

But Carrie nodded. "I know we haven't been a family for very long, but you're more important to me than any building. Whether you stay and help us turn the town around or leave for greener pastures, we'll still be sisters."

"What she said," Meredith added.

Avery sucked in a breath. She'd never expected to find this kind of connection but was smart enough to realize the precious gift her sisters were offering her. She'd made some stupid mistakes but couldn't continue to punish herself for them.

"Magnolia is just green enough for me," she told them. "I'm not going to sell, but I do want to stay." She swallowed, then continued, "I need to face what happened in California. Even if Gray chooses to believe the worst about me, I can't keep doing that to myself."

"What do you need?" Carrie asked without hesitation.

"I want to try to talk to Tony's wife," she said, heart pounding at the thought of it. "To apologize once and for all for the part I played in her being hurt. Maybe it won't make a difference to her, but it will give me some closure."

"I'll go with you," Carrie said, then threw a pointed look at Meredith.

"I hate planes," she said, then rolled her eyes when Carrie continued to stare. "Okay, fine. We're going to San Francisco. Can we at least tour Alcatraz while we're there?"

"You'd come with me?" Avery was stunned.

"Yes," both women answered.

Meredith winked. "We can use the ungodly long flight to plan how you're going to fix things with Gray when we get back."

"I don't know if that's possible." Avery shook her head. She was done taking life's punches without fighting back. This was Avery 2.0 and she planned to make the most of her new start. "You're right. I'm going to try. I love him and I know he's worth the risk."

"So are you," Carrie told her and those three little words were like a balm to Avery's soul. Hope blossomed in her chest, soothing the dull ache that had taken residence there. Maybe Niall Reed had been a world-class jerk while he was alive, but in the end he'd given her the gift of her sisters. For that she'd always be grateful.

"How's it hanging, Grayson?"

Gray turned at the sound of Malcolm's deep voice. "Did you really just ask me how it's hanging?"

Mal grinned as he approached the park bench where Gray sat. "The young folks don't use that expression any longer?"

"Not at all," Gray said, then inclined his head toward the crowded playground. "Especially not in front of a bunch of kids."

"Good point." Mal rubbed a hand across his jaw. "Mind if I join you?"

"Sure." Gray patted the bench. "No one else seems to want to talk to me today."

"You look like someone peed in your Wheaties," Malcolm explained as he took a seat.

"No one says that anymore, either." Gray crossed his arms over his chest. "Besides, I look the same as always."

"Except mad as hell," Malcolm told him, none too helpfully as far as Gray was concerned.

The mayor waved at Violet when she turned her attention toward them. The little girl waved back, then glanced at Gray before returning to the sandcastle she was building with a towheaded boy.

Mal chuckled. "Your daughter looks just as grumpy."

"She is," Gray confirmed. "She's mad at me."

"Any particular reason?"

"Avery moved out of the carriage house, and I suck at braiding."

"You should watch YouTube videos."

"Really?" Gray sat up straight, then turned to face Malcolm. "I tell you Avery left and you focus on braids?"

"I raised boys," Malcolm answered with a shrug. "From what I understand, hair is important to little girls."

"It's not about the braids." Gray gritted his teeth and tried not to yell. "She misses Avery."

"Look at all the moms pretending not to watch us talking," Malcolm said, propping an ankle on the opposite knee and leaning back against the bench. "Do you always get this much attention?"

"You aren't going to address Avery moving out?"

"It's none of my business," the mayor answered with a sniff.

"Uh-huh." Gray had already heard from most of his buddies at the fire station that he'd been an idiot to believe his ex-wife's version of Avery's breakup story. Lucas's wife, Jennie, had made a special trip to the station to lay into him. He'd discovered pregnant women could be extremely intimidating when they wanted to. "Why do I feel like there's a big fat *but* coming my way?"

"You were always a good kid," Malcolm said. "I remember when your mama moved back here with you and your brother."

"I was a handful," Gray admitted.

"True," Mal agreed. "Most boys are." He stifled a laugh as they watched Violet stomp away from the sandpit after the boy building with her tossed aside the dandelion she'd placed on top of their castle. "Some girls, too."

"I love that girl."

"I know," the older man agreed quietly. "She's lucky to have you."

"Did you talk to Avery?" Gray couldn't help but ask. "Do you know what happened?"

Malcolm's lips thinned. "Yeah. She stopped by to see me right before she left for California."

The breath rushed out of Gray's lungs like he'd just taken a gut punch. "She's gone?"

The mayor didn't answer, but one thick brow lifted. Gray felt all sorts of unspoken judgment in that small movement.

"I'm a single dad," Gray said. "Violet has to be my top priority."

"Do you think Avery would have it any other way?"

Gray sighed. "Stacy will use Avery's past against me in court."

"What do you know about her past besides the garbage your ex-wife fed you?"

"Avery didn't deny any of it."

"She shouldn't have to," Mal countered.

"Damn." Gray ran a hand through his hair. The older man was right, of course. He'd had a knee-jerk reaction to Stacy's bombshell and had gone in guns blazing when he confronted Avery. He understood there were two sides to every story. Why hadn't he forced himself to calm down and find out Avery's?

She'd gone out of her way to connect with his daughter. There had never been one moment he'd doubted her affection for Violet, even when she would have denied it. Had he taken the easy way out? Instead of facing something difficult, he'd assumed the worst so he wouldn't actually have to put in the work to get through that kind of challenge. "Are you going to tell me what actually happened?"

"Not my story to share," Malcolm answered as he stood up. "Just know that woman loves you and she loves your daughter. She'd never do anything to purposely hurt either of you."

Regret churned in Gray's stomach as he watched Malcolm walk away. He couldn't believe Avery was gone. As angry as he'd been during their last conversation, the past few days had been horrible without her. It was like a dark cloud hovered over him, blotting out the brightness she'd brought to his world. He put on a good face for Violet, but inside he felt like he'd never recover.

Stacy had claimed he was too black-and-white in life—there was no room for any mistakes in light of his high expectations. She'd accused him of holding the people who loved him to unreachable standards. At the time, he'd paid no attention to her words, too righteous in his own heartbreak and betrayal.

Now he wondered if she'd actually been on-target with her charges. Becoming a father hadn't been part of his plan at the time, but he'd embraced the role with the whole of his being. He'd wanted to create the perfect life for Violet any way he could. But what if his daughter grew up feeling like she had to be perfect to earn his love?

Of course she had his heart unconditionally.

Too late, he understood Avery did, as well.

CHAPTER TWENTY-TWO

AVERY GAZED OUT the window of the rental car, toward the well-appointed brick house in a posh neighborhood outside San Francisco.

"I can do this," she whispered.

"Absolutely," Carrie agreed and reached over to squeeze her hand.

"Are you sure we shouldn't have stopped for a drink on the way?" Meredith asked from the back seat.

Avery shook her head. "I can't talk to Tony's wife when I've been drinking."

"I meant for me," her youngest sister clarified. "I'm a nervous wreck right now."

Avery felt the corner of her mouth twitch into a smile. "How do you do that?" She glanced back at Meredith. "You manage to make me feel better with your asinine comments."

"It's a gift," Meredith answered with a wink.

Carrie rolled her eyes, but even she smiled. "Are you sure you don't want us to go up to the house with you?"

"I need to talk to her on my own." Avery drew in a deep breath, then handed Carrie the keys. "But if you hear plates crashing against a wall or—"

"A gunshot?" Meredith suggested.

Carrie wagged her fingers toward the back seat.

"Enough from you," she said, then gave Avery an encouraging smile. "You'll be fine. She invited you here."

"Right." Nerves zipped through Avery until it felt like her skin was electric. But this was what she needed to do for closure. She'd called Sofia Monteroy from the kitchen table at Niall's house two nights ago with her sisters flanking her. Their presence gave her the strength she needed to punch in the number. Sofia had answered on the second ring, sounding strangely unsurprised to hear from Avery. They'd spoken for less than a minute when Sofia had asked Avery to come by her house.

Without explaining that the meeting would require a cross-country flight, Avery had accepted. She wanted to apologize in person. Thanks to the support of Carrie and Meredith, she was about to get that chance.

She walked up the cobblestone path that led to the house, her stomach pitching when the door opened as she got to the porch.

"Please come in," her ex-boyfriend's wife told her, stepping back into the house. Sofia looked different than she had that day in the office. Her light brown hair was cut in a stylish bob and she wore a silk shirt and fitted jeans. A diamond solitaire on a gold chain hung around her neck and her makeup was both subtle and elegant. Worry lines bracketed her mouth. Avery couldn't help but wonder if they'd been there before she discovered her husband's adultery and the accident that occurred in its aftermath.

"Thank you," Avery murmured. It was surreal to enter Tony's home, or the house where he'd once lived. On the phone, Sofia had immediately offered that they were indeed divorcing. The only question Avery had cared about asking was whether their son had recovered and relief had pounded through her when Sofia confirmed that he was doing well.

"My boys are at a friend's house," Sofia now explained as she closed the door and then led Avery into a formal living room. The interior of the house was modern, with cream-colored furniture and very few personal photos or knickknacks as decoration. "It seemed more appropriate that they not be here."

"I'm glad to know that Mark's doing better," Avery said as she lowered herself onto the edge of one of the leather chairs that flanked the sofa. "Once again, I'm so sorry. I never meant—"

"You paid his hospital bill," Sofia interrupted, taking a seat on the couch.

"As much as I could afford," Avery confirmed. "If you need anything else—"

"You weren't the only one. I discovered soon after confronting you that Tony was a serial cheater."

Avery bit down on the inside of her cheek. Her heart had healed from the betrayal, but somehow it still hurt to learn that a man she'd thought she loved had been even more duplicitous than she could have imagined.

"I'm sorry," she said.

"You keep apologizing." Sofia inclined her head. "What for?"

"For the pain I caused you," Avery answered without hesitation.

Sofia laughed. "You or my husband?"

"For my part in it. I appreciate your willingness to meet with me. I understand this is awkward." Avery offered a shaky smile. "It means a lot to me to apologize in person."

"Tony and I met at Stanford," Sofia told her, tucking a lock of hair behind her ear. "It was love at first sight on my part, although it took a little longer for him. We dated over a year, and then on the eve of graduation, I found out he'd slept with one of my sorority sisters."

"Why didn't you break up with him?"

The other woman shook her head. "I believed him when he told me it was a drunken mistake and she'd come on to him. He said he barely remembered the next morning, and nothing like that would ever happen again. Until I found out about you, I thought he'd been faithful to me. To our marriage. You can understand my devastation."

"Of course." Avery swallowed against the sick feeling that rose in her throat, hating her part in causing that kind of pain.

"Now I understand he's a master manipulator. Not just of me. All the women in his life. And you aren't the only one with regrets."

Avery nodded, afraid she'd be unable to speak without bursting into tears. She couldn't help but compare what her ex had done to her father's actions. Of course, she had no reason to believe that Tony had fathered children with any of his mistresses, but the selfishness and disregard for everyone else felt eerily similar. She felt a pang of sympathy for her mother, whose protests that Niall didn't matter to her rang so hollow.

"You're not to blame," Sofia said quietly, "Even though I wanted you to be."

Tears stung the backs of Avery's eyes and she didn't bother to blink them away.

"I tried to take him back," Sofia admitted, swiping at her own cheeks. "I want a happy home more than anything, but I deserve better than a liar and a cheat. My sons deserve more. How can I raise good men if the example they have of marriage is so dysfunctional?"

"I think you're doing the right thing," Avery offered. "Not that my opinion matters."

"You matter." Sofia flashed the barest hint of a smile. "It's why I asked you to come here. You wanted to apologize, and I needed to tell you I don't blame you anymore. For any of it."

"Thank you," Avery whispered.

"It isn't fair you lost your job," Sofia continued. "Tony's given me all kinds of excuses for his behavior but taken little personal responsibility and been forced to face no consequences in his professional life. From what I understand, your career at Pierce and Chambers was ruined. I'd be willing to help you fight to get your job back or if you decide to file a wrongful terminati—"

"I'm not going back." Avery drew in a breath. "I've actually moved to North Carolina. I have family there." The words felt right as she spoke them and the bands that seemed to constrict her heart loosened.

Sofia's delicate brow arched. "You flew all the way from the East Coast to meet with me?"

"My sisters came with me," Avery answered with a nod. "They're in the car waiting." She glanced toward the front window of the house. "I should go."

"I have an older sister," Sofia shared as they both stood. "She's been my rock through all this. I don't know what I'd do without her."

"I know just what you mean."

She said goodbye to the woman and walked out of the house. The weather was cool today, with gray skies that spoke of impending rain. Although she'd only been in Magnolia a short time, she missed the sunshine and the smell of honeysuckle on the morning air.

Carrie and Meredith both climbed out of the rental car as she approached.

"Well?" Meredith demanded. "It doesn't look like she punched you in the face."

"She was lovely," Avery answered. "Sad but lovely."

Carrie reached out for a quick hug. "And how are you?"

Avery let out a soft sigh. "I'm ready to go home."

GRAY SAT ON the front porch step outside Stacy's condo the following evening as the moon rose in the midnight sky. He'd been there for almost an hour when his ex-wife's sleek Mercedes pulled into the driveway.

Stacy got out and approached him with a warrior glare, heels clicking on the stamped concrete walk. She wore a navy wrap dress that hugged her slim figure with her hair down in loose curls.

"You're going to scare the neighbors," she told him, tucking her phone into the sparkly clutch she carried. "You seem like a stalker."

"Where were you tonight?" Gray asked as he straightened.

"Why is that your business?" She elbowed her way past him toward the front door.

"Violet was waiting, Stace. She had her little overnight bag packed and was so excited because you promised to take her for frozen yogurt after dinner."

Stacy shoved her key in the lock, then turned toward him. "The Froyo place isn't going anywhere. We'll go the next time I have her."

"That's not the point." He massaged a hand against the back of his neck. "This was your night. If you want the custody agreement to stay the way it is, you have to honor it."

"Something came up with work," she told him with a sniff.

"That's bullshit and we both know it."

"Don't swear at me," she snapped. "You have no idea what goes on in my life."

"And I don't care," he countered. "But you're hurting our daughter and I'm not going to let it continue. I want to work together, but if you won't then I'll fight you, Stacy."

"I'm the mother," she reminded him. "No court is going to be in your favor."

He knew she was likely right, but he ignored that fact. Whatever it took, he'd make it happen if it would protect his daughter.

"Please. You name the terms."

"What about your girlfriend?"

He closed his eyes and let an image of Avery drift into his mind. After the visit from the mayor, Gray had tried to track down both Carrie and Meredith, but it appeared they'd gone to California, as well. No one seemed to know—or at least be willing to share—why the three sisters had left together or when they were returning. *If* Avery was coming back with them.

He'd screwed up big-time by pushing her away. He loved her, and his daughter loved her. Nothing else mattered. Life would never be perfect, but he understood now he had to be willing to face the damaged parts of himself to have the life he wanted.

The life he wanted included Avery.

"My relationship is none of your business."

Stacy placed her hands on her hips and leaned forward. "I'll make it my business if you don't back off on custody."

He shrugged. "It won't stop me. Why can't you see that this is what's best?"

"What makes you think I don't?" She took a step toward him, then shook her head. "Don't you think I know I'm not a good mother?" she asked, her voice cracking on the last word. "It's like I have no maternal instinct." She dashed a tear from her cheek with a violent swipe, as if angry to be showing any measure of vulnerability. "It's always come so damn naturally to you."

"I don't think you're a bad mother."

"Liar," she muttered. "I can't be perfect the way you are, Gray. I couldn't live up to your standards when we were married, and we both know I'm failing miserably now. But I love my daughter."

"I know."

"How is that girlfriend of yours so fantastic with Violet? She seems about as motherly as a box of crayons."

He chuckled. "Avery isn't worried about being perfect or maternal when she's with Violet. She's just herself and that's enough. It would be for you, too. Our daughter needs the best of you, Stace. Not some arbitrary mom standards that you've read about on social media or you think that I expect of you." He took a step forward and gentled his tone. "This wasn't how either of us planned things to go, but we have to figure out how to make it work."

She sniffed and looked away. "You think changing custody will do that?"

"I think it would make things easier on all of us. I promise I'm not trying to push you out of her life. But if you make a commitment to her, honor it. We can come up with a generous visitation and make it flexible if that's what you need. You and I will submit a parenting plan together."

A muscle worked along Stacy's fine jaw. He could see how difficult this was for her and he remained silent, giving her the time she needed. Finally, she lifted her face to meet his gaze. "Those things I said about Avery weren't all true."

A dull ache spread through his chest. Not because Stacy had lied to him. The blame was with him for believing her and doubting Avery. Damn, he hoped she'd give him another chance. He couldn't imagine what he'd do without her in his life.

"I'm sorry if I messed things up for you."

"I'll fix it," he answered, sending up a silent prayer that was possible.

Her features softened. "It's what you do." She dabbed at the corners of her eyes. "I'll have my attorney call yours in the morning to set up a time to meet. If we can come up with a plan that works for both of us and is right for Violet, I'll agree to submitting the custody change."

He let out a slow breath. "Thank you."

"Good night, Gray." She turned and let herself into the condo, leaving him alone in the dark. He looked up at the stars dotting the night sky like a blanket woven from a thousand pinpricks of light.

Where was Avery at the moment? In California or returned to Magnolia or someplace in between? Was it possible she was gazing up to the same starry sky?

As relieved as he felt about Stacy's willingness to work with him on the custody change, a weight still settled on his heart. Now that he'd had a taste of a full life with Avery at his side, he wasn't going to give up on his chance at love.

Not without a fight.

CHAPTER TWENTY-THREE

AVERY SPENT AN additional day in San Francisco with her sisters. Neither of them had ever been to California so they'd toured the city's most famous sights and then had dinner with her mother. She'd thought it would be strange, but her mom seemed to enjoy getting to know both Carrie and Meredith. Okay, it was still strange, at least for Avery, but she'd come to realize her rigorous pursuit of some ideal existence had cut her off from appreciating the good things in the life she had.

Maybe her mother finally understood that, as well. Melissa hadn't batted an eye at Meredith's snarky asides or the awkward pauses as Carrie tried to steer the conversation from potential emotional land mines. On that count, it felt like they were walking through a war zone.

But they'd managed it, and Avery had even texted Gray while they were waiting to board the red-eye home. She'd typed in and then deleted at least a half dozen messages before settling on a simple can we talk? His answer had been an immediate and succinct yes. She'd waited for more and, when nothing came through, she'd sent a thumbs-up emoji. The little icon seemed wholly inadequate, but everything she wanted to tell him needed to be said in person.

They were all tired and slightly punchy by the time they touched down in Charlotte the following morning. Carrie had driven to the airport, so they piled into her Volvo station wagon and started the drive toward Magnolia.

"It feels like the seasons changed while we were gone." Avery turned her head to gaze out the car's passenger window at the bright orange and gold leaves of the trees lining the highway. "How does that happen so fast?"

Meredith thumped a hand against the back of the headrest. "Don't forget, you were out of commission for a while before we coaxed you back from the brink of heartbreak."

"That wasn't coaxing," Avery said over her shoulder. "That was being hit over the head with a sledgehammer."

"It worked," Carrie reminded her. "I wouldn't call it the brink of anything. You were writhing in the depths of despair."

"Dramatic much?" Avery muttered but chuckled just the same.

Meredith leaned forward as much as her seat belt would allow. "You're just lucky we're not only your sisters, but also your bosom friends."

Carrie lifted her gaze to the rearview mirror. "You're an *Anne of Green Gables* fan?" she asked Meredith.

Avery turned in her seat just as Meredith made a face. "Isn't everyone?"

They both looked at Avery for confirmation. "Depths of despair and bosom friends," she repeated. "I get it. I'm not going to color my hair green in solidarity, but I read the series."

"We should start a book club," Meredith said, sitting back again.

Avery blinked, keeping her gaze trained on the front window. Out of the corner of her eye, she saw Carrie try and fail to smother a smile. "I'd like to wrangle an invitation to one of Julie's toys for women parties," Carrie said.

"You need it," Meredith agreed.

"What's that supposed to mean?"

Meredith draped one foot across the console between the two front seats. "You're uptight."

"I am not," Carrie argued and slapped at Meredith's flip-flop. "Get your foot off there. It's dirty."

"You only think that because you're uptight."

"I *am* not."

Avery's mouth curved into a smile as she listened to her sisters' affectionate bickering. Having been raised an only child, she had no means to compare their nutty dynamics to siblings who'd grown up together, but she figured they were doing okay. Meredith and Carrie gave her a sense of belonging to something bigger. They might each have an individual history but they'd remain connected going forward, no matter what life threw at each of them.

As they drove into Magnolia, Carrie turned at the water tower and headed into downtown.

"Are you stopping at the gallery?" Avery asked.

"The bakery," Carrie answered. "I'm hungry."

"Me, too," Meredith offered from the back seat. "I hope she has the carrot-cake muffins today."

Carrie pulled into an open parking space and turned off the car.

"I'll wait here," Avery told them, unwilling to return to life in Magnolia until she spoke with Gray. "I'm more tired than hungry."

She frowned as her sisters shared a look.

"We're going to eat inside," Meredith told her. "It will take a while."

"How long does it take to eat a muffin?" Avery asked. "Besides, you can order everything to go. I miss Spot. I want to get out to the rescue and see her."

The other two women climbed out of the car, and Meredith immediately opened the passenger door. "You need to come in with us. People will talk if we're not together."

Avery laughed softly. "No one expects us to be together all the time."

"Come on," Carrie coaxed in her gentle voice. "Meredith has been particularly annoying today. I need a buffer."

"What you need," Meredith said as she nudged Carrie's arm, "is someone to stop me from reaching across the table to smack your pretty face when you say something stupid."

"See?" Carrie held up her hands in entreaty.

"Codependent much?" Avery unbuckled her seat belt. "I'm sure you could have managed ordering breakfast without my supervision."

She darted a glance up and down the street after slamming shut the car door. It was Saturday morning but the sidewalks seemed particularly quiet. There was no reason to think she'd run into Gray so soon. Of course, part of her was desperate to see him but she needed to gather her thoughts, come up with all the reasons he should give their relationship another chance.

Yes, she'd had over four hours in the air on the way back to think about her list but the possibility of rejection still made nerves flutter across her skin.

Carrie and Meredith flanked her as they headed for Sunnyside's entrance, each of them looping an arm with one of hers. "I'm not a flight risk," she said with a laugh. "You two are acting weird."

"You have no idea," Meredith answered as she held open the bakery's door.

What was that supposed to mean? Avery was preoccupied studying her youngest sister as she entered so it took her an extra moment to register what waited for them inside the bakery.

"Welcome home!" a chorus of voices shouted.

Avery felt her eyes grow wide as she took in the crowd of people staring at her. From Malcolm to Josie to a host of other residents she'd gotten to know throughout her time in Magnolia. They were smiling at her, eyes shining with affection like she'd just returned home from some holy crusade instead of a few days on the West Coast.

"What did you two do?" she asked her sisters, who'd stepped forward to face the crowd at her side.

"Not us." Carrie grinned. "Our only job was getting you here."

Her brain working overtime to figure out why she was on the receiving end of all of this fanfare, Avery's gaze snagged on a tall figure making his way to the front of the crowd.

"Hey," Gray said as he came toward her. That one syllable sent longing fluttering through her belly.

"Give her something better than *hey*," Malcolm shouted with a laugh.

"You complete me," a voice from the back called.

"You make me want to be a better man," Mary Ellen suggested with an enthusiastic nod.

"You have bewitched me, body and soul," Joe from the diner added.

"Jane Austen didn't write that line," Julie Martindale informed him, shaking her head. "It's not in the book."

"Works for my wife," Joe shot back.

Avery pressed her lips together to keep from grinning as Gray squeezed shut his eyes in evident frustration. "This was a terrible idea," he said softly.

"It's working for me," she told him, restating Joe's words in her own way.

As he drew closer, Meredith and Carrie stepped away. "Is it?" he asked, hope filling his gaze.

She nodded.

"But you're going to need to do better than what they said," Meredith told him before Carrie yanked her toward the crowd.

"I'm sorry," Gray said, glancing over his shoulder and then back at Avery. "For acting like an idiot."

"Forgiven," she answered immediately.

He massaged a hand along the back of his neck, gazing at her with a sexy half smile that made her toes curl. "You're going to let me off that easily?"

"Only if you'll do the same." She bit down on her lip, then said, "I'm sorry for being scared to stay and fight for us. I should have told you everything about my past at the start."

"I should have trusted you." He reached out and smoothed a strand of hair away from her cheek. "I know you, Avery. I know who you are in your heart, and I know you're one of the best things that ever happened to me."

She shook her head. "Violet is the best."

"I love you for saying that."

"I'd never hurt either of you. You mean the world to me."

"You *are* my world," he told her. "You make everything better, brighter. I love you with every bit of my imperfect heart."

"Imperfect?" she whispered with a laugh. "Are you sure that's the right word?"

"You meant to say *perfect*," Malcolm called, earning a round of laughter from their audience. "Women want a perfect love."

"Imperfect," he repeated, ignoring everyone else. His eyes darkened, the intensity in his gaze stealing her breath. "I'm not going to list my imperfections for you but I have plenty. I'm going to make mistakes but the one thing I can promise is that I'll never stop loving you or working to be the man you deserve." He laced their fingers together. "If you'll give me another chance?"

Emotion swelled in Avery and she wrapped her arms around his waist and pressed a kiss to the base of his neck. It was difficult to find the words to speak but he had to know she'd give him a million chances. She'd missed Gray so much. Missed being in his arms, talking to him and sharing the tiny moments of their days. Magnolia was the place she belonged, but he was her home. She'd never let him go again.

GRAY DREW BACK, waiting for Avery to respond to his question. Based on the way she'd nuzzled against him, he was betting on a yes. He still wanted to hear it out loud.

"Answer the boy," Julie hollered from the front of the crowd. "He's so nervous I can see his butt cheeks clenching."

"Why didn't I do this in private?" He let out a put-upon groan as Avery giggled.

"Are you nervous?" Her eyes danced as she stared up at him. "And how tight are your pants?"

"Is it time, Daddy?"

Gray smiled as Violet tugged on the hem of his shirt. She stayed behind him even as she peeked around to look at Avery.

"Don't start with the shy act," Avery said, crouching down and opening her arms. "I know it means you want something."

Violet launched herself at Avery with a laugh, and the certainty of his love settled over him like a warm blanket. "I did my own braids," she announced. "Crisscross and everything."

Avery pretended to examine them closely, then nodded. "They look pretty darn good, kiddo. I suppose this means you don't need me anymore."

"I still like yours better," Violet answered, almost cautiously. Gray understood that for his daughter, those words were as close to a grand gesture as she could offer.

"I'll braid your hair anytime you'd like." He watched as Avery dabbed at the corners of her eyes, knowing she must also realize the significance of the words.

Suddenly there was a high-pitched yip from behind him and he turned to see Spot come barreling toward them. Lucas was supposed to be holding the dog until Gray gave him the release signal, but clearly the animal wasn't going to be separated from her human any longer.

"Look at my pretty girl," Avery said as the dog rose up on her hind legs to bestow sloppy kisses on her cheeks. "I missed you. Have you been a good girl while I was away?"

So far he'd been heckled by his friends and upstaged by his daughter and a dog. This romantic gesture wasn't exactly turning out the way he'd planned, but Avery didn't seem to mind.

Her smile stretched from ear to ear and she radiated the kind of happiness he'd hoped to give her. That he wanted to offer her every day for the rest of their lives.

"What's this?" she asked as she reached for the small velvet box attached to Spot's new collar.

"Daddy, now," Violet screamed as if he were across the room and not standing two feet from her.

Avery paused, her fingers frozen in midair, and he could almost hear the collective gasp go up from everyone watching.

Nothing about their love affair had gone according to any sort of plan he might have created, so he was used to winging it by now.

He dropped to his knees in front of Avery, pulling Violet onto his knee and scooping up Spot into his arm like she was a furry football.

"I have something to ask you." He cleared his throat when Violet elbowed him in the ribs. "We have something to ask you."

"About another chance?" she asked, her voice gentle. "My answer is yes. All the chances."

He nodded and then shook his head. "I'm glad to hear that, because the question we've moved on to now is just a tad bit more serious."

"You're gonna freak her out," Violet told him. "Like she's in trouble."

"Listen to the girl," Mal shouted.

"You're not in trouble," he clarified. "But I will be if I mess this up any more."

She shifted so that her knees grazed his and gave him a slow smile. "You aren't messing anything up."

"I had a plan," he explained, his mouth suddenly dry. "A solid one."

"I'm sure."

Spot, who was gently mouthing Gray's wrist, gave a low whine and then farted. "It involved your dog behaving."

"Good luck with that."

"And everyone else watching in respectful silence," he said over his shoulder.

"Get on with it," Meredith commanded.

"You can do it, Daddy," Violet said, squeezing his arm with her small hand.

He dropped a kiss on the top of his daughter's head and undid the box from Spot's leash before letting the dog down on the floor. Spot immediately climbed into Avery's lap and stared at him with her liquid brown eyes.

"You were going to ask me something," Avery reminded him as she patted the dog's head like she had all day to wait.

Gray didn't want a moment longer. "Will you marry me?" he said in a rush of breath. "It doesn't have to be soon. We can have a long engagement or a short one. Whatever you want. Just say yes, Avery. Please. Make me the happiest man in Magnolia and say yes."

Violet plucked the box out of his hand, flipped it open and gave it back to him. "You forgot the ring."

Right. "Thanks, sweetheart." He took the ring, a round solitaire in a platinum band, and held it up toward Avery. "Will you say yes?"

"Yes," she whispered and the bakery erupted in a cacophony of cheers and wolf whistles.

Trying to ignore his trembling hand, he slid the ring onto her finger, then leaned in to kiss her.

"Did you ever doubt I'd say yes?" she asked against his lips. "I love you with every part of me, Grayson Atwell. Forever."

"Forever," he repeated. "I love you forever."

"Just remember..." Violet wagged a finger between them as they separated. "No brothers. Only sisters."

Gray opened his mouth and then shut it again. He could handle just about anything at the moment, other than discussing potential future siblings with his precocious daughter.

He glanced at Avery to see her smile go wide once again and grinned right back at her. They straightened and he lifted Violet into his arms. Family and friends surrounded the three of them, with Spot barking happily at their feet.

In the midst of all the revelry, a sense of peace filled Gray. All the poignant and corny movie lines in the world couldn't capture the breadth of his feelings for Avery. He simply loved her with everything he had and knew deep in his heart it would always be that way.

EPILOGUE

One month later

"S<small>TOP HIDING</small>."

"I'm not hiding."

Avery shared a look with Meredith before placing her palms on the enormous oak desk in the gallery's private office and leaning forward. Carrie sat on the floor, knees drawn up to her chest.

"The opening is a huge success. Everyone's amazed at your talent."

"They're just being nice," Carrie said, continuing to stare at the floor.

Meredith snorted. "Since when has Julie Martindale ever been nice if there isn't something in it for her?"

Carrie let out a choked laugh. "She dropped off a handwritten invitation to one of her parties the other day and was extremely friendly."

"She wants your money," Meredith argued. "Although, someone with that much inventory should have a smile on her face."

"Once again, we're getting off topic," Avery told her sisters. "People want to congratulate you."

As if on cue, there was a knock on the door. Butterflies danced across Avery's stomach as Gray entered the office. Would the thrill of him ever diminish? She didn't

THE MAGNOLIA SISTERS

think so. In the past few weeks, her life had taken on a glow of happiness she never could have expected. They still had a long way to go as far as untangling Niall's estate, but she had no doubt she belonged in Magnolia, building a life with Gray and Violet.

She glanced down at the diamond sparkling on her finger as she took a step toward him. It felt like a cliché, but she loved gazing at her ring and what it represented. They were planning a wedding for just before Christmas and she relished the time they'd truly be a family.

"She's coming out," Avery told Gray, slipping her hand into his.

They watched as Carrie straightened from behind the desk, smoothing a hand over her printed maxidress. Her dark hair was down around her shoulders, and she kept tucking it behind one ear in a gesture of obvious nerves.

Meredith stepped around the desk and patted Carrie on both cheeks, maybe a little harder than necessary in Avery's opinion.

"Ouch." Carrie drew back. "What was that for?"

"You need some color in your face," Meredith explained with an innocent smile. "You look like you're going to pass out."

"I'm not going to faint," Carrie murmured. "I'm stronger than that."

"We know you are," Avery assured her. It had taken a lot of coaxing to get Carrie to agree to open the gallery for private group-painting sessions, but already she had a half dozen parties and events booked. Meredith had come up with the idea to kick off the reopening of the studio with a showing of Carrie's old paintings. They both hoped a positive response to her work would encourage her to return to her art on a deeper level than teaching classes.

"You're sure no one is making fun of me?" Carrie asked, her worried gaze darting between Gray, Meredith and Avery. "What if they think I'm trying to capitalize on Dad's fame?"

"You're talented," Gray reminded her, his voice gentle. "You always have been. Now is the time to let the world know it. Tonight isn't about Niall. It's your moment, Carrie. You need to claim it."

Avery's heart swelled with gratitude as she watched her sweet, sometimes shy sister consider Gray's words and then nod in agreement. "I've missed my paints," she whispered.

"You might want to invest in new ones after all this time," Meredith said, giving Carrie's arm a playful nudge. "But first, you must greet your adoring public."

Carrie rolled her eyes even as she laughed. "Let's go, then. I know Mer-Bear will eviscerate anyone who dares to criticize me."

"Damn straight, Princess," Meredith agreed and then led the way out of the office and down the hall toward the gathering.

"Thank you." Avery leaned in to press a kiss to Gray's mouth. "Your support means a lot to Carrie."

"She deserves all the support she gets." Gray cupped her cheeks between his palms. "But if I'm honest, I can't wait for this night to be over so I can take you home and have you all to myself."

Violet was spending the night with her mother. To Avery's surprise, Stacy had come around to the idea of Avery being part of Violet's life without too much convincing. They were still going forward with a modification of the custody arrangement, and although the new plan made Violet's scheduled nights with her mom more infrequent, Stacy seemed motivated to honor her duties.

Avery and Gray only spent the night together when Violet wasn't with him, although they did their best to find creative ways to steal intimate moments at other times.

"I can't wait," she whispered.

"Are you sure you don't want a Halloween wedding?" he asked with a laugh.

"We can wait a few weeks longer."

"I'd wait forever," he promised, kissing her again. "That's how much I love you. I'll admit I'm anticipating Christmas like Ralphie dreaming of that Red Ryder BB gun."

She grinned at him. "Now I know you're desperate for me."

He pulled her closer to him. "Would you like a demonstration?"

She broke away with a laugh. "Later, my love. Right now is about supporting Carrie."

"I hope she truly embraces her gift," he said as he took her hand and followed her to the front of the gallery. "Your father did a number on her self-confidence."

"We'll make sure she gets there." Avery wasn't yet sure how'd they'd accomplish it, but she knew that she and Meredith would find a way to make Carrie's long-buried artistic dreams a reality once again.

They entered the gallery space, which was crowded with locals and visitors alike. An art opening featuring the works of Niall Reed's daughter had proved to be a huge draw.

Avery also knew without a doubt that Carrie had more talent than she even realized. People gathered around the paintings, as if mesmerized by the composition and style, making it clear she wasn't the only one to feel that way.

She kept an eye on Carrie, who seemed to grow more relaxed with every passing minute. She spoke to everyone who approached her with the same kind smile and charming focus. Avery couldn't imagine that Niall had ever been so authentic in how he'd dealt with people.

The gallery remained packed for a while longer, but eventually the crowd disappeared.

"We've sold everything," Meredith announced when it was just the three sisters remaining in the empty space. Gray had offered to drive Julie home when it became clear she'd had a few too many glasses of champagne. Carrie would drop Avery at his house after they locked up.

"I can't believe it." Carrie pressed a hand to her chest. "Who bought it all?"

Meredith checked the receipt book. "A variety of people, really. But the same man purchased several of the larger pieces. A Scott Dylan."

Carrie frowned. "Are you sure that's his name?"

"He's the Boston real estate bigwig I told you about," Avery said. "His company is going to develop the empty space at the end of the block. They're the ones who wanted to buy all the property, but when I explained we weren't selling, they offered a lease agreement. It's our big influx of rental income and by the amount this guy spent on your paintings, they're flush in cash."

"Okay, I guess," Carrie said but her brows drew together as if she were working out a puzzle.

"I can't wait to meet this Scott Dylan." Meredith did a funny little hip sway. "Maybe he's cute, too."

"You have the name backward," a deep voice announced and they all turned to see a tall, muscular, sandy-haired man standing in the doorway that led to the back of the building. "It's Dylan Scott."

"No," Carrie whispered on a frantic puff of air.

"Wait." Avery's brain went into overdrive, trying to figure out why this man—or at least his name—seemed familiar, certain she'd never met Dylan Scott before.

He was a man who a woman wouldn't easily forget. Well over six feet, with broad shoulders, lean hips and an intricate tattoo peeking out from under the sleeve of his fitted black T-shirt, Dylan looked more like a leader of some dangerous biker gang than the head of a prominent real estate development company. "Do we know you?" Avery asked.

"Not you," Meredith said, poking her from around the back of Carrie's stiff frame. "But Carrie did back in high school. Remember when we talked about how long it's been since she had great—"

"Shut up, Meredith," Carrie said in a hiss of breath.

Dylan only chuckled. "It's been a while," he announced in that gravelly voice that sounded like whiskey and sin. "But it's good to be home. I missed this town."

Avery's breath caught at the intensity of this man's focus on her sister. Obviously Magnolia wasn't the only thing Dylan Scott had missed.

* * * * *

SPECIAL EXCERPT FROM

H HARLEQUIN
SPECIAL EDITION

*Harrison McCord was sure he was the rightful owner
of the Dawson Family Ranch. And delivering Daisy
Dawson's baby on the side of the road was a mere
diversion. Still, when Daisy found out his intentions,
instead of pushing him away, she invited him in, figuring
he'd start to see her in a whole new light. But what if
she started seeing him that way, as well?*

*Read on for a sneak preview of the next
book in Melissa Senate's
Dawson Family Ranch miniseries,*
Wyoming Special Delivery.

Daisy went over to the bassinet and lifted out Tony,
cradling him against her. "Of course. There's lots
more video, but another time. The footage of what the
ranch looked like before Noah started rebuilding to the
day I helped put up the grand reopening banner—it's
amazing."

Harrison wasn't sure he wanted to see any of that. No,
he knew he didn't. This was all too much. "Well, I'll be
in touch about that tour."

*That's it. Keep it nice and impersonal. "Be in touch"
was a sure distance maker.*

She eyed him and lifted her chin. "Oh—I almost
forgot! I have a favor to ask, Harrison."

Gulp. How was he supposed to emotionally distance
himself by doing her a favor?

She smiled that dazzling smile. The one that drew him like nothing else could. "If you're not busy around five o'clock or so, I'd love your help in putting together the rocking cradle my brother Rex ordered for Tony. It arrived yesterday, and I tried to put it together, but it has directions a mile long that I can't make heads or tails of. Don't tell my brother Axel I said this—he's a wizard at GPS, maps and terrain—but give him instructions and he holds the paper upside down."

Ah. This was almost a relief. He'd put together the cradle alone. No chitchat. No old family movies. Just him, a set of instructions and five thousand various pieces of cradle. "I'm actually pretty handy. Sure, I can help you."

"Perfect," she said. "See you at fiveish."

A few minutes later, as he stood on the porch watching her walk back up the path, he had a feeling he was at a serious disadvantage in this deal.

Because the farther away she got, the more he wanted to chase after her and just keep talking. Which sent off serious warning bells. That Harrison might actually more than just like Daisy Dawson already—and it was only day one of the deal.

Don't miss
Wyoming Special Delivery *by Melissa Senate,*
available April 2020 wherever
Harlequin Special Edition books and ebooks are sold.

Harlequin.com